Toni Jordan was born in Brisbane [...] University of Queensland with a bachelor of science. Her debut novel, *Addition*, was a Richard and Judy Summer Read, won best themed fiction from the UK Medical Journalists' Association and was published in 16 countries. She lives in Melbourne where she teaches creative writing and writes a weekly newspaper column.

Praise for ADDITION

Grace Lisa Vandenburg counts. The letters in her name (19). The steps she takes every morning to the local café (920). The number of poppy seeds on her orange cake, which dictates the number of bites she'll take to eat it. Grace counts everything because that way there are no unpleasant surprises.

As Grace struggles to balance a new relationship with old habits, to find a way to change while staying true to herself, she realises that nothing is more chaotic than love.

'Toni Jordan has created such a real character in Grace that you are cheering her on . . . Jordan's voice is distinctive, refreshing . . . Her debut novel is juicy and funny, just like its protagonist . . . this is a gem' *Sydney Morning Herald*

'Bringing a quirky humour and a sympathetic view of diversity to her story, the author sustains the momentum to the end of this engaging romantic comedy' *The Times*

'Interesting, funny and engaging' *Harper's*

'Brimming with sarcastic humour' *Guardian*

'An empathetic journey, both heartbreaking and hilarious' *Good Reading*

'Sensuously written, fabulously entertaining . . . a first novel that takes your breath away' *West Australian*

Fall Girl

Toni Jordan

SCEPTRE

First published in Australia in 2010 by The Text Publishing Company

First published in Great Britain in 2011 by Sceptre
An imprint of Hodder & Stoughton
An Hachette UK company

First published in paperback in 2011

1

A CIP catalogue record for this title is available from the British Library.

ISBN 978 1 444 72387 8
eBook ISBN 978 1 444 72386 1

Printed and bound in the UK by Clays Ltd, St Ives plc

Hodder & Stoughton policy is to use papers that are natural, renewable
and recyclable products and made from wood grown in sustainable forests.
The logging and manufacturing processes are expected to conform to
the environmental regulations of the country of origin.

Hodder & Stoughton Ltd
338 Euston Road
London NW1 3BH

www.hodder.co.uk

To Bobo
Thanks for all the coffee

From the beginning it is the glasses that give me trouble. They have a mind of their own. When I practised back at Cumberland Street they behaved perfectly yet now, in the sittingroom of the mansion, they are heavy and uncomfortable. They pinch my nose and won't stay still. When I raise my head to look at the Streeton landscape on the opposite wall they sit so flat against my face that my eyelashes brush against them when I blink. When I bow my head in contemplation they slide down my nose. I am continually propping them back up the bridge with my middle finger.

This erratic spectacle dance is not a good sign. I have worn these glasses before without this problem; perhaps I have bent them, squished them in my purse or against the arm of a chair without realising. Still, all this fidgeting makes me look nervous. This is an important interview. It would seem odd if I wasn't nervous.

Finally Professor Carmichael appears in the doorway. 'Dr

Canfield?' he says, and he introduces himself, bestows a handshake.

I am following him down the fine wide corridor two paces behind and this is when the glasses earn their keep. I think fast, on my feet. Ruby would be proud. Daniel Metcalf himself is standing across from the doorway to the boardroom. He is leaning against a grandfather clock, mobile against his ear, finishing a call before we go in for the interview. I bend my neck in a sharp movement to rifle through the papers in my briefcase, checking I have everything I need. The glasses fall. The heavy tortoiseshell frames bounce on the Persian runner and clatter against Daniel Metcalf's left boot. They are outdoor boots, scuffed and water-marked.

We kneel at the same moment. Our knees almost touch. He sets the phone on the floor; it makes muffled sounds that he ignores. He picks up the glasses with his thumb and index finger as if they might bruise and folds each arm closed with a clack. Down the palm of his right hand, from the inside tip of his index finger to the folds of his wrist, is a straight white scar raised like a thread.

'Sorry,' I say. I bite my bottom lip and tilt my head down.

'You should be,' he says. He rests the glasses in the centre of his palm, raises and lowers his hand to gauge their weight. 'In the wrong hands these could be a deadly weapon.'

'Just as well I'm not the wrong hands,' I say.

My father often says that the very rich surround themselves with objects that increase in value, while the average person selects things that decrease in value. This house contains, among other assets, the Streeton landscape, the clock in the hall, the antique dining table with gleaming French polish, and Daniel Metcalf. He too is worth more with every year that passes. He is not as tall as the clock and easier to transport than the table. He does not wear glasses: even a minor weakness such as this can be fixed with money.

I would recognise him anywhere from the photos in the social pages. He is thirty-four and his hair is brown and slightly too long. He could use a shave. He is not nervous or awkward. He's wearing jeans and a striped linen shirt that is either the work of a very expensive designer or else needs an iron. I learned long ago that immaculate suits and shiny shoes are for men who rely on the opinions of others for their livelihood.

I do not know him, but I do not need to. I can tell the way he votes, the restaurants he frequents, who cuts his hair. I knew the house would look like this and would be located here in Toorak among the other mansions. People everywhere play the roles they are assigned. Being very rich is like belonging to an excessively controlling cult.

The light in this room is calmer, more refined than outside. It is softer, as though nervous about resting on an antique. On the other side of the table, Professor Carmichael is on Daniel Metcalf's right. Carmichael has a young face for a man in his mid-seventies, with pink skin like a baby's stretching to the top of his head. His age and general level of disapproval are revealed, though, in the saggy baggy skin of his throat, which could fold over itself and conceal a small Volkswagen. Before he began administering the trust, Carmichael was a researcher in pure mathematics at a sandstone university on the other side of the world. He appears to have no connections in science these days, no friends or colleagues at the universities I have chosen. Since his retirement due to ill health this is his only professional commitment. Apparently he was a friend of Daniel Metcalf's father, so this job is a lucrative debt of honour.

Carmichael fulfils his obligations without diligence. The decision has always been his and seems based on very little. Daniel Metcalf himself is a rubber stamp. His attendance at these final interviews is a formality. For a Metcalf, twenty-five thousand dollars is tax-deductible small change.

On Daniel Metcalf's left is a dowdy woman, mid-fifties, seventy-five kilos with cat-green eyes. She has a notepad in front of her and a pen in her hand and keeps her head down. She is the secretary, Mrs Tesseraro. I can disregard her.

We sit on redwood chairs with curved legs and crimson velvet seats and backs, evenly spaced around the table. For a moment I find it hard to concentrate on the three people across from me: every wall of this room holds rows of soft leather books, probably bought by the metre for their patina. The faces blend in.

I force my eyes back to Daniel Metcalf. He has a bearing that betrays his pedigree. His clothes might be casual but he belongs in this house in a way the others do not, a pharaoh flanked by two bumptious high priests. For an instant I try to imagine him somewhere else: a student squat, a hospital, a playground. It's no use. He doesn't belong anywhere but here.

The opulence of the room makes me thirsty. I blink a few times, then catch his eye.

'This could be the Toorak and district public library,' I say. 'Have you read all these books?'

'I get people in to do that. It's a big job best left to professionals. Most of that wall is poetry and it's not going to appreciate itself,' he says. 'They're not damaged, I hope?'

I realise I am fiddling with my glasses, twirling them by one arm. 'They're bulletproof,' I say. I rest them on top of my head then slide them down like I am dropping the visor on a helmet before a joust. 'I should do something about it. Laser surgery or something. Without these I'm blind as a bat.'

At this moment I don't feel like a real scientist. Ruby taught me elegance, and part of every job is to make best use of the assets available. I chose my outfit carefully today: tight khaki trousers,

4

tailored, with a flat front and snakeskin belt. A sleeveless fitted top with a slight khaki shimmer that highlights my green eyes. Open-toed black heels. I am wearing classic styles, solid colours. I straightened the curl from my hair this morning but I ought to have dyed it last night. It is too red for a serious person.

Now I think I might as well have worn a tracksuit and a stained lab coat. Daniel Metcalf does not seem interested. He is sitting back in his chair, still holding his mobile.

Carmichael clears his throat ostentatiously. 'Dr Canfield. Your application. We have some concerns.'

I lean forward. I am alert, alarmed, shocked. My pulse is beginning to race.

'My paperwork,' I say. My eyes dart from Daniel to Carmichael and back again. 'Everything was in order?'

'Yes, yes,' Carmichael says. 'Your academic achievements are exemplary. Your university webpage was very helpful, all those links to your research papers. The media coverage, the awards. And thank you for sending us your thesis.' He rests his hand on a tall pile of paper beside him. 'I confess I haven't finished the entire document, but, ah, very impressive.'

I am beginning to hyperventilate, just a little. I rub my hands together, twisting the fingers, curling and looping. Any moment now they will mention the tiger.

'My referees, then? Did you speak with them? It's hard with the time differences. And they're so busy.'

'No, no problem with your referees. I spoke to them both,' Carmichael says. 'Very distinguished. One so young, and Professor Weldon soon to be announced a Nobel laureate, indeed.'

'A Nobel prize?' I say. 'He didn't mention that to me. He is notoriously modest.'

'I was honoured to speak with him. He was familiar with my

work and said some kind words about a particular theorem of mine. He spoke glowingly of your potential. And your post-doc. Harvard. First rate.' Carmichael plucks the skin of his throat like someone playing a jazz riff on the double bass. 'That's not the problem.'

All the while I am speaking to Carmichael I am watching Daniel from the corner of my eye. He seemed bored before but now he is sitting forward. He is frowning and his hands are on the table in front of him. The corner of his mouth twitches. He stretches one arm over to Carmichael's folder and angles it so he can read my application. He is becoming interested. This is good.

'What exactly is the problem, then?' I say. This is a demand, not a question. I steel myself.

'The project you have submitted for support is not related to your previous work. It's entirely unconnected to your career so far,' Carmichael says.

'The trust encourages that. It says so on the application form.' I rifle through my papers then stab the document with my finger. 'Here. "Researchers should not be discouraged from nominating novel projects in areas that are unlikely to receive funding from their universities or from other sources." Novel projects. That's what it means.'

'I know what it means,' Carmichael says. 'Dr Canfield. Please understand. Twenty-five thousand dollars is a considerable sum.'

Daniel Metcalf has been absorbed in Carmichael's folder, flicking the pages, running his finger down my CV, but now he speaks. 'What the professor means,' he says, 'is that we like to verify the sanity of anyone who applies for money. It's a little quirk we have.'

For a long moment I freeze. I look down at my notes, lift my glasses, pinch the bridge of my nose. I wait, then I make a decision. It is time to go. I gather my folders and papers, then I lift my briefcase up onto the table with a thump. I'm upset. I'm not thinking about scratches on antiques.

6

'Dr Canfield?' Carmichael says.

I stand. 'You're right. It must sound crazy. I'll withdraw the application.' I purse my lips and narrow my eyes. 'Forgive me for wasting your time.'

Daniel frowns and stands as well. He looks a little bemused. 'Please sit, Dr Canfield. Maybe we could waive the sanity rule just this once.'

I glare to show I have nothing more to lose, then shove the papers in my briefcase and fumble with the clasp, which refuses to click. I can't speak. Now the bag won't close because of my haphazard stuffing. I blink faster. Soon it will look as though I am about to cry.

Daniel walks around the table and takes the briefcase from my hands before I throw it out the window. 'Sit down. Sit and tell me what you're thinking. Carla, a glass of water for Dr Canfield.' He places the briefcase next to me and perches on the side of the table.

That's when I look into Daniel Metcalf's eyes with something like a plea. I am deciding whether to push him aside and bolt for the door or do as he says. I sit. I take a deep breath, compose myself. 'I'm twenty-nine years old,' I say. 'I've been an evolutionary biologist since I was twenty-one. Since my post-doc I've done the right kind of research. I've had good jobs and great papers in the right journals. And now...I thought this was my chance. I know this project is unorthodox, but it's been my dream. Since I was a little girl.'

'You honestly want to find a Tasmanian tiger in Wilsons Promontory National Park?' Carmichael's voice is on tiptoes, like he's breaking bad news. 'Dr Canfield, they are extinct. And it's been thousands of years since they lived here in Victoria, even when they weren't extinct. Do you know how many tourists visit that park? Campers and hikers, for weekends and longer? It's teeming with people. And you've wanted this since you were a little girl?'

I don't look at him. He can say what he likes. It's not his money. I keep my eyes on Daniel, who shrugs.

'It's different,' he says. 'Most little girls want a pony.'

The secretary places a coaster on the table in front of me, and a glass of water. I sip it, steady myself. I'm not done yet.

'This wouldn't be the first unorthodox application you've awarded. Your trust is renowned for it, for giving people a chance. There's a science grapevine, you know. We talk.'

Carmichael sniffs. I've said the wrong thing. 'You're mistaken,' he says. 'We are, ah, lateral in our choices, but prudent. This is one of the oldest privately funded trusts in Melbourne. We have a reputation to uphold.'

'What about the year we gave it to that guy who wanted to know if dogs bark in different accents?' Daniel says.

'That was excellent research,' says Carmichael. 'Cutting edge communication theory.'

'And the snowflake guy? Professor Eng?'

Carmichael flutters his eyelids several times, to the rhythm of the *1812 Overture*. 'Completely valid. It was the first proper statistical study of the unproven assumption that snowflakes are unique.'

'And Dr…what was her name? Pace? The one who wanted to select people at random and force them to get divorced.'

'We didn't fund that in the end, if you recall.'

'Didn't we?' Daniel leans back in his chair and folded his arms. 'It seemed like a great idea to me. My married friends are always debating if it's better for the kids if they stay together and fight constantly, or get divorced and fight constantly.'

'She couldn't get ethics committee approval.'

'Shame,' says Daniel.

They've almost forgotten I'm here. Carmichael stacks his papers in a pile, pushes his chair away from the table. But Daniel Metcalf isn't finished. He pulls out the chair next to mine, he sits. He looks right into my eyes as though he was seeing me for the first time. 'Tell me about your project,' he says.

I open my folder and begin to fumble. 'Well. We can ignore the executive summary and skip straight to page four of the application.'

'No,' he says, and he puts his hand flat on the pile of paper. 'Just tell me.'

'Well.' I brace myself. 'Everyone thinks Tasmanian tigers became extinct in the thirties. Yet every year there are reported sightings, some here in Victoria.'

'It's utterly ridiculous. It's impossible there's anything there,' says Carmichael.

'Let her finish, Aldrich,' Daniel says.

'I know it's a long shot,' I say. I reach out and lay my hand on Daniel's knee, an unconscious-type gesture. 'But what about the vu quang ox? It lives on the Vietnam–Laos border. It's an entirely new genus, only found by zoologists in 1992. This is not a small animal. This is a hundred-kilo bovine we didn't know about twenty years ago. And what about the okapi? That's a miniature giraffe not known to science until 1901. Or the Chacoan peccary. That's kind of like a pig, found in Paraguay, but everyone thought it was extinct until 1975. Now we know there's three thousand of them.'

'Three thousand pigs,' says Carmichael.

'It's not just pigs. What about Leadbeater's possum? Considered extinct until 1961. The central rock rat? Went missing for twenty-five years, then just showed up again. The mahogany glider? We thought it was extinct for a hundred years, until a few turned up in 1989. A hundred years. That's seriously missing.'

'You're right.' Daniel shrugs. 'That's not just nipping down the shops for some milk without telling anyone.'

'There are all kinds of animals that have come back from alleged extinction,' I say. 'They're called Lazarus species. It's all here,' I thump the table. 'In my application.'

'My dear Dr Canfield,' Carmichael begins. 'Giraffes, pigs and, er, oxen are irrelevant. No one has seen a live Tasmanian tiger in over seventy years. They no longer exist.'

I look down as if just registering my hand is on Daniel's knee. I yank it away, embarrassed. Now, a sudden and awkward change of subject. 'Professor Carmichael. Have you seen the pyramids?'

'What?'

'Egypt. Big pointy things.'

'I have dedicated my life to science, not aimlessly wandering the globe.'

'So how do you know they exist?'

'That is hardly the same thing.'

'It's precisely the same thing,' I say. 'Do you know the pyramids exist because you've seen them on television? Well, how did people know before then? Maybe you've spoken to people who have seen them. There are dozens of eyewitnesses who've seen a Tasmanian tiger. I've got brief records of interviews, but with the trust's money I could go down there, really take the time to talk to people who've seen it. Maybe the pyramids don't exist either. It could all be one giant conspiracy theory cooked up to sell...pyramid-shaped things.' I take a deep breath, but my conviction fades. 'Like those weird Japanese watermelons.'

'Or Toblerones,' says Daniel Metcalf.

'It's a shame you didn't want the money to research watermelons, Japanese or otherwise,' says Carmichael. 'That would be a stronger case. Value adding in agriculture is a very hot topic. Watermelon cultivation, especially if you focused on reducing water usage, would be a fascinating project. Watermelons could become a leading export crop. A pyramid shape would pack easier. For cheaper transportation.'

'The watermelons aren't important,' I say. 'What's important is this: there are over thirty species of mammal at Wilsons Promontory. It's more than fifty thousand hectares surrounded by thousands more in farmland. We don't know what's there. Behind my application are solid field techniques. I could bundle in some PhD students, do a broad taxonomic survey of the whole area.'

'And what does that mean, precisely? A "broad taxonomic survey",' Daniel Metcalf says. 'Pretend for a moment I know nothing whatsoever about science and that I haven't read your application.'

I think fast. 'It's like a census, but for animals. To find out exactly what's there. We collect bone fragments and spoor. Measure and take casts of scat. That sort of thing.'

'I think I'm beginning to understand,' he says. 'This is fascinating. It definitely beats the snowflake guy.' He stands. He rubs his arms, like he's unused to sitting for such a long time. 'Well, Dr Canfield...what is your first name?' he says.

'Ella,' I say, with just the right pause. Not so quick that it may appear I have something to prove. Not so slow like I couldn't remember.

'Well, Ella. This is easily the most entertaining of these interviews I've attended.' He offers me his hand. 'There might be some additional questions I need to ask. Some points I need to clarify. Can I call you?'

This is, of course, the outcome I wanted and expected. I feel a blush creep up my cheeks. He is a head or so taller than me. With our hands pressed together I can't feel the scar on his palm, but for a moment I imagine it under my fingertips, smooth and raised.

'Of course.' I fish in my pocket for a business card with my other hand. 'My mobile is there. That's the best number. I'm often at the museum or with my students and the university switchboard is hopeless. Half the time they can't find me at all.'

'That would be handy,' he says, still holding my hand, 'if you didn't want to be found.'

'But I do want to be found,' I say.

I walk down the drive of the mansion. It is now late in the afternoon and dark clouds are gathering. The sky gives the grass an iridescent tinge. In the centre of the lawn is a stone fountain spurting water from the mouth of a cupid. It is surrounded by beds of mauve flowers growing in formation. I have driven past often in the weeks leading up to this but now that my task is over I can relax. This house is a two-storey Edwardian island on an expanse of bore-watered green sea. The satellite photo shows a tennis court floating on one side and a classic rectangular pool adrift on the other but I can't see either from here. The tortured limbs of the pear trees poke over the wall. The pears are ornamental. This means they have strong branches, glossy leaves and soft flowers just as a useful tree does, but produce no messy undisciplined fruit. The wall is rendered, at least eight feet tall and it circles the entire compound. For security. There are unscrupulous people out there. You can't be too careful.

On the street I reach the car that I have borrowed for the day. It is especially nondescript, utterly without style. I wait until I am around the corner and out of sight before I take off the glasses. They are not frames I would have chosen for myself: they are not elegant and I don't recognise the name of the designer. I wore them because carrying a prop is one of my father's rules. The heavy frames hold plain glass. My eyesight is perfect.

What I remember of my first time is this: the heat of the footpath and the pain from a small blister under the strap of my pink plastic sandal. I remember being frightened. I'm not sure of the date or the time. It was summer. Perhaps it was late morning. I may have been seven or eight. Ruby drove, but I couldn't see her. She must have been keeping me under surveillance from the cafe across the street. Ruby was always watching, peering through keyholes or around corners or spying across the street with her opera glasses. I loved her opera glasses. I thought them sophisticated, like something Audrey Hepburn would keep in a black silk evening purse. They were burgundy enamel and gold trim with a squat little handle. Ruby kept them close. She knew there was usually something to observe.

I waited around the corner where the end of the arcade met the narrow side street. I sat on a concrete planter filled with dirt and brown scratchy palms and there I swung my legs and waited for a shopping woman to walk by accidentally. It was confusing, the arcade. It was dark inside on the sunniest day; a cave, if caves were lined with Spanish tiles that clicked under ladies' heels. A woman might leave a shop that sold twisted glass sculptures or hand-made hats. She might pause to look in a window with gold lettering on the pane, a shop stocking corsetry or embossed paper, and she might turn left instead of right. It was easy to end up here with me instead of safe in the corridor to the car park.

I knew the words to say, knew how to intersperse them with sobs. I had practised for days with my father and Ruby, over and over. I was excited, had barely slept last night but now that it was time to begin I was shaking. My breakfast lay heavy in my stomach. Maybe I would be sick. What if I forgot everything? What if I let everyone down?

I took a deep breath. Remember the rules. Rule one is easy. Never ask for money.

'The whole world asks for money,' my father would say. I would sit in his study opposite his desk, dark wood with a green leather top, and he'd lean forward and tell me the rules. My father was old, even older than Ruby. His hair was thin and white. He was important, I knew, but was never too busy to answer my questions or tell me stories or let me sit beside him while he worked. Sometimes I would lie on the floor and draw pictures for him, which he would solemnly frame and hang behind his desk.

There in his study we had important conversations and he would never laugh or make me feel like a child, though sometimes he let me sit in his leather chair and he twirled me around until my head spun. Other times he paced around the room, hands clenched behind his back. I swivelled my head to watch him, tall and dapper. He always wore a sports coat and silk cravat. When he was telling me something serious he would tap the desk with his pinkie ring. There was nothing my father didn't know.

I was the youngest. Sam was four years older and already on his way, selling leather jackets out of the back of a van on weekends to marks who didn't mind that the jackets were obviously stolen. They were beautiful jackets, or at least the sample the mark felt and tried on was beautiful. The jacket the mark actually bought was sealed in tough plastic and, when opened at home, was found to be one piece of soft leather wrapped around a bundle of unsewn scraps. Sam, everyone acknowledged, had great potential. He showed the knack even then.

My father had gone through the rules with him years before, and with my cousins. He was the patriarch, and so it was his duty.

My father turned up his nose at shrieking television commercials and door-to-door salesmen. 'Buy this, borrow that. You need this trinket. Interest free. No deposit. People always want to sell you bits of rubbish that do nothing but weigh your life down,' he told me. 'We're not like that. We never ask. The secret to having people give you money is to act as though you don't want it. Make them talk you into it. Hold your head high, Della. We're not beggars.'

It seemed like hours but must have been only minutes before a woman came. She couldn't miss me. My head hung low, face in my hands, red curls over my eyes. I was wearing my favourite dress. I can see it now: blue and purple paisley with straps that tied on my pale shoulders. It was important to look respectable, not scruffy. This was rule number two. Look successful. Worthy of trust. You are not a people apart. It could just as easily be them in your position.

My mark was plumpish, I saw through my fringe. She wore dusty brown shoes with a stocky heel and a plastic buckle. She wore tan slacks and a dull pink cardigan over a floral shirt. She carried shopping bags: one from a linen store, another two from the department store. I couldn't see if she had jewellery. Her handbag was balanced on one shoulder. The zip was a little open at the far end.

She stood in front of me. 'Hello?' she said. 'Are you all right, dear?'

Maybe I couldn't do it. I was too young for this, not ready. My hair was in pigtails, but one was higher than the other and the ribbons didn't match; not the usual way Ruby did my hair, but this was a rule. Carry one prop, or wear one thing, that makes you feel your character, a prompt that you are not your usual self. One visible, obvious thing that reminds you who you are supposed to be.

I shivered a little: a nice touch, but it was easy. Ruby had taken my jumper. It looked better, she said, if I was a little cold. It looked better if I showed off my thin arms.

'Are you lost? Where's your mum?' The woman touched the back of my hand. Her skin was warm and papery.

'Gone away,' I managed, then I sniffed and it all came out in a rush. 'Mum's gone away and Dad said I wasn't supposed to make any noise so he gave me money for the bus and the movies but I've lost it and now I don't know how I'm going to get home. I don't know how I lost it. It was right here and now it's gone.' I turned the pocket of my dress out, feeling the seam as if the money might magically reappear. I kept my head low and raised only my eyes to her. Puppy dog eyes, like I'd been taught. Sam said my eyes gave me an unfair advantage.

She folded her arms. She clucked. I saw the lines on her cheeks, the way her mouth turned down at the edges.

'Disgraceful. Your age. Out in the city on your own.'

I threaded my fingers together. 'I told Daddy I was big enough.

I said I'd be all right. 'Cos Mummy's gone away and Daddy cries all the time and I'm supposed to be quiet.'

She raised her head like I'd struck her. She shifted her weight from one leg to the other, then rubbed her chin with the palm of her hand. 'We need to find a policeman,' she said.

I gave a small start and a cry. No problems faking this.

'No. No, please. I know where the bus leaves from. I can do it, really I can. If I come home with a policeman…I want to be a good girl. I want to show Daddy I'm grown up. I want my mummy.' I put my head in my hands again and gave a sob. I'd gone too far. No one would believe this. I stood. I'd go home, practise harder. Then I heard the sound of the zip opening.

'Here,' she said. 'Here, take it.'

My heart stopped. It was crisp and new and blue. Ten dollars. Much more than a ticket to the movies and bus fare.

'Here,' she said again. She held the note between her fingers, waved it as though fanning a fire.

'It's too much,' I whispered.

That's when she smiled, and touched my shoulder. 'A little extra for a drink at the movies and an ice cream. But you can't talk to strangers. Other than me, just now. In the future, I mean.' And the ten dollar note was stiff between her outstretched fingers, swaying in the air.

I am not a gambler, though some in my family are. I could not live with the thought my fortune depended on the fall of dice or the actions of some unconnected other—a jockey, a dealer of cards. But one thing I do know. To become a gambler, you must have one big win at the beginning. One taste of victory, to spend your life trying to replicate.

Sometimes I wonder what would have happened to me if I had

failed that first time, or even if it had been difficult. If no one had stopped. If that woman had given me nothing or twenty cents or a sharp talking to. My life might have turned out differently. I might have become a vet or an architect or a chef. Instead it does not matter how many marks I have taken or how much money I have made. I have spent the last twenty years in the thrall of that waving note.

Ruby did not believe in the rules the way my father did. She did not lecture me across a handsome desk. She believed in planning and lists and organisation. She was cautious and calm and believed every job should be considered on its own merits and that no rule ever suits all situations. She humoured my father in the way he wanted me trained. After all, I was not her child.

In the Mercedes on the drive back to Cumberland Street, she went over some of the things I'd been taught. She didn't say how well I'd done. She didn't smile. I had met her expectations, that was all. For Ruby, it was all about the lesson.

'So, Della,' she said, when we stopped at the lights. Her pencil skirt was so tight she could barely move her legs to work the brake. She was wearing her driving slippers and her crocodile-skin pumps were beside me on the seat, like a burnished bronze living thing. 'You must remember two things: the woman's face, so you can recognise her if you see her again, and the things you said. Some people sketch the face and write down the conversation, but what's the point of that? If you run into that woman again, odds are you won't have your notebook with you. Commit it to memory. Memory is the most important tool of your trade.'

I folded my arms and stared out the window. I knew this. I didn't need to hear it again, not from Ruby. I had ten dollars, folded and sweaty in my hand. I was sick of lessons, especially the never-ending memory games. We would sit on the leather couch with piles of photos ripped from magazines and newspapers on the coffee table in front of us. Dozens of photos of anyone. I would see each one for only an instant. Then the next day or the day after or days later my father and Uncle Syd would move all the furniture and spread groups of thirty or forty photos over the diningroom floor. I would have to pick the ones I had seen before. I learned to notice the shape of lips, frown marks, lashes; most of all, the curves of the ear. Other days we practised details, like objects in a room, or numbers like bank accounts and safe combinations. Ruby was right when she said that memory is my most important tool. They taught me well. I never forget a face. I never forget anything.

'Della?' Ruby frowned. 'Go over it in your mind and remember it. Now, I said.'

I tightened my lips but still I did as she said and went over the conversation in my mind, each sentence, each gesture. I remembered it all.

'Good. Now don't think about the words. Think about what you felt. What parts of it were true?'

I closed my eyes, ticked off each thought on my fingers. 'That I didn't want her to find a policeman. That I didn't have any money. That ten dollars was too much.'

'Just so,' Ruby said. 'And this is why you were successful. People always think that success in this business is about lying but it's the opposite of that. It's about telling the truth.'

'I told her I miss my mummy. That was the truth.'

Ruby stiffened in her seat as she turned off the main road up over the railway tracks. Her cheeks showed a faint blush under her makeup. The car inhaled, paused for a breath as she pressed the clutch in to change gears.

'Well,' she said. 'That sounds nice and melodramatic Della, but I doubt it. I doubt you can even remember your mother.'

I closed my eyes, tight, then opened them. I swung my legs more violently against the seat. My shoes banged against the glove compartment, leaving little-girl scuff marks on the wood trim. I wanted to throw the ten dollars at her head but couldn't bring myself to open my fingers.

'I didn't like it anyway. I didn't like doing it,' I said. 'It was wrong to take the money off that lady. I'm going to toss it out the window.'

If I had thought for hours I could not have calculated a better way of hurting her. *It was wrong to take the money off that lady*. Now I cannot envisage a time I thought that. It was like being young enough to believe in Santa or sleep with a teddy bear. Now I think of Ruby as a young woman trying her best to love my father and fit into a family and bring up the children of a woman she had never met. Of all the things I said during my childhood, my wilful adolescence, my arrogant teens, this is the one I regret most. This is the one I ought to have swallowed.

People often mistook me for Ruby's daughter, and sometimes for her younger sister. She was slender with a model's bearing, high cheekbones, coiffed hair the same auburn as mine, but sleek instead of my wild curls. She still has it set twice a week at Luigi's, in the High Street, where she makes appointments under another name and always pays cash. She taught me a certain refinement, a sophistication. She knew neither of us should wear pink or navy on account of our hair. Her eyes are a cool brown instead of green like mine.

She never laid a hand on me except that one day. When we pulled up outside Cumberland Street at the end of the long drive, she opened her door quickly and came around to mine. She yanked me out by my arm. Her crimson nails dug into my skin. She left the car door open and dragged me into the house, along the narrow hall, through the sittingroom and the library and into the kitchen. The kitchen is as large as a flat, with pale green-washed panelled cupboards and four sinks made from stone and hooks from the ceiling hung with saucepans and frypans and utensils of all kinds. The pantry, where the trapdoor opens, is the size of my room and filled with glass jars of peaches and pickles, bags of potatoes and bowls of walnuts. Ruby and my Aunt Ava are still compulsive preservers.

She opened the trapdoor by the hidden rope and led me down the stairs to my father's study. She banged on the door with the side of her fist, the rhythmic knock that let him know it was her. The door opened; he'd pushed the button hidden inside the top drawer. He was concentrating. He had his jeweller's loupe wedged to his eye and a velvet bag lying on the desk before him. I remember the bag vividly, the plush burgundy against the green leather of the desktop, its pile brushed in a sweep by his fingers.

'Lawrence,' Ruby said.

He looked up from his desk. My father was also an observer: he must have noticed the way she said his name, the look in her eye, the way she gripped my arm. The loupe fell. He caught it before it hit the desk.

'Well,' he said. 'My little girl is back. How did it go?'

She spun me in front of his desk and folded her arms. 'Tell him. Tell him what you said to me in the car.'

He raised one eyebrow, laced his fingers. I could see his pinkie ring gleaming in the lamplight.

'I just thought that maybe it wasn't right, taking money from that lady,' I said, after a time. I spoke to the carpet. I could not lift my eyes from my shoes. 'I thought maybe I shouldn't have done it.'

He stared at me for a moment, and his face turned grey. He wiped his brow with the handkerchief from his top pocket and I knew this was to stall before he spoke, that he was waiting until he was composed. When he was ready, his voice was soft. 'Come here Della,' he said.

I wished I could melt down into the rug but instead I walked around the desk and stood in front of him. He had never punished me before, not properly, not once. One of my paintings was framed behind his desk: a gentle meadow with yellow sunbeams raining from clouds. I remembered the day I drew it, how happy I had been to give it to him.

He pulled me into his arms and sat me on his knee, then he opened my fist to find the ten dollar note, folded now, hidden. He sighed as though he was wounded. The shame that I had said this to him was such a weight on my shoulders I felt I could barely raise my arms. All I wanted was to say sorry and take it back, take it all back.

'I can see you did very well, Della. But I think you forgot rule number four,' he said finally. He bit his bottom lip, then he said, 'What is rule number four?'

'To watch, until the mark is out of sight,' I said. 'To never look at the money until you can't see the mark anymore.'

'That's right,' he said. 'You didn't, did you Della? You didn't watch her walk away.'

Sometimes you think a job is over, but it's not over. I'd been told this. But that day it was true. I hadn't been able to take my eyes off my ten dollars. I've never made that mistake again.

I shook my head. My father raised his eyebrows at Ruby.

'I watched her,' Ruby said. 'Five-eight or five-nine. Early forties. Medium build. Light brown hair with grey roots, short, wavy. Just over twelve stone. Bad varicose veins on her calves. I watched her walk to the end of the street and turn the corner. She walked tall. She was proud.'

My father straightened my skirt, and bent a little to pull up my white socks. 'Della, listen to me very carefully. There are two types of people who give us money. The first type are greedy people. They think they can get something for nothing, or profit from other people's misfortune. They are opportunists. Look. See these stones?'

As he spoke he lifted with one hand the burgundy bag and five rectangular emeralds skidded on to the desk. They were twinkling, beckoning things of beauty. I had to restrain my fingers from touching them. My father picked one up between his fingers and turned it so it caught the light.

'Greedy people will buy these stones because they think they are real. They will rush to give me four or five or ten thousand dollars, write out their cheques or count out their cash and shove it into my hand. I won't be able to dissuade them, though I will show suitable reluctance to take their money. They will buy them because they think they are worth many times that. They think they are stolen gems, smuggled from a country at war with itself, where people slave and die to find them. Sometimes even children have to dig in deep holes to find these jewels. Do you think it's fair, that children have to do that?'

'No,' I said. No, it was not fair. Every child should have a room like mine and a father like mine and not have to dig in a hole. I was the lucky one.

'And by the time these buyers realise the stones are not real, if they ever do realise it, the cheques are cashed and the account is empty and untraceable and I have vanished. They won't go to the police, either because they are too embarrassed or because they would have to admit they were trying to commit a crime. Now, don't people like that deserve to be punished?'

I nodded. Of course. Of course they did.

'The second type of people who give us money might be rich, or they might not be. They can be old or young, or honest or not. But they have one thing in common. They need to feel better about themselves. That woman walked down the street with her head held high after she gave you that money. She would have felt better about herself as a mother, because *she* would never leave her children alone in the city. She would have told the story of how she met you to all her friends, who would have praised her generosity. Ten dollars is a small price to pay to awaken that woman's compassion, Della. You gave her a gift. Never forget that.'

I looked up at my father's wise eyes, then down at the note folded in my palm. I placed it carefully on the desk next to the stone.

'You can have it,' I said. 'It can go in the kitty, with everyone else's.'

'Of course it'll go in the kitty,' said Ruby, and she walked around the desk with her hand outstretched.

My father shut his eyes for a moment, and pursed his lips. While Ruby waited he opened the bag to return the emeralds then picked up the note, spread open my fingers and placed it back in my hand. He curled my fingers into a fist around it.

'This one time you may keep it. Buy something that you fall in love with, Della. We define ourselves by possessing things of beauty. But I want you to think carefully about this. Remember, who makes the laws of this society?'

'The rich and the heartless,' I said.

'And why do they make these laws?'

'To protect their own privilege, which is the result of the luck of their birth and generations of oppression of the weak.'

'And what do we think about these laws?'

'We reject them,' I said. 'Utterly.'

He stood then, and set me on my feet, and walked over to Ruby and squeezed her empty hand. 'You did well today Della. No lessons this afternoon.'

Ruby opened her mouth to object and I ran in case he changed his mind, as fast as I was able back up the stairs to the kitchen. It was late afternoon now but I did not stop for a biscuit. I ran down the hall to the front of the house and up the grand staircase all the way to my attic bedroom. I did not look back although I could picture Ruby standing there, one hand on her hips, watching, thinking my father was too easy on me. All at once I was exhausted. In my room I lay on the bed, I curled into a ball. I fell asleep almost instantly.

The next day Ruby drove me to my father's friend Felix's house. In Felix's backyard was a long corrugated iron shed with rows and rows of trestle tables spread with piles of things: televisions, jewellery, toys. Not secondhand rubbish taken by drug addicts when people are at work. New. Still in boxes from broken shipping containers or backs of trucks or department stores.

While Felix and Ruby chatted and sipped tea, I walked the aisles with Timothy, Felix's son, who was Sam's age and who stayed half a step behind me, hands folded behind his back. He wore a child-sized apron, the pocket filled with pens, and he nodded at my choices like a miniature shopkeeper. I picked up this and touched that, thinking how best to spend my ten dollars, wondering which thing of beauty would define me. I came home with colouring books of fairy-tale princesses and a purple tin of imported chocolates, each one individually wrapped in foil the colour of emeralds.

We are all in the diningroom at our home on Cumberland Street, at our usual Thursday night family meeting where everyone takes turns discussing the work they are doing and the tasks they need the rest of us to do. My father sits at the head of a table not dissimilar to the one in the Metcalf mansion, but Cumberland Street is not aloof or pretentious. Our house is one of us, part of our family. It has been our home since before any of us can remember, although it is old now and has seen better days. The grounds were once a smallish apple orchard with privacy and space but the trees are uncared for and litter the ground with their fruit, wizened and sharp-sour. None of us is a farmer.

How Cumberland Street came to belong to us is a story my father is fond of telling. Over one hundred years ago, there was an ancient forefather who was a canny speculator. Through his friendship with a member of parliament, he knew in advance the direction a new rail line would take south toward the bay, and he showed remarkable foresight in buying up all the land along the proposed line. When the information was finally released to the public, he sold the land for a fabulous sum. It was an ingenious scheme and his only expense was a generous gift to his good friend the politician.

With the profits he bought Cumberland Street. A house this size would be impossible to find now but in those days homes were built for large families and servants and weekend parties. The land alone would be worth a fortune. But it is ours, free and clear, and we will never let it go.

There are no farms around here anymore. The outskirts of town have reached us. Neighbours encroach. Every few weeks a leaflet appears in the letterbox from a local real estate agent asking if my father wants to sell. He snorts and throws the leaflet in the bin.

Cumberland Street is large enough to be a private hotel or small hospital. It has a dumbwaiter, open fires and a warren of rooms painted different colours and wallpapered with stripes and spots and florals. The carpets don't match and the tiles are from other countries, from far away. Halls go nowhere, doors open upon themselves. It is a maze of extensions from different eras, the results of windfall jobs over decades. There are at least a dozen bedrooms in the main house and a number of liveable sheds under the apple trees where things can be hidden. There are cellars and shelters that only we can find, with doors buried flush to the ground under drifts of leaves. For us as children it was the most magical place to play, a land of hiding places and secret nooks.

Here in the diningroom is where we eat and work, although my father still has his study hidden under the trapdoor in the kitchen. On the sideboard are the dirty dishes piled from dinner. In one corner is the old blackboard we have always used for planning. My father won't be convinced to use a new-fangled whiteboard. Paper is, of course, out of the question. On a small side table is my father's ivory chess set. This is how he teaches us the importance of strategy. We all learned to play like demons when we were very young.

'For the love of God, Dad,' I say. 'A Nobel prize?'

My father is like a football coach, all diagrams and plans and assigning roles. He has chalk in one hand and the other dances across the buttons of his old-fashioned adding machine, the kind that feeds a trail of paper all over the table. He chuckles and twirls his pinkie ring. All the men in our family wear pinkie rings, genuine stones, as expensive as they can manage. It is an old grifters' tradition so that, if the worst happens, family and friends are never burdened with the cost of a funeral.

'I didn't say I *had* a Nobel prize, Della. That would be foolish. I just hinted to your professor of an announcement that might possibly be expected in the next few weeks. I told him in the spirit of collegiate solidarity, in the strictest confidence.'

'He'll blab it all over town.'

'No doubt, seeing as he swore on his mother's grave he wouldn't tell a living soul. It's no matter. Your professor will tell the story with such conviction that not one in a hundred people will pipe up and admit they've never heard of me, or rather, the name you chose for me. The rest will just nod because they don't want to be thought fools. Besides, you'll have the money by then. No one will care.' He pats my hand. 'Small fibs are no good Della. People see through small fibs in no time. Stun them into submission. Lie only if you must, but if you must, make it a colossus.'

This from the wisest man I know, the man who taught me to be cautious. Ten, even five years ago he would not have taken such a risk. He would have considered the consequences: that Carmichael would know the Nobel committee never inform candidates in advance, or that someone else was likely to win, or that the announcement itself was months away. It would take only two or three phone calls to unwind our story. It will be all right of course, but it is only my father, with his skill, his experience, who could get away with this. I worry about the bad example he is setting for my cousins.

'I've been in this business since before you were born.' He winks as though that will appease me. 'There're surprises in your old man yet. But the interview: how did it go?'

'Good. Fine. Metcalf asked a question that surprised me. Wanted to know what a broad taxonomic survey is and I wasn't expecting anything technical. I'd only done a few hours of research, on the net. I winged it.'

'Interesting. It's a rare millionaire who will reveal his ignorance on any topic. Well, I'm sure your answer sounded sufficiently scientific, which is all that matters. Jargon intimidates everybody. More importantly,' he says, 'is our wealthy young man interested in you?'

'Yes and no,' I say. 'The beginning went well. Meaningful eye contact. Then he seemed to pull back during the interview and took a while to re-engage. No lifted shoulders or open palms, not that I could see; but I did get a long handshake at the end. And he asked for my number.'

My father smiles. 'All right then.'

I learned long ago that my family was not like other people's. We all live together, for a start, here in the house in Cumberland Street. We always have and we always will. All around us in the dining-room are reminders of our work and our legacy. One wall is covered in framed photos of my father, smiling, arm in arm with the wealthy and famous: long-dead politicians, movie stars, captains of industry.

Ruby sits on my father's left. She is in her fifties now but still embodies elegance, right down to the scarlet polish on her fingernails. There is the air of a retired ballet dancer in the way she sits, in the swan line of her neck. She makes notes on a pad in front of her, small ticks like our unofficial secretary.

My Aunt Ava and Uncle Syd sit next to me. Syd looks like a younger version of my father but without his dapper charm; instead Syd is earthy, stocky. He always wears a waistcoat, winter or summer. When not working or helping around the house he tends the orchids that are taking over the conservatory on the western side of the house, cajoling their twisted dry stems to produce lyrical flowers. My Aunt Ava is crumpled and small with worry lines on her face that belie her mischievous nature. Many marks have been fooled by her kindly little old lady persona.

My brother Sam is at the foot of the table, opposite my father. His hair is not as red as mine, more a dark blond, and he's wearing jeans so creased he might have just crawled out of bed. His hair is messy to match his clothes. Sam looks relaxed, as though he's daydreaming, but I know underneath he is sharp as a blade, focused on our work, thinking of our future. One day all of us, and this house, will be his responsibility but for now he dresses like a hobo, rebellion forcing its way to the surface like an underground stream.

On the other side of the table, next to Ruby, my four cousins sit together. They are Aunt Ava's and Uncle Syd's children. First there is Beau, the youngest, crossing and uncrossing his legs, wriggling in his seat. It is hard for him to sit still for any length of time but he forces himself to concentrate the way he forces himself to read the great stacks of self-help books that tower beside his bed. My cousin Beau is only interested in small stings. This is a mistake, we always tell him. It is just as difficult to convince a mark to part with a small sum as a large one; sometimes more so. The only benefit to these baby pickings is that they are safer. With police resources stretched and the community outraged by violent crime, Beau's stings are unlikely to be investigated even if he is discovered.

Next to him is Greta. She is doodling on a pad. She is bored, I can tell. We have not spoken about her at all tonight. She is going out after the meeting, and her skirt is slightly shorter than I would wear, her cleavage just a little lower.

Then there is her twin, Anders, who has come straight from the gym in T-shirt and sweats. Even in these baggy clothes the curves of his muscles are visible: the rounded forearms that rest on the table, the line from his shoulders to the base of his skull. He is smart, but in our line of work his strength often comes in handy.

Finally there is Julius, in his grey, fine wool suit and open-necked white shirt. The shirt is stark against his skin because it is black, instead of pale like ours. Julius has been my closest ally, as usual, and success in this job is shared equally by him. When I say Daniel Metcalf asked for my number, Julius gives me a grin and a wink.

The chair on my father's right is still empty. This was my mother's chair.

It is rare for us all to be together around the dining table like this; our work necessitates much travel, domestic and international. This is more difficult now than when my father and mother were young and passports easy to obtain, identity checks less thorough. My father had the foresight to set up many names for the six of us when we were babies, so our identities rotate between the names he chose then. New identities can still be created. We have done it in special circumstances, but it is expensive and we are forced to deal with traders in forged documents, an evil we try to avoid. My father abhors these people the way he does drug dealers. He would disown any of us, I'm sure, if we became drug dealers.

'They think they're the cat's pyjamas,' he sometimes says, pursing his lips. 'These glorified shopkeepers, with their scales and their little baggies. "Can I gift wrap that for you, sir?" "Would you like a pint of milk with that?" Where's the finesse? The creativity?'

'Metcalf won't stand a chance,' Julius is saying.

'Anyway, it doesn't matter if he is interested or not,' I say. 'This is a good sting. He'd fall for it if I looked like a troll.'

Anders tenses his square jaw but says nothing. Quite a few wealthy older women around the city have invested in his landscaping business. Sam once joked that if Anders added up every twenty per cent share he had sold, it would come to about ten thousand per cent. Greta smirks and admires her new bracelet, twists it in the light to watch it gleam. She is the beauty of the family. She has long golden hair and a movie-star smile which she deploys strategically every few months selling time-share units on the Gold Coast.

'Don't play it too cool,' she says.

'I can understand that Della doesn't want to play up to Metcalf,' Sam says. 'She's already got a boyfriend.'

'Sam,' I say. 'What is that lump on your neck? An extraordinarily large pimple?'

'Methinks she complainth a lot, or whatever,' he says.

'I hope you're not losing your nerve Della,' my father says. 'Now that you're in a relationship.'

'Timothy is not a relationship,' I say.

'He's a good catch, Tim is,' says Greta.

'You shouldn't pander to any irrational jealousy on Timothy's part,' my father says. 'Flirting is part of the job description. If you were born with the voice of Melba you'd be singing in Carnegie Hall by now. There's no shame in making the most of your gifts, but they're only the bait. You still need a hook, line and sinker.'

'They could have the reception here, couldn't they Dad?' says Sam.

'Samson,' says Ruby.

'Ah, well. He has to ask her first, you know. Properly. Then nothing will be too good for my little girl.'

'Sam,' I say. 'Shut it.'

'Laurence,' says Ruby. 'The job at hand.'

'Yes, yes.' My father frowns, and limps over to the blackboard, where the top line reads: Metcalf Trust. He adjusts the total hours of work that we have done for this job, adds up my time at the interview today. On the other half of the blackboard is a figure in a circle. The projected return.

'It's not a lot of money, but it hasn't been a lot of work.' He tosses the chalk in the air and catches it, then he turns back to the board and calculates as he speaks, adding lines and multiplying by our daily and hourly rates, adding expenses. 'Julius. Your times?'

Julius flips open his small black notebook. 'Two days for the grant application, a day and a half on Della's webpage, half a day on the PhD. Just under four total.'

'Good job, Julius,' my father says. 'It's a nice little return. Good job, Della.'

'My bit's easy,' says Julius. 'Sitting in front of the screen, feet up, eating Cheezels. Playing computer games between attacks of technological genius.'

My father assigns the roles. It is usual for the person who first had the idea to be the mechanic, as I am in the Metcalf job. I am the one who must drive it, who must actually perform the sting. The other roles will vary depending on the job, but often we have a wall man for lookout and perhaps a chiller, to calm things down if they get overheated and to help the mechanic escape. On this job, Julius was in support. I could not have done it without him.

'Maybe Della'll buy Timmy an engagement ring with her share,' says Sam.

'Maybe you could rent a girlfriend with your share,' I say.

'You do make a very handsome couple,' my father says. 'I know Timothy's parents are very fond of you, Della.'

'I thought we had a rule,' says Ruby. 'No congratulations until the cheque is cashed.'

'And me, Della?' says Beau. 'How did I go? What did he say about me?'

Beau was my other referee, the one that wasn't the Nobel laureate. 'He said you were young. That's all.'

'Too young? Did he think I wasn't convincing?'

I sigh. 'He's hardly going to say that, is he? You were fine, just fine.'

'Can we return to the job at hand?' says Ruby. 'Does anything still need to be done?' She twirls her pen around her thumb.

This job began on a rainy night almost two years ago. Julius had just received a bank deposit for his biggest job yet, which involved an oil company keen to avoid publicity about a spill near a remote colony of endangered birds. There had been no spill near the rare bird colony, of course, but the site was difficult to reach and the company knew itself well enough to think the story was likely, and besides, in circumstances like this it's imperative that the company does not visit the sites. If there were travel records to show they had inspected the leak, their plausible deniability was shot.

So they did not question Julius's cover: a corrupt wildlife worker, or his Photoshopped evidence and fake WWF press releases. They just arranged the transfer of funds from their standard blackmail account. Julius promised the company reps the problem would go away if they paid him. It did. Julius gave a generous gratitude payment to the executive who approved the fee, but this was merely insurance. Large companies are usually safe to sting. They are unlikely to beef because the staff aren't harmed individually, and the damage to their share price if the truth came out would be a greater loss than the money that had been scammed. To the oil company, it was money well spent.

This was not really new, but a modern spin on a charity scam my father might have run in his teens or twenties: a team of earnest youngsters knocking on doors, holding collecting buckets for some widows' home or an orphans' trip to the seaside. My father and his colleagues would have carried an oversized money thermometer with them from town to town. They would have tacked it to the wall of a public building in the town square and watched their money rise.

These days we have no giant thermometers but Julius has watched his takings rise just the same. He now makes more than my father and almost as much as Sam. Because we all grew up together my four cousins are like siblings to Sam and me but I am closest to Julius, who is only a few months my senior.

I was just learning to crawl when Uncle Syd and Aunt Ava first brought him home from Nigeria. Julius's father had been a business associate whose success was too conspicuous and who had not paid the right money to the right people. He feared for his family. Julius, wrapped in a red cotton sack with only his false adoption papers and passport, was presented to my aunt and uncle just as they were leaving Lagos to come home and, despite their three children already waiting back in Australia, Ava could not resist him.

Now it seems like he has always been here. Skinny and quiet at first, he is now the star among us, the one I know will succeed with his technology when the face-to-face stings of the rest of us are dead like dodos.

We all went out to celebrate on the night Julius received the oil company payment. A new place: we never go to the same bar twice, and we travel a long way from home. As we toasted Julius and the rare birds, in the booth behind us was a drunk man of about fifty with his arm around a much-younger, giggling girl. The man was balding, with a shiny patch near the top of his brow where a skin cancer had been removed by laser. He was buying expensive champagne and making sure the whole bar knew. I know now it was Dr Eng, the snowflake researcher, with one of his assistants. It's not just me: we all eavesdrop, the whole family. It's amazing what you hear. Stock tips, horse tips, juicy bits of gossip that come in handy. I leaned my head back against the booth.

What a rort. So rich they don't even care where the money goes…the administrator is rubbish…no procedures. Just a tiny notice in a few journals that no one reads…hardly any applications…no progress reports or reconciliations. Then he said, *Metcalf.*

Metcalf is a famous name in this city. Straight away I became interested. Unlike my cousins, I am more at home in high-society stings. I can and do play almost any role, but times like that in the Metcalf mansion seem the closest I can manage to being myself. Perhaps it is Ruby's influence, the way I find myself drawn to the beautiful things of life. Expensive things. Whatever the cause of this feeling, I know the one defence we have against the sordidness of life, the dirt, the base animal nature of humankind, is beauty.

The next day I walked down to a distant corner of our property, where my father kept his filing system in a shed that had been used for packing apples since the last century. The shed still has a clean smell that seeps from the old wood. The musty paper has not taken over yet. My father has files on hundreds of the world's wealthiest families and individuals and companies. These days my Aunt Ava is responsible but when we were children it was our job to update them, liberate old *Newsweeks* and *Financial Reviews* from cafes and dentists' surgeries using sad smiles and stories of late assignments, then cut out anything on everyone who was anyone. It was our favourite job, this cutting and filing, the way other children make scrap books of pop singers and soap stars.

Yet the filing system was also my greatest worry when I was a child. It seemed so incriminating. It kept me up nights. When I couldn't sleep I would creep down to the shed at first light to test the lock, check the windows. Once, in a blind moment of fear after waking from a nightmare, I took matches from the kitchen and sat shivering for an hour in the half-light next to a pile of apple leaves I'd heaped against the side wall of the shed. I wanted to dispose of this evidence forever but I couldn't bring myself to do it. When I told my father, he only laughed. 'Circumstantial, my dear', he said. 'People collect the strangest things. Teddy bears and teaspoons and cola cans. Would never stand up in a court of law'.

The day after I overheard Dr Eng, I found the hanging file labelled Metcalf. It was bulging with the history of the mining company and the family. Arnold and Frances Metcalf, both deceased in a car accident on the way to a skiing holiday. Two of their three children had fat files: business and fashion magazine articles and interviews on Celeste's move to Sydney and the international success of her swimwear company; women's and gossip magazine stories and photo spreads on Gabrielle's marriage to a media heir and her three adorable children.

At the back of the file was one slim folder on Daniel, the baby of the family. It held nothing but torn sheets of social pages, Daniel with his arm around one pretty girl after another. At first glance he is not quite handsome. His nose is too big and bends to one side like it's been broken. His eyes are too deep set and his jaw is too prominent. I have met many men like him in the course of my work, wealthy and idle, and at heart they are all the same. The folder contained only one page of words, ripped from a weekend newspaper. It was one of those 'Sixty seconds with...' pieces, the kind that became popular when editors realised they could fill a page by printing verbatim answers received by email instead of despatching a journalist to spend an entire day interviewing a subject.

There was no clue as to why this piece was written. Daniel had no book coming out, no show that needed tickets sold. Among the lame questions, like 'My best trait is...' and 'I am happiest when...', and the witty replies was one that caught my eye. 'The strangest thing that has ever happened to me was...'

Daniel's answer was: 'The time I saw a Tasmanian tiger in Wilsons Promontory National Park when I was eight years old.'

That was just the beginning. It took some time, still, for the two ideas to gel in my mind. To find the details of the trust by looking through the university archive, to speak to past winners and entice them to say more than they should. To devise an application he would find impossible to resist. At the beginning I thought it impossible. Ridiculous. Then slowly I became intrigued, and that's always a good sign. If I can intrigue myself, it's also possible to intrigue a mark.

Tasmanian tigers are remnants of a bygone age. They were marsupials: related to kangaroos and koalas rather than tabby cats, although they did have stripes on their lower back, hind legs and tail, and they did hunt smaller, weaker animals. And, as every Australian school child knows, in 1936 the Tasmanian tiger went the way of the passenger pigeon and the dodo. There is a grainy black and white film of the last of them in Hobart zoo, pacing in her small wire enclosure as if she knows the end is near. The film was taken in 1933 and in 1936 she died and that was that. Her species had been hunted to extinction and her home destroyed. The Tasmanian government had, at one time, paid £1 for each head brought in.

In a stunning example of efficiency, the government declared the tiger a protected species a full fifty-nine days before the last one died in captivity, of neglect. Her full name was Thylacine, or *Thylacinus cynocephalus*. Although she lived in Tasmania until the 1930s, she had been extinct in the rest of the country for perhaps two thousand years.

At the beginning of my planning I almost gave up on the idea. I thought it was impossible that anyone would believe something so ridiculous. Then I remembered my father's favourite quote, from H. L. Mencken. 'The men the American public admire most extravagantly are the most daring liars; the men they detest most violently are those who try to tell them the truth.'

I've always suspected that Mencken was sad about this, but my father certainly wasn't. He taught me that this applies not just to Americans but to us too, and to people everywhere. It is ridiculous to claim that this animal may be alive, I thought, but I will dare.

There will be no ceremony for the awarding of the cheque. It will be handed over in a plain envelope by Carmichael alone in the room where I sat today. My bank account, in the name of a two-dollar company called the Victorian Tasmanian Tiger Research Trust, is ready. By this time on Monday I will have deposited the money. By Friday next week I will have withdrawn it and closed the account. It will be like Dr Ella Canfield never existed. I will never see Daniel Metcalf again.

The Metcalf job is the last on the agenda for discussion tonight. We have already talked over an upcoming job of Beau's involving fictitious invoices for internet advertising to be sent to large disorganised companies, and briefly, a job of my father's. This one took little planning: it is one more in the series of counterfeit emerald scams that he has run since he was a young man. This time he is selling a pair of antique earrings that are, I imagine, exquisite green tourmaline or cubic zirconia. The jewels themselves have not arrived yet but my father has a glossy photo of them, and an unscrupulous purchaser already lined up. I have never asked him where the stones come from and he would not tell me if I did. *Need to know basis*, he would say. He might wink. *Can't have my little girl in the firing line if it all goes pear-shaped*.

After my father and Ruby and Aunt Ava and Uncle Syd retire, the six of us kids sit for a while in the drawingroom among the gilded mirrors and the ancient rugs of animal skins. These old chairs are not comfortable so Sam is lying lengthways on the couch, smoking a cigar. He dislodges the antimacassars with his feet and they crumple on the floor. Greta and Beau sprawl in front of the fire. Anders and Julius each have a tub Chesterfield, and I lie on the daybed and we sip balloon glasses of my father's cognac and talk of stings past and future and of the glory days of our childhood, those times when my father and Ruby and Ava and Syd would come home in the old Mercedes all glamour and furs and throw cash in the air for us children to collect like leaves.

Or the nights we would pile in the cars and drive to the city, to the restaurant of a friend of Uncle Syd's, and we would take a private diningroom at the back and eat oysters and lobster, even the littlest of us, and wear bibs and wipe our mouths on them and our parents would let us drink lemonade out of champagne glasses so we could toast their success.

As the night becomes colder Julius feeds the fire with dried apple wood. Now we are reminiscing about the wonderful times we had on holidays when we were children. One, my favourite, was a driving holiday along the coast with just my father and Ruby and Sam and me. We were free and the days were warm and long and my father would let us kids pick the next day's destination from a map he kept folded in the glove compartment. We spent our days picnicking from a huge wicker basket or fishing or listening to my father's stories about our family's heritage or walking along the beach. At night we slept under the stars.

Tonight we have stayed up too late with all these memories, and on the way up the stairs to our bedrooms we tiptoe drunkenly and whisper so as not to wake our sleeping parents. On the landing, Sam puts his hand on my shoulder.

'It's a nice little return, your scientist caper,' he says. 'Good job, Della.'

I watch Sam tumble into his room and sag on the unmade bed without closing the door or taking off his shoes, then I turn to go up another flight to my attic bedroom. The window looks west towards the city; I stand under the tilt of the roof and rest the crown of my head on the low ceiling. I close my eyes.

These are my father's words, I know. It is precisely what he said earlier tonight. For the last few years it seems that all my jobs have been small ones. Safe. Modest. I have not celebrated with champagne or lobster, not for many months. There was no needle in Sam's voice yet still I feel it. Good job, Della, on your nice little return.

In the morning I sleep in, my head fuzzy from the cognac and the late night. On waking my hair is curly and even redder. No one in my father's family has hair like this. It must come from my mother's side; it takes the serious business of the day to straighten it and calm the colour. I have missed breakfast. By the time I hobble to the kitchen, still in my dressing gown and slippers, the kippers are long finished and the eggs are poached and eaten and everything is cleared away. On the stove there is a small pot of porridge wrapped in a tea-towel. This I know is meant for me.

I have just picked up my spoon when a head peeks around the corner: wide white smile, soft blond fringe. Even from here I can see his dimple. His expression is a fraction too cheery for this time of the morning.

'Good morning princess,' he says.

I take a deep breath. 'Timothy. What a surprise.'

He frowns. 'Really? I've been looking for you. I've dropped around several times, left messages with the cousins.'

'You're right. It's not really a surprise.'

'Are you busy? Because I've been wanting to talk to you.' Timothy pulls out a chair and sits beside me at the long pine table. He is dressed for work: short-sleeved, crisp ironed shirt, the top pocket filled with pens, navy trousers. His BlackBerry in a holster on his belt. He is bright-eyed, bushy-tailed. I am bushy-eyed and bright-nothinged. His face is solemn; his fingers drum the table. 'It's important,' he says.

I lean across the table, rearrange the bowl and the salt and pepper grinders. I take the napkin off my lap and fold it carefully.

'Porridge? It's still warm. I can sprinkle some brown sugar on top.'

'No thank you, Del. No porridge.' He fumbles on the table top towards my hand.

'Then how about some tea?' I jump to my feet, chair grating on the tiles, and pull my dressing gown tighter around me. 'Ruby would never forgive me if I had a guest and didn't offer them any tea. Or juice? There's probably fresh juice left over from breakfast. You've been up for hours I bet. You must be ready for a break.'

For a moment his eyebrows go up, but then he shakes his head. 'No thanks. No juice. I just want to talk to you.'

I open the fridge door and pull out a flat white plate. 'Ooh, look. There's pancakes.'

'No, no, I don't want anything. I've already eaten breakfast, hours ago. Deliveries come early, you know, it's not office hours, my line of work. Wait, pancakes? What kind?'

I poke them through the plastic wrap. 'Blueberry.'

He nods, and I busy myself heating some butter in a cast iron pan, chatting aimlessly about whatever comes into my head: the last of the summer blueberries, sealed in glass jars in the pantry; my Aunt Ava, who seems to survive only on desserts and claims not to have eaten anything green since 1979; whether home-made butter tastes better than store-bought. He wants to talk to me. I've suspected this for some weeks now, ever since I woke up early one morning in his bed in the bungalow at the back of his parents' house to find him staring down at me, gooey eyed. I am just setting down the plate of pancakes when he takes my arm and guides me into a chair.

'Della,' he says, and I hold my breath but he gestures across the room. 'That old fridge. It's on its last legs. Let me get you a nice new one. Double-doored. Titanium. Ice dispenser. Still in the carton. Make life much easier for your father at cocktail time.'

I exhale. 'That's it? That's what you wanted to talk to me about?'

'Ah, no.'

'Timothy.' I rub my fist against my temple, then pick up the tea towel and bustle around with dishes in the sink. I don't look at him when I speak. 'We have a good arrangement. We've had a good arrangement for a while now. Fun. No strings. Don't spoil it.'

'I'm not trying to spoil it,' he says. 'I'm trying to make it better.'

He stands, but just then my mobile phone sounds from the

pocket of my dressing gown. I mutter an apology, move back toward the sink. Before I answer, I know it's Daniel Metcalf.

It is fatal to sleep with a mark. Despite his intimations and teasing, my father knows that this is perhaps the only unbreakable rule. In our business, it's true, a certain element of the lure is essential. A heightening of tension. Some might call this a seduction but it is not. It is many things: the building of a connection between a man and a woman that forms the basis of trust; the exchange of money for intimacy, which is worth more and is rarer; and the sleight of hand that shifts the mark's focus from the mechanics of money to the hint of promise.

But to sleep with a man and vanish with his pride as well as his money is the surest path to disaster. I must live somewhere. I cannot entirely disappear, and there is the family to consider. The mark must not feel so bereft that he wants to destroy me, not so burned or so proprietorial that he will spend his (usually ample) resources on tracking me down. That line cannot be crossed.

Meeting men is not easy in my line of work. There's an entire conversation to be had when you meet someone new, about who you are and what you do. I could lie, of course. But then it would all become rather like work.

Timothy is trustworthy. He is from a reliable family, the son of my father's friend Felix the Fence. He is attractive in a boyish, earnest sort of way. We often played together as children, not usually at his house with deliveries and pallet jacks and customers coming and going but here, around the apple trees with Sam and the cousins. Our arrangement has been good for both of us, but I have an idea it is coming to an end.

'I hope I haven't caught you in the middle of chasing some wild animal,' Daniel says.

I picture him cradling the phone in his hand, the shiny metal lined up along the white scar on his palm.

Timothy is alert now, swivelled around, leaning on the back of the chair with his chin resting in his hands. 'Daniel?' he mouths. 'Who's Daniel?'

I look at Timothy, the frown between his eyebrows, dumpling cheeks squeezing his eyes almost closed. I jerk my head towards the kitchen door and turn away as best I can. 'Actually I'm at home, catching up on some dull paperwork without any student interruptions.'

The next thing I know Timothy is standing beside me; he is pretending to rinse his hands in the sink but his head is on an angle, his ear close to the phone. For a moment I tell myself that I care for him very much as a life-long friend, that he feels anxious and awkward and that I must be gentle. In fact I'd like to stick his eavesdropping head under the tap. I move to the other side of the kitchen and turn my back.

'Perhaps I can distract you,' Daniel says. 'Ella, look. I've been thinking about your tiger. Perhaps insanity is contagious. Let's sit down, have a coffee. Discuss it.'

Discuss it. This is not good. I've spoken to the other successful applicants; it does not work this way. This is a delaying tactic. By the next day or two I should have the cheque, feel it in my hand.

'Daniel, look.' I sigh, more resignation than despair. *Ella look*, he says, so *Daniel look*, I say. Mirroring his words from my mouth is an age-old trick to build rapport, used by everyone from desperate car salesmen to gold-medallioned Lotharios. Age-old, clichéd, yet it works. 'I've been trying to get someone interested in this idea for years. I've missed out on more grants than you'd believe. I know there are a lot of worthy projects around. If this is your way of saying you've awarded it to somebody else, just tell me. I'm a big girl.'

I feel two fingers coaxing their way along my spine, sliding down the silk of my night gown. Timothy's arm slides around my waist and I can feel his mouth on my other ear. I fight the urge to shake my arm like a fly has alighted on it, and cup my hand around the phone. I try to concentrate.

'I'm sure you are,' Daniel says. 'It's not that at all. In fact I've been thinking over the terms of the trust. I've been busy lately, with stuff of my own. I've been neglectful. I didn't realise that this is the thirtieth anniversary of my parents' first awarding the prize. I'm thinking now I should mark it with something really special. To honour them.'

'Della,' Timothy breathes. 'You know how I feel about you.'

I frown and bend my head toward the phone. 'What a lovely gesture. Are you thinking of a plaque?'

'I need to talk to you,' says Timothy. 'About our future.'

'I'm thinking of increasing the amount,' says Daniel. 'Dramatically.'

My head jerks up—I can't help it. 'That certainly would be dramatic.' How much money in a millionaire's 'dramatically', I wonder.

'I'm not normally insistent,' says Timothy. 'Normally I'm very patient. But sometimes a little caveman is required. I want you to know I'm not afraid to be forceful, to get what I want.'

I shake my head at him. 'Go away,' I mouth.

'Della. I really wish you'd listen,' he says. 'It's very hard to be forceful when you won't hang up.'

Daniel is speaking but I can't hear him. 'Will you shut up? Just shut up.'

'Sorry?' says Daniel.

'Not you. One of my colleagues.'

'So, me? You want me to shut up? And I'm,' Timothy makes

imaginary quote marks in the air, 'a "colleague".' He stomps back to the sink and leans against it. 'You're making me feel like I'm not as important as whoever's on the phone.'

'Clearly I've called at a bad time,' Daniel says. 'But I'd need to discuss this with you. Face to face.'

I wave my hand at Timothy, the kind of pacifying sweeps you offer a crying child. 'I see. Professor Carmichael too?'

'No, Ella. Not Carmichael. Just you and me. I'm feeling quite a connection to your project. I'm intrigued. I'm thinking something more personal.'

'Personal,' I say.

'Personal?' says Timothy.

'Let's get together this afternoon, at the university. What time are you free?'

My mind goes blank for an instant, and when I look up Timothy is in front of me, hands on his hips, mischievous smile on his face. 'You know, when we were kids, you could never resist it when I tickled you. Whenever you were tickled, you'd cave straight away.'

I back away and mouth 'don't you dare', but he's already giggling and he makes a sudden grab for my ribs. I hold the phone with one shoulder. With both hands I grab Timothy's ears and pull hard until he squeals. He drops to his knees.

'Ella?' Daniel says. 'Are you there? Are you all right?'

'Yes, fine. I'm fine. I'm just checking my diary,' I say. 'It... squeals. It's a squealing diary.'

'A squealing diary,' Daniel says. 'Of course.'

'This afternoon, this afternoon.' I mentally run my virtual finger down the appointment column of my imaginary squealing diary, then I let go of Timothy's ears and with one hand grab his nose tight between my thumb and forefinger. He groans. I hold the phone again. 'I'm so sorry. I just can't do it. I've got my hands full.'

'Monday morning, then. I'll come to your office, at the university. I want to see the biologist in her natural habitat. You're in the Zoology Department, right? What's your room number?'

I let go of the nose; Timothy sinks to the floor. 'My room number is…now, is it 216 or 316?' I say. 'Actually maybe it's 361. I'm terrible with numbers. They've just moved us all around in there. I used to have a window looking over the garden. Now I'm in a broom cupboard.'

'Don't worry. I'll ask at reception. I'll see you Monday at ten, Ella.'

Under seventy-two hours. It's too tight. I open my mouth again but he has gone and the phone is cold in my hand. Then I look down to see Timothy on his back on the kitchen floor, holding his nose, looking like he's about to cry.

'That was completely unnecessary,' he says. 'You might have broken my nose. I was trying to be playful.' I bend over and offer a hand, intending to help him up, but he goes on. 'A squealing diary, Della?' he says. 'Nice one. Classy.' So instead I kick him in the ribs.

'And that,' I say, 'is for messing with a defenceless girl with one brother and three male cousins. For God's sake, Timothy. That was a mark. I'm working. What on earth has got into you?'

'Sam said you'd like it. Be playful and persistent, he said. Women like that. Act like George Clooney, he said.'

I should have recognised Sam's sticky fingerprints on this. 'Timothy. Trusting Sam for advice about women? Just don't, please.'

Timothy grumbles to his feet, prodding his nose with one finger. He picks up his BlackBerry, which has fallen from the holster, and holds it to his ear. 'And anyway, I know a mark when I hear it. I heard the way you said "personal". That didn't sound like a mark to me.'

'I'm reeling him in, you idiot. He's super rich. This one could be worth a fortune.'

He drapes one arm over my shoulder. 'And that's another thing I admire about you Della. You never give up. You just keep trying. Just because you've had a few years where the deals have been smallish. It's been a bit…lean, recently, I know. You don't let it get you down.'

'Smallish? Lean?' Bloody Sam again, blabbing my business all over south-eastern Australia. 'What would you know about big deals anyway, Timothy? Half the things you sell get change from a hundred.'

'There's no use getting snippy about it,' Timothy says. He pats my shoulder. 'But maybe it's worth handing this one over to Sam. You know, if the mark really is as rich as you say. Handball it to the full-forward.'

'Sammy, a full-forward?' I say. 'Half backward more like it. And if you don't get out of here right now, I'm going to shove that phone where it will never be seen again.'

'Threats, eh?' He smiles like a Labrador. 'I know what's really going on. It's Freudian. You can't keep your hands off me. Besides, what are you going to do? Run mini-scams forever? Until you're a little old lady, panhandling other pensioners for their small change? In the next year or two I'll be taking over Dad's business. I've got big plans, Del. Big. Together we could really make it into something. Maybe it's time you thought about settling down.'

I may be a smallish woman wearing nothing but my pyjamas but when Timothy sees the look on my face, he runs. In the hall, he passes my father.

'Hello, Mr Gilmore. Goodbye, Mr Gilmore,' he says as he runs.

'Timothy, dear boy,' my father says. 'We don't see enough of you these days. Will you be staying for lunch?' He turns his head as

Timothy bolts past. 'That's a "no", I expect.'

'Just keep running,' I yell after Timothy, and then I hear the long sequence of clicks that tells me the front door is opening, 'if you know what's good for you. Keep running and don't stop.'

I walk up the stairs and on the landing I kick open the door to Sam's room hard so it crashes against the wall. He is lying on the bed on his stomach, shirt off, headphones on, practising a new signature upside down on a white pad with blue lines. A waste of time. There's no need for it anymore, not with the quality of the scanners we have. But Sam shares with my father a nostalgia for the old days of the pen-and-ink man, and signatures are Sam's speciality.

His room is a disaster as usual: bed unmade, three old safes in a jumble in a corner, stamps and inks for making government documents, papers piled up in various states of senility, assorted dumbbells for his incessant flexing and preening. In the middle of the room is a pile of basketball clothes from last night's game and a pair of exhausted runners. It stinks to high heaven in here.

Sam looks up with an angelic smile and takes his headphones off. 'What?' he says.

'What have you been saying to Timothy?'

'Nothing. Just some friendly advice about how to manage my little sister. The poor boy's in lerve.'

'Do not talk about me with Timothy again, ever, or I swear I'll let the air out of your girlfriend and nail her to an apple tree.'

'No need to thank me, really. All this romance warms my heart.' He waves his hand with regal grace. 'Della, seeing a man. Who would've guessed? I thought you'd taken holy orders.'

'You are a skunk.' I wind the headphone cord around his neck. 'If I didn't need you downstairs in five minutes for an emergency meeting I'd smack you into the middle of next week.'

'Emergency meeting?' He worries a finger under his noose.

'Don't tell me. You want me to work this weekend?'

'Yes. But not just you.' I step back to the landing where my father is waiting. 'I'm going to need everybody. We have a problem, and we have an opportunity.'

By nine Monday morning, as Daniel Metcalf's black Beemer pulls out of his driveway and purrs around the corner into Toorak Road, we are watching. We watch him sidle around a tram then queue at the lights at the entrance to the freeway, and then we watch him drive all the way through the city. The university I have chosen is the city's oldest, built back when the land was newly stolen and a gracious seat of learning was considered the height of old-world glamour. It sprawls with entrances and accesses like a small city, yet we watch Daniel find a park with spooky ease. He parks at exactly the right entrance, on Royal Parade between the Percy Grainger Museum and the Conservatorium of Music.

For this job we need two wall men, responsible for keeping one eye on the mark while scanning for potential trouble. Beau is the first, the one who waited for Daniel outside his house and followed him on the drive. From his car on Royal Parade, Beau whistles into his mobile.

'He has good parking karma, I'll say that for him. It's been a while since I've seen parking karma that good.'

'Right,' I say. I am inside the Zoology building, with my mobile. 'Thanks for that. I'll make a note.'

In the last twenty minutes of Daniel's drive, Anders will have entered the Zoology building by the front door. He is wearing the uniform of the university's Property and Campus Services Division, who really should deadlock their storage cupboards. Anders wears steel-capped boots and a set of keys hangs off his belt loop. The navy and fluorescent-yellow shirt is slightly tight around his chest; the trouser legs were let down by Aunt Ava very late last night but are still a little short. Anders carries a long thin aluminium strip and walks with the hip roll of someone who has not much to do and all day to do it. He looks sleepy but works fast. Using a tool from his collection, he will open the dinky locks on two glass display cabinets in the building's foyer. Students and academics will walk back and forth past him—they will not give him a second glance.

Anders does not suffer from nerves and has no fear of discovery. He knows the magic power of the uniform, a lesson his father taught him; for one whole year when my Uncle Syd was young, before security tags on clothing, he made a good living wheeling racks of expensive frocks right out the front door of department stores. Not only are people in uniform never questioned, but no one ever looks at their faces. To make doubly sure of his anonymity and freedom to do as he pleases, and also in cases where a uniform is not appropriate, Anders knows to carry a clipboard and pen.

The first display cabinet he will have opened is where the department displays its publications, showing off its successes to visitors and students and staff. *Zoology members in the news*, it says.

White scientific papers are displayed there, glued onto blue cardboard. He will have removed two and replaced them with papers that look identical except that the lead researcher is now Dr Ella Canfield. They cannot be overlooked, unless you have seen them a hundred times, in which case they look the same as they always have.

The second cabinet is the building directory, a wide panel with dozens of flat aluminium strips bearing names and room numbers etched in black. There are plenty of empty spaces and into one of them he will have slid the strip he brought from home, with my name and room number. While he does this, he will be noisy and showy, banging the glass with the strip. When he walks out he will stomp his feet. This, too, is learned. Bystanders mistrust anyone who acts furtive. As he steps out the front door, he will turn to the left to wait at the back of the building for the precise moment to undo his work. As he turns, if our timing is correct, he will see Daniel Metcalf walking up the slope.

When Daniel reaches the door, he will hold it open for a woman coming out. She is in her early fifties but could pass for younger. She is wearing a tailored tweed suit, black pumps, black glasses suspended around her neck by a chain. The woman will smile at him and flutter her eyes. He will smile back. There—a connection is made. He is a stranger here, uncertain, perhaps looking down from time to time to check a map of the university that he holds in his hand. She belongs here, knows her way around. It is natural that she will speak.

'Can I help you?' she will say. She could be the Dean's secretary or an administrator, but she is not.

'I'm looking for Ella Canfield,' Daniel will say.

'Oh,' Ruby will say. For this job, she is our steerer. It is her task to appear unconnected but in reality steer the mark towards me.

She will give a sniff as if she knows me well but thinks me beneath her, and she might gesture Daniel along the corridor. 'Dr Canfield. If she's not in the lab borrowing equipment or in the field, you'll find her in her office. Second floor. Near the lift.'

Daniel Metcalf will not think twice about this advice. He will not ask for me at the window marked *Information*, but as he walks past the directory on the wall he will see my name displayed.

My family is a team of professionals who work together like cogs in a beautiful machine. Everything hinges on the next few minutes; this is why my job is the most exciting in the world. I almost feel sorry for Daniel Metcalf.

This incursion would have been more difficult just a few years ago when universities were bustling places filled with researchers and ideas. Luckily for us, thinking is no longer valued. Universities have been transformed from crowded rooms with too many academics squeezed into a tiny space to understaffed halls with many empty or half-empty offices occupied by casual and sessional lecturers whom no one recognises by sight or even by name.

In the Zoology Department, one such empty room is 257, near the lift on the second floor. Near the lift is good: there is less chance of being seen filing in and out than if we had chosen a room at the far end of the corridor. I have already cased the building. This involves checking the exits but, more importantly, visiting the bathroom. I did the same at the Metcalf mansion on Friday, before I was shown in to see Daniel. Even when you anticipate no problems you should see if there are bars or locks on the windows of the toilets, and whether you could fit through these windows if the need arose. Jobs can curdle very quickly. It is smart to be prepared.

A desk and a chair and a peeling paint job were already there when we arrived; no one noticed the delivery woman who brought the extra boxes in at 8 am. The room is now decorated with framed newspaper clippings, a joke farewell card from Harvard, some academic citations from obscure institutions. There is a coffee mug that says 'Ella', two photos of an elderly couple and one of three blond children who will prove to be my mythical parents, nieces and nephew, piles of papers and copies of journals, a jar of Belgian chocolates wrapped in foil, an umbrella.

The delivery woman's overalls are folded in a box under the desk: now I am wearing tight tailored pants and a black short-sleeved top. I typically don't reveal much skin, just shape. Over the top, I wear a lab coat—perhaps not strictly accurate for an office day, but expected by a layman. Around my neck is a blue cord that should be attached to a security pass, but the pass is in the top pocket of the coat so no one can see it is laminated cardboard. This is a barely adequate solution but we had no time to obtain a real one. Anders fixed my glasses for me last night. One arm was crooked, that was the trouble. They sit easier now.

With twenty seconds to spare, I open the door of my new office and stick three aluminium name strips on the front door with double sided tape. One is etched: Dr Ella Canfield. The other names are underneath this, and are crudely written on torn strips of paper: Elvis Aaron Presley and Dr A. B. Snowman. I answer the door at the first knock.

Daniel gestures to the signs on the door. 'You share your office with illustrious company,' he says.

I frown, and look up and down the corridor to make sure it's empty. Then I grab the strips with the fake names and roll them into a ball. 'My colleagues, next door. They're marsupial researchers. My project is a source of constant amusement to them. Apparently they don't think much of my chances.'

He stands in front of the desk and I close the door then lean with my back against it. 'Look, Daniel. Would you mind if we went somewhere else? If Larry, Curly and Moe from next door find out about this I'll never hear the end of it.'

'Knock on their door and invite them in,' he says. 'I'm sure you could convince them there really are live Tasmanian tigers right here in Victoria. Tell them about the ox. And the watermelon. You're very persuasive.' He moves toward the door and stops only a metre away, but I stay put.

'I've tried. They won't listen.'

'Show them your documents.'

'I've gone through everything. There are records from the Wilsons Promontory Management Committee dated 1908, where they discussed the benefits of catching tigers in Tasmania and releasing them in the park for hunting. Evidence of all the other imported animals that were released in odd spots in the nineteenth century by the Acclimatisation Society. It's absolutely plausible that they were once in the park, and when you add the sightings, it becomes possible. I've explained my whole theory to them.'

'Sounds convincing to me. What did they say?

'They asked if I would help them with a grant application to catch the tooth fairy.'

'Jeez. Scientists,' he says and shakes his head. 'I wouldn't want anything to do with that fairy. No head for business at all—cash flow all in the wrong direction and the tooth inventory always increasing.'

'I'll let them know.'

'Mind you, she's not alone. There're poorly run businesses everywhere. Look at the Easter bunny—runs that business like a charity. One hundred per cent market share, certainly, but where's the revenue? They'll all need government bail-outs eventually. Worldwide markets, you see. Too big to fail.'

He says this in a flirty way, and that's when I know I've got him. I am slightly disappointed. I had expected more of a challenge, considering the stupidity of this whole idea and the number of women someone like him must attract. It turns out he's as pathetic as the rest of them. I twist a curl of hair around my finger and smile, suddenly coy. 'So I should sell my shares in Santa?'

'Well, the margins in the gift business are rubbish anyway and I hear he's been paying the reindeer a Christmas bonus for years now. As for their super: let's just say I wouldn't mind being an elf on the verge of retirement.'

'I'm so glad you're here to tell me these things. I never would have figured it out without you.'

'I'm from a long line of businessmen. It's in the blood. Perhaps I should knock next door and give your colleagues some advice.'

'Not a chance,' I say, and I raise my arms as though I'm barring the door. 'You're all mine. With any luck they've never heard of your trust. The last thing I need is more competition.' I blush a little, though by this stage it's probably unnecessary.

'Ella,' he says. 'Competition should be the least of your worries.'

I take off my lab coat and bundle him out. I know the hall is empty, otherwise I would have heard Sam, a spruced-up second wall man in his cleaner's uniform, speaking loudly on his mobile right outside my door. At the end of the corridor is the lift. As the doors open, an older lady scientist exits: late sixties, white close-cropped hair, lab coat, small jade earrings. I hold the doors for her, then we walk inside. The lift doors close. And all at once I begin to feel nervous.

This feeling is not the normal nerves that I know and love, the sudden rush of butterflies, the adrenaline that brings out my best performance. As the lift begins to move, a nauseated feeling that might be dread overtakes me. I stand, arms at my side, legs stiff, eyes toward the door. For a moment I feel I'm going to faint.

I've been in lifts before, obviously. I have travelled in this very lift several times since Friday lunchtime but now I am conscious of what an enclosed space it is, how isolated from the rest of the world. A small steel bubble.

The denim of Daniel's jeans has fine ridges like corduroy that make sonic waves in the atmosphere. The satchel, carried across his body, is a smooth brown leather that echoes good sense and calm. The face is tanned; his skin looks slightly rough even under the stubble. He leans one shoulder against the wall of the lift, hands behind his back, eyes to the ceiling. I close my eyes. I should have eaten breakfast, I think, and then I remember that I did. Perhaps I shouldn't have. I swallow. I think of the old lady scientist who left the lift as we entered. She had an unfriendly look in her eye. Suspicious. That might be me in forty years, still sneaking around, pulling the same stings. My legs feel wobbly underneath me. There are perhaps two hundred floors to go.

Then the door opens again and I feel the breeze against my face and all is well. I've had some strange reaction to the air in the lift, lack of oxygen, or too much, or something. I feel myself again; or at least the self that I am today. In fact now that the feeling has passed I think it was a good thing, that creeping dread. It's an extra awareness. A sixth sense, warning me to be on my toes. Although this job seems in the bag I will be careful. Everything will be all right.

Down the corridor I stop in front of the glass display case as though something has unexpectedly caught my eye. 'Well,' I say, after a moment. 'They finally put them up.'

Daniel slouches so that he is at eye level with me. 'Posters with scientific papers on them. Well well. The biologist as rock star. More people would notice if they were stuck on poles in the city.'

'Here,' I say, and I tap my finger on the glass right above my name, so he can't miss it. 'They finally displayed them. My papers.'

'That doesn't usually happen?'

I straighten and shrug. 'A university department is just like a family. I was popular enough at the beginning but now I'm the black sheep, I guess. But I probably shouldn't be telling you that.'

'Why not?'

'It's a lot of money. I'm sure you want the grant to be awarded to someone…Well.' I pause. I am shy here, diffident. I am saying something that will count against me but I can't in all good conscience not mention it. This will speak to my honesty, my integrity. I look bashful. 'Someone more establishment than me.'

'Not necessarily,' he says. 'Sometimes I become interested in unexpected things. Sometimes I think I'm the only one who notices.'

I hold the main doors open for him; he nods and allows himself to be ushered out. We are nearly out of doorway when I hear a voice behind me, sharp and close.

'Excuse me. Just one moment.'

I turn. It's the elderly lady scientist, the one with the jade earrings I saw on the second floor. She must have followed us down in the lift. She does not look friendly. I can almost hear her say: Who are you? What are you doing in the building? I'm calling security, right now. This could be the end of everything. From the corner of my eye I see Ruby in a doorway to the right; she is too far away to intervene without breaking into a jog, which would look strange. I need to make a judgment, right now, from the look on the woman's face. I can excuse myself to Daniel and hope he keeps walking. Anders would keep an eye on him, but it is risky, disruptive.

'Yes?' I say.

'I think you might have dropped this. Outside the lift.' She puts out her hand and in her palm is the ball of paper, the screwed-up name plates of Elvis Presley and Dr Snowman. Her lips are pursed, her eyes are narrowed. She knows that no one would miss a ball of paper. She is making a point about littering, about inappropriate behaviour in the departmental corridors. She is only just restraining herself from folding her arms and tapping one foot.

'Thanks.' I put the ball of paper in my coat pocket.

After she leaves Daniel says, 'Not a friend of yours?'

'I told you. I'm not the most popular person here.'

'I find that hard to believe.' He flashes me a smile that I'm sure is his most charming.

It's all I can do to not roll my eyes; this is almost too easy. I smile. 'Would I lie to you?'

Outside the air is still, the grounds are perfect and there is a peace that comes with being in the sun where no one is rushing. This campus has a crack team of gardeners that make it perpetually photo-ready, unlike our garden at home which is well on the way to being reclaimed by the apple trees. We are walking to the student cafe because I tell Daniel that there I won't run into any of my colleagues and I don't want to share him. This is perhaps as overtly flirtatious as I want to get on this job and maybe it's too far, but he only smiles and admires the gargoyles.

'But you were at Harvard, didn't you say?' he says. 'There must have been some wonderful buildings there.'

'Oh yes. Beautiful old buildings.'

'What exactly was your research project? For your post-doc?'

My mind goes blank for a moment, and then I see Sam, still in his cleaner's uniform. He left the Zoology Department by the stairs while we were in the lift and he is here now, sweeping a path ahead of us, keeping a lookout.

Correction, pretending to sweep a path. Leaning on a broom, which is as close to proper labour as he can get. He's good at this kind of surveillance, though. It comes naturally to him. Daniel will never know that we're being watched.

'Skunks,' I say, looking at Sam. 'I worked on skunks.'

'The right thing to say here, I think, is "that stinks". What kind of skunks?'

'Oh, just your common garden-variety skunk. The one with the striped tail. *Pepelepewicus stinkicus*.'

'Surely skunk research isn't very useful to your career back here in Australia?'

'You'd be surprised.'

As we round a corner, we almost run into two young people: a tall lanky African man, smooth coal-black skin, angular arms; and a girl who could be Scandinavian with slim hips, gold hair and blue eyes. They are carrying books in their arms, ambling the way people do when they do not have proper jobs. They might be students but they are not. They both look younger than their years. When they see us, they smile.

'Dr Canfield,' they say together.

'What a very pleasant and unexpected surprise,' says Julius.

'Joshua. Glenda.' I turn to Daniel. 'Mr Metcalf. Joshua and Glenda are my two new PhD students. The ones who will be involved in my project.' I smile wistfully, which involves biting my bottom lip. 'Should I obtain funding, of course.'

'Sir I am very pleased to be making your acquaintance,' says Julius.

'Mr Metcalf,' says Greta, flicking her hair and resting one hand on her hip. 'Hello.'

Greta's shoes are strappy sandals with high heels that stretch her long brown calves to best effect, not shoes appropriate for a young researcher. She's been selling time-share to aimless husbands for too long.

'Mr Metcalf is considering giving us a grant,' I say. 'For the tiger project.'

'Really?' says Greta. 'That's wonderful!' She clasps her hands like she's praying. Her eyes are impossibly wide and her gaze doesn't leave Daniel's face. Julius and I might not even be here.

'Without the generosity of people such as yourself, sir, the course of scientific research would be considerably retarded,' says Julius.

'It's the least I can do,' Daniel says. 'After all, without science, we'd all still suffer from the common cold.'

'We mustn't judge science too harshly,' I say. 'It's been pretty busy getting rid of polio and smallpox. I'm sure the common cold is on the list.'

'Have you always been interested in evolutionary biology, Mr Metcalf?' says Greta.

'Fascinated,' Daniel says. 'All those eras. The Jurassic I know. Full of dinosaurs and Attenboroughs. Then there's the Prosaic and the Heimlich. See? Just as well it's not my job. I'd be hopeless.'

'It is the most important profession in the world, science,' says Julius. 'Back home in my village in Kenya, sir, I lived in a grass hut with all my aunties and uncles and cousins and walked five miles every day to bring water from the well. And even then I dreamed of coming here to Melbourne to work with an academic of such renown as Dr Canfield.'

'Goodness Joshua,' I say. 'I'm blushing.'

'Me too!' says Glenda. She is, actually. Perhaps she's unwell. 'I'm just so passionate about biology. I love everything about it. Just thinking about it makes me go all tingly.' She bites her bottom lip in a far less subtle way than I did earlier, and inhales again.

'Perhaps you're allergic to something,' says Daniel.

Greta does seem quite peaky today. Flushed in the face, breathing heavily. It might have been better for us all if she had skipped this job. Sometimes people think they're doing the right thing with this soldier-on mentality when really they let everybody down and get in everybody's way and detract attention from what it is that the mark is supposed to be looking at, which, as I'm going to make very clear to her when we get back to Cumberland Street, isn't actually Greta or her heaving chest. Now she's giggling. She sounds like she's having an asthma attack and if she sticks her rack out any further she'll poke him in the eye. In a moment she's going to ask him to give her mouth to mouth. This is just making my job that much harder.

'Glenda is one of our star pupils,' I say. 'She's a very talented field researcher. It's such a shame that she's taking a long trip away in just a few weeks. Six months in the Mojave Desert, isn't it Glenda? To study coyotes. You'll have to be careful.'

'Coyotes. Yes. But I'll be back, after that,' she says, and smiles again. 'Back to good old Melbourne. Where I live.'

'We're all very proud of Glenda,' I say. 'The way she works so hard and travels so well, considering her disability. Anyhow, we must keep moving.'

'Disability?' says Daniel.

'It's nothing,' says Greta.

'How very very brave of you Glenda,' I say. 'But it certainly is something.' I lean closer to Daniel and raise one hand to the side of my face. 'Claustrophobia. She can't bear to be enclosed. In a room. At all. Or even to stand too close to people. Always likes to be outdoors, preferably completely alone. You're doing very well

Glenda, even talking to us now.'

'I'm fighting it,' says Greta. 'I'm getting better.'

'It's a wonder you can catch a plane,' says Daniel.

'Six valium and a hip flask of bourbon,' I say.

In the student food hall we sit on plastic chairs bolted to the floor while back in the Zoology Department the others are working like an army of ants stripping a carcass back to pure white bones. Name plates are being taken off doors and building directories. Offices are being packed up. Fake papers in glass cabinets are being replaced with the originals.

Daniel and I have coffees in front of us, surprisingly good, from one of the neon-flashing stands that sell curries and bubble tea. A campus security guard wanders in from the rear entrance and walks around for a few minutes, but he is aimless, on routine patrol. He doesn't look at us. It is still early for lunch, even for students; they are chatting in groups and in queues ordering food so we have one sticky-surfaced plastic table all to ourselves.

'So,' I say. Casually, like I'd be just as happy talking about the weather. I stir my coffee. 'You mentioned something on the phone about increasing the amount of the bursary.'

He takes a sip of his long black. 'A quarter of a million dollars,' he says.

I cannot help it: I splutter indelicately into my espresso. The very wealthy Daniel Metcalf is sitting right in front of me, but I'm not concentrating on him. I'm not seeing the students milling around, or feeling the warmth of the cup in my hand. A quarter of a million dollars. That is certainly champagne and lobster territory. That would shut Sam up, possibly for years. This would become a famous sting, one that would enter into our family folklore like the time my father, just starting out, only twenty-two, mortgaged a vacant warehouse in the city that he didn't actually own and bought the Mercedes. This Metcalf deal would be my moment of glory. This would be the time that Della took money from right under the nose of the one of Melbourne's richest families without them even noticing it was gone.

'Well. A quarter of a million dollars. That *is* dramatically more.' Students are beginning to file in, congregating around the juice bar, the lolly shop. They all look so young. They're at the beginning of their careers, of their lives. 'But. Well. I don't know how to say this. I don't want you to be offended.'

'You'll find I'm very hard to offend.'

'Are you sure you have the authority to make that kind of offer? Don't you need to get someone else's approval?'

This is an old trick too, favoured by telemarketers. If you want someone to give you something, make them feel like they are weak or frightened if they don't. Dare them to hand it over. There is a risk to it, though. Sometimes the mark gets snippy. But not Daniel Metcalf. He just smiles.

'Promise. I'm the chair of the trust. Professor Carmichael is just my advisor. It's completely up to me how much I give.'

I drain my coffee and settle my handbag on my shoulder. Now is the time to let him talk me into it. 'I believe you. But...' I stare into the middle distance, listening to imaginary thinking music. I shake my head. 'No.'

His eyes narrow. 'No? As in, you don't want a quarter of a million dollars?'

'No. As in, I'm having second thoughts about this whole project—which you'll agree is completely crazy and might ruin my career. I guess I'm saying, I don't know if I'm brave enough.' I bite my bottom lip and lean forward across the table towards him, resting on my forearms.

He shakes his head. 'Ella. I thought you said you'd had this dream since you were a little girl? They laughed at Archimedes when he discovered the spa. They laughed at Copernicus when he namcd a comet after a dead rock and roll singer. They laughed at Einstein when he invented the theory of avoiding your relatives.'

'Funny. But you're proving my point. Archimedes was murdered by the Romans, Copernicus didn't publish until right before his death, from fear of the reaction, and Einstein was sentenced to eternity emblazoned on the T-shirts of nerds around the world. Besides, it's not just that. There are practical issues. I can't possibly manage that kind of money. I've seen colleagues win these big grants. A quarter of a million dollars brings a whole host of issues I don't want to deal with.' Now my feet are flexed so I look like I'm ready to stand; a sprinter in the starting blocks waiting for the gun.

He frowns. 'It's a very unusual person who can turn down that much money.'

'Daniel, look. It's not that I want to turn it down, obviously. But I applied for this grant so I can get out in the field and do real research. Not convene meetings with heads of departments or deans. Not write new and better proposals, or calculate reconciliations of how the money's spent, or do publicity to promote the trust, or hire an accountant. The thing that was so appealing about this in the first place is the blessed anonymity. You just give me the money and I do the research. I'm not interested in a circus.'

He shakes his head. 'No reconciliations, no accountants, no heads of department. Once I hand the cheque over, it's yours.'

'You hand me a quarter of a million dollars. Just like that.'

He stretches his legs out under the table, and I feel his foot brush against mine. 'I'd need a bit more information, sure. I'd need to see precisely what you want to do, and how you want to do it. First hand.'

'First hand?'

'Yes. Let's say, this weekend. Take me to your research site, in the national park.'

The lobster was lying in front of me on a white platter of bone china, next to a cut-crystal champagne glass filled with the palest amber liquid, tiny bubbles swelling to the surface. I could almost smell its yeasty caress.

With just four words—*let's say this weekend*—the lobster and the champagne vanish to reveal stained laminate and a lingering smell of fried noodles. A one-hour meeting I can manage. And a written application, with Julius's help. But pass myself off as a serious scientist, with four days' notice? And camping? I'm pretty sure that happens in the outdoors. Tents. Sleeping bags. Gear. This is impossible.

'This weekend? You can't tell me you've got nothing on this weekend. Planning on watching a few DVDs, were you?'

He shrugs. 'There might be a few things I need to cancel.'

'Won't those few things be a bit miffed, to be dumped at such short notice?'

'I'm sure they'll get over it. I've decided. This weekend.'

Now my reluctance is not just for show—I really must pull out, and in a feasible manner. Immediately. I dread to think what they'll say when I get home. Sam will never let me hear the end of it.

'No,' I say. 'This is too hard. It's too much. I'm out.'

Daniel stretches across the table with his right hand and holds my wrist, firm, warm. He doesn't speak. I'm pinned. Then with his other hand, he reaches down into his satchel on the floor beside him. He lets go of me and pulls out a cheque book. He puts the cheque book on the table and turns the pages. He starts writing.

'Ella, this is a cheque for twenty-five thousand dollars made out to your research fund. I'm going to hand it to you right now. You can keep it, if you like. Or you can hand it back to me, and this time next week I'll write you out a cheque for two hundred and fifty thousand.' He tears the cheque from the book, a sound that seems so loud in my ears that I can't believe everyone in the food hall doesn't stop and stare. 'It's up to you.' He holds the cheque between his fingers. Holds it out to me.

I shut my eyes and when I open them I am a child again, sitting in my favourite dress on a planter on a hot day. In front of me is a middle-aged woman holding a ten dollar note between her fingers and all I can see is this note that has the grace of a fish's tail, like a salmon hovering in a stream. The water in the stream is cool ripples like emeralds and I swear I can hear it tinkling gently. For a moment when I look across the table at Daniel Metcalf, it seems like he's under water.

'One weekend,' he says. 'Just so I can satisfy myself that this project is run professionally and seriously. You can bring your PhD students. Glenda will still be around then? She won't be in the Mojave Desert chasing coyotes?'

Maybe I'm tired. I've been doing this since I was six. Around me, students are jostling each other, talking about their lectures, thinking about their futures. Maybe it isn't too late for me to start again. To do something else. This is the kind of sting that could buy someone a new beginning. This is my career, after all. My career is to become someone I'm not, become an expert on something I've never tried before. I slip the different Dellas on and off like white silk gloves.

I don't think about national parks, or about camping, or about equipment or even about science. I'm not thinking about Greta, either.

'Wild horses wouldn't keep her away,' I say.

It isn't until I get to the car, where Beau is waiting, that I start to feel sick.

All the way back to Cumberland Street I don't speak. After suburbs and freeways and intersections of trying to tempt me with questions like: And then what did he say? and What was the look on his face then? and receiving the briefest of answers, Beau gives up and switches on the radio. Beau is a safe driver, as we all are. This is another of my father's rules. We travel just under the speed limit, we always indicate, we check for broken tail lights and worn tyres. There is never any excuse to pull us over.

By the time Beau swings into the driveway I have been staring out the window like it was a competition sport for about twenty-five klicks, and changed my mind back and forth a dozen times.

Wilsons Promontory National Park. The Prom, they call it, like it was a high school dance. I've never been there and neither has any of my family. I've heard of it, of course, and I've seen it on TV. It's been a favourite holiday destination for Melburnians for decades, this wedge of land barely attached to the bottom of Australia's coastline like a comma reluctantly added to a rambling sentence. On travel shows hikers and surfers and fisherfolk rug up against the elements and sleep under the stars enjoying the majesty of the great outdoors. It always makes me wonder why, if this camping business is so entrancing, these people sleep in houses at all. They all have perfectly serviceable backyards. Knock yourselves out, tentophiles. I try to recall everything I've heard about this park and before I know it we're home, at Cumberland Street.

I am barely out of the car when I see something that makes the Prom drop right out of my head. The front door is ajar.

My heart begins to race. Something terrible has happened, to my father, to my family. The front door is never left open. There is a line of deadlocks and chains attached to this door and they are meant to be used. The door is plywood over steel, made to my father's specifications before I was born. In our home there can be no unpleasant surprises.

I look around the side of the house. There are no strange cars parked in the drive, nothing on the street. The house is still, although an army of police or worse could be hiding behind the apple trees and sheds and sunken patios without us noticing. I look at Beau. He shrugs and says nothing. It would be prudent to climb back behind the wheel and drive off. That is the plan we've rehearsed, but it would mean leaving them all behind.

'Keep the motor running,' I whisper. He nods.

From the drive, the house looks the same as always. It is tall, three storeys plus my attic. It is old. The fireplaces are brick and the rest of the house is timber, whitewashed, some planks running in one direction, some running in the other. On the right hand side I can see the conservatory but there is no movement there and the glass is dirty and streaked. I creep on to the patio, flatten myself against the front wall, dodge the peeling white cane furniture, a variety of faded cushions. Limp plants in painted terracotta, in mosaic, in plastic of all colours. There are cast-iron garden ornaments scattered at random, here a rusted rooster, there a dented lizard. There are no obvious footprints, the door bears no marks of boots or a battering ram. The hinges are intact. I peer down the hall. Along the faded Persian runner are piles of cardboard boxes. As I creep further along I see our livingroom full of picks and shovels, and hessian sacks and ropes and crates and nets.

'Dad.' I speak quietly at first, but when he doesn't reply I try again, louder.

Finally he appears from the kitchen, tea towel over one shoulder. Ruby is close behind him. 'Ah. My warrior queen returns,' he says, arms outstretched. 'Tell me, what did our young Master Metcalf say?'

'Dad. The front door was open when I got home. Wide open. Anyone could walk in.'

'Was it? Odd.' He looks especially spiffy today. He is wearing a new silk cravat in blue and green tucked under his white shirt and tweed blazer, and his hair has a brilliantine shine. I think he has even lost a little weight. He walks to the end of the hall and closes the door after Beau comes in. 'That must have been your brother,' he says. 'I'll speak with him directly.'

My brother. Sam is sloppy about many things, but not about that. 'Dad,' I say. 'The locks.'

'The locks? Of course.' And only then does he deliberately fasten each of them. 'No need for that look on your face, young lady. If you saw the door was open you should not have come in. You should have gone directly to the safe house, and taken Beaufort with you. It might have been a drill, to rehearse our movements if we should become compromised. It behooves us to practise now and again.'

First Sam was to blame for leaving the door open. Now he has almost convinced himself it was deliberate. I bend down to look in one of the boxes. 'And what is all this stuff?' I say.

'This?' He chuckles in a way that sets my teeth on edge, and takes my shoulders to move me aside. 'No peeking. Not yet. This is the apex of my career, Della. This is the grandest, most magnificent scheme I have ever devised.'

'You talk to him,' Ruby says. 'He won't listen to me.'

I sit on the arm of the couch and rest my elbows on my knees. I'd never noticed before, but the leather is cracking and this part of the frame is coming away from the back. After all these years it might be ready to collapse under our weight. 'What scheme?'

'Ah,' he says, folding his arms. 'That would be telling.'

'Yes, Dad,' I say. 'It would be telling. That's why I would be asking.'

'See?' says Ruby. 'He's impossible.'

'No sense being premature about these things. Things must progress to their natural fruition. I just need a little longer to finalise my stratagem,' he says. 'Beaufort is helping me, aren't you boy?' He winks at Beau, now standing in the hall.

'Yes, Uncle Laurence,' Beau says, and I can see him stand a little taller and straighter with this knowledge that he has and I haven't. He folds his arms, too, the mirror of my father, and looks at me with something like defiance. I see now I should have answered his questions in the car.

'That's not how it works,' I say. 'That's not how you taught us. Every job is raised at the weekly meeting and we all decide whether to proceed. We don't go off by ourselves, you always said. It's not smart and it's not safe. That's one of your rules.'

He avoids my eyes. One of the cardboard boxes is partly open; he bends over and folds closed the flap so I can't see what's inside, then when he straightens again he holds one hand on the small of his back and puffs like he is blowing out candles.

'Ask him how all this junk got here,' says Ruby.

I don't need to ask him. The look on Ruby's face tells me.

'Dad. Did you have all this stuff delivered here? To our home address?'

He is fussing around his boxes and for a moment it seems he doesn't hear me. 'Hmmm? Once in a lifetime opportunity, this is. The normal rules do not apply. Ruby worries for no reason.' He drops his voice to a whisper. 'It's the change of life. Makes her edgy.'

Ruby throws her hands in the air and stalks back to the kitchen.

Our home address is never used for business, not ever. We have worked from post office boxes and self-storage units and vacant lots and empty houses and shops waiting to be leased, but we never use our home address for a job. We must be untraceable. And we are *so* careful. Uncle Syd is responsible for our props department, and only the most innocuous or easily hidden are allowed to stay here. Uniforms, decals for vans in the names of telecommunications and utility companies, identity tags, spare mobile phones and scanners and printers, paper of all types: these can stay, if they fold flat or have an innocent purpose. But nothing else.

Even in the glory days of the eighties when my father sold pallet upon pallet of slimming tea and we went to Portsea for a holiday with the profits and ate at posh restaurants every night, the tea never came here. It was always stored in a dusty anonymous warehouse where we would sit at trestle tables in a familial production line, one day packing and addressing and stamping boxes to be sent all over the world, the next day processing cheques and money orders and cash. The only slimming tea that made it here to Cumberland Street were the packets that Ruby brought home in her handbag and sipped religiously every night.

None of my father's jobs ever came here. The engine additive that doubled fuel consumption never came here. The insurance company brochures, the investment prospectuses, the deeds and flyers for the land on the Queensland island that was under water at high tide. None of it ever came here.

Nothing bigger than we can carry in our pocket or flush down the toilet, that is the rule. All my life I have followed the rules. And now he says the normal rules do not apply.

He teeters over to where I sit on the couch. My arms are folded. I glare.

'Don't concern yourself, my dear,' he says, and he tousles my hair the way he did when I was a child. 'I just need a little more time, and then I shall make a presentation that none of you shall soon forget. There's life in your old man yet.'

I open my mouth to lecture him, tell him that the rules are for him too but then I stop. For the first time I notice that his eyes are wet with fluid that looks thicker than tears and the bottom lid is puckered away from the eyeball. Rheumy eyes. Old-man eyes.

Tonight will be an extraordinary family meeting. I will present my revised plans for this increased offer from the Metcalf Trust. It is not too late to back out. It will be a long night and I should be relaxing. If we vote in favour of proceeding I'll barely have time to breathe for a week. I feel too restless to walk, too edgy to drive to the pool for a swim. I have already visited the library and my floor is covered with every book on evolutionary biology and camping that I could borrow. I try to read but until I know for certain that we will vote in favour of my plan, my attention wanders. Every so often I pace. I fluff my pillows, idly dust the window ledge with a tissue. I sit here in my bedroom, sketching plans and ideas.

I have spent my whole life in this room. It is still painted pale pink with bluebell wallpaper along the cornices. Almost everything was bought from Timothy's father—smart buying for furniture and clothes and other sensible things. Not so smart for electricals: one of the apple sheds is full of thirty years of broken toasters and laptops and stereos that bear the manufacturer's serial number, which is traceable. We can't take them for repair.

Here are my computer, printer and scanner. The shredder is in the corner. There is no rubbish bin. As soon as something is shredded, regardless of the inconvenience or the weather, it is walked to the compost heap and stirred among the vegetable peelings and rotten fruit. The wardrobe is cheap veneer with sticky-tape marks from the posters of pop stars I stuck to it in my teens. Inside it are business suits for when I'm a banker, furs for when I'm a millionaire, shabby peasant skirts for when I am a hippy who owns priceless oceanfront land down the coast and isn't worldly enough to know what to do with it but just requires a wealthy 'friend' to pay a bribe to a planning official, usually played by Beau. He's a brilliant planning official. The bed is single for a little girl, country-style American oak with worn spots where it hinges to the bed head; the dresser is white reclaimed timber that was once merely distressed but is now hysterical. The bedside table is faded antique Queen Anne. The gold curtains clash with the teal carpet. The real crystal chandelier sparkles on the fake cane chair with cheesecloth cushion, on which sits a pile of teddy bears from my childhood.

Now I think how old this house is; that everything in it is old too. All the furniture is wearing and splitting and the curtains are thinning and the wallpaper is lifting and the carpet is a palette of mysterious stains. My father has a short attention span for household effects. We might have a painting for some months that he declares he loves, then suddenly it will vanish. *That old thing? Bored with it, my dear, bored with it*. Once we had a dinner service handed down, if not through generations of our family, then certainly through generations of somebody's. Hand-painted Japanese ladies waving fans on bridges, porcelain so thin the light shone through. Ruby loved it. She would sip tea from a fragile cup and rest a biscuit on the matching saucer. She loved that dinner service, but it just vanished overnight. *Can't stand it another minute*, my father said. *Either it goes or I do*.

I have lived in this house for so long I have not noticed it decaying around me. I am wearing, too. Slipping in and out of different names and lives grates away at my skin. I think about Daniel Metcalf, who is the one person all the time. How simple things must be for him. Like everything in this house, like everything in this room, nothing in my life matches.

'I don't like it,' says Sam. He leans back in his chair and scratches his stomach.

'I've met him. It's legit,' says Greta. She gives me a wan smile. She is supporting me in any way she can, after our little altercation earlier in the kitchen. At first she tried to defend her behaviour this morning with lame explanations about his money and the way he looked. I had calmed down by then. No threats were involved. I just carefully explained that if Daniel's attentions wander we will all get nothing and we will all miss out and everyone will know who is responsible. This is business. It is not personal.

And it is a wonderful business. We have taken from many of his kind over the years, a small way towards balancing the score of inherited privilege. I have only met Daniel Metcalf twice but I know him well, or as well as I need to. I have met many of his type: idle, with a sense of entitlement that seeps from their pores. No direction. So bored that spending a weekend in the forest with a bunch of scientists seems like a harmless lark.

'He's just another rich guy who doesn't know which end is up,' says Julius, who often seems to read my mind. 'You know how much we've made from people like that over the years. Rich people. Dumb as planks. It's the inbreeding, you know. They've got the IQ of a floorboard. Metcalf won't even know he's been done.'

'You should have heard him today, at the uni,' I say. '"Glenda will still be around then? She won't be in the Mojave Desert chasing coyotes?" I could barely keep a straight face.'

'Now Della,' my father says. 'I know it's tempting to make sport with these fools. But it's not their fault, remember.'

'No one just gives away that much money,' says Sam. 'Not even someone stupid. Something smells.'

Sam is not normally like this. He is normally up for anything. He's the one who sees possibilities, not problems.

We have been talking for hours. The blackboard is filled with lines and arrows and lists and figures. It is dark outside now and the brocade wallpaper does not help the light in here. There are three empty bottles of merlot and ten dirty glasses, and take-away pizza boxes in the middle of the table next to the crystal candelabra and months of raised mounds of set candle wax. I drove to the shops and picked up the pizzas myself. I had a sudden fear my father would ask for home delivery.

He had only one slice, despite Ruby's urging, and no dessert. Perhaps he is feeling unwell. Also on the table are camping-store catalogues downloaded from the web and my piles of books from the library. Occasionally someone reaches for one and flicks through it, as if they were in a dentist's office.

'There are all kinds of charitable trusts, when you know to look for them,' Julius says. 'Family trusts, trusts set up by private philanthropists, by big business. Trusts that give money for poetry, classical music, art history. There's nothing strange about it at all. We've just never targeted it before, that's all. I'm seriously thinking about being a violin prodigy from some third-world country for my next job.'

'I didn't know you could play the violin,' says Beau.

'I've hurt my arm. Lifting water from the well. Maybe I need the money for an urgent wrist tendon cartilage elbow stem cell operation to save my career. An arthroscopic hemi-orthomolecular tendonectomy. And here's a genius recording I made earlier.'

'I think we can lighten up on the well, Julius,' I say.

He shrugs. 'Feeding the goats then. It's got to be exotic or they won't buy it. I can't say I hurt it on my Wii Fit.'

'Della,' says Ruby, 'what do we really know about Metcalf?'

'What's to know?' I say. 'Daniel is just another over-privileged under-disciplined rich boy.'

'Now now, Della,' says my father. 'Let's not be prejudicial. Young Metcalf has not had the benefit of your upbringing. He was never trained to live by his wits. He was not brought up to live the rare and wild life of the fox or the eagle. He is imprisoned by values that are not of his making. He is a battery chicken in a gilded cage. He is a gelding with a golden bridle, tamed with a bit of iron.'

'I don't think he's a gelding,' says Greta.

'If we're the fox, I'm pretty sure he should be a rabbit,' says Beau.

'It doesn't matter what he is,' I say.

'Unless we're an eagle. Then he could be a chicken. But he'd have to be a small chicken if an eagle was to grab him, because the eagles around here aren't that big,' says Beau. 'Maybe he's a quail.'

'I don't think he's a quail either,' says Greta.

'It doesn't matter, it doesn't matter,' I say. 'For all I care he can be a bloody Tasmanian tiger. All that matters is the money.'

'I can't believe you can look at him and only see the money,' says Greta. 'What's wrong with you?'

'Perhaps Della has not space in her affections for any other man,' says my father. He winks at Sam. Ruby rolls her eyes.

'All right,' I say. 'It was funny the first hundred times or so. Memo to all of you. This business with Timothy has gone far enough.'

'It'd be better psychologically if you saw Metcalf as a chicken,' says Beau. 'Positive visualisation.'

'I am not going to think of Daniel as any kind of bird whatsoever,' I say. 'I'm not going to think of him at all. He's a mark. That's it. He's not one of us.'

'There's nothing insulting about being a chicken,' Beau says. 'They can be quite intelligent, you know. They talk to each other. If a predator is coming, they can tell another chicken what kind it is. A fox, for example.'

'"Daniel?"' says Sam. 'That's twice you called him Daniel.'

'You're an idiot,' I say. 'That's his name. And you. Forget about the chicken.'

'It's not easy being continually underestimated, Della,' Beau says. 'I know. I can see it from the chicken's point of view.'

'Metcalf is certainly a famous name in Melbourne society circles,' says my father. 'It would be a feather in our cap to lighten the young man's pockets just a little.'

'I'm for it,' says Uncle Syd. 'We should trust Della, whatever she calls him. She knows what she's doing.'

'Me too. My granny was a scullery maid for the Metcalfs during the Great Depression, cleaning silver and lighting fires. This is decades of back wages,' says Ava. 'And Samson. You shouldn't tease your sister in that way. It's an important part of her job, to make men fall in love with her.'

'I don't think it's *that* important,' I say. 'I do have a brain, you know.'

'Don't you remember the Kowalski sting, Della? Milton Kowalski, he was in love with you. I think he proposed, didn't he? And before that, the vicar who was responsible for the parish investments? And he gave investment advice to the whole congregation, remember? That church was loaded. What was his name?' says Beau.

'I thought he was going to faint every time he saw you, the reverend. The way he ran his finger around the inside of his collar like it was suddenly too tight. Incredibly phallic, it was,' says Uncle Syd. 'Don't make a face, Della. You've never objected to playing the femme fatale before.'

'I'm not objecting. It's just that there's more to it than that.'

'You're frightened of him,' says Sam. 'Metcalf. I can see it in your eyes. You've been frightened of him since you first met him.'

'I'm not frightened of anybody, much less a Metcalf. I'm reeling him in.'

'You don't have to tell me,' says Aunt Ava. 'I was young once. I made a good living out of my face and figure in those days. Having men fall for you is an occupational hazard in this business, Della. Just keep your eye on the ball.'

'I'm not on the game, you know,' I say. 'I make a living the same way you all do. I don't work lying on my back.'

'Just as well, or we'd all starve to death,' says Greta under her breath.

'Excuse me Greta. It's not that easy to meet someone, you know?' I say.

'Stick to your own circle. You've got heaps of men to choose from, just in the people we know,' says Greta.

'Really.'

'Certainly,' my father says. 'What's wrong with Tony? He's always asking me about you.'

'Which Tony?' says Greta. 'The SP bookie? Or the financial planner who does the money laundering?'

'There's lots of guys down at the track,' says Beau. 'Carl, Louis. The guy with the eczema, what's his name? The one who trains greyhounds. He's got a great car.'

'Thanks so much for the advice,' I say. 'Really. You all need to get a hobby.'

'There's Omar the loan shark,' says Anders. 'I could get you his number.'

'Decoupage. Bongo playing. Anything,' I say.

'You've made the right choice anyway,' says Greta. 'Tim's the cream of the crop.'

'As fascinating as this little digression is, if we could get back to the matter at hand?' says Ruby. 'We need to discuss if this job is even feasible. It wasn't set up as a long con. There's a tremendous amount of work to be done in a limited amount of time. Now. Metcalf has already seen me, and Greta and Julius.'

'Do I have to sleep outside? Because I don't know if I can do that,' says Greta. 'There are bugs outside. There's no chance I can stay in a motel for this job, thanks to you Della, thanks to you giving me claustrophobia. Great idea, that was.'

Greta's right. It was impulsive and amateurish of me to give her claustrophobia just because I was annoyed with her. If I had known we'd be spending the weekend with Metcalf I'd have given her something else. Leprosy, perhaps.

'Della. Ruby's right. Be realistic. This weekend is under four days away,' says Sam. 'You've never been camping. You don't know the first thing about animals. And as for science, for God's sake. People study for years to become scientists. You've never even been to school, none of us has. This will be intense. Lots of time with him. He'll ask a lot of questions. You won't be able to pull it off.'

'Or you don't want me to pull it off,' I say. 'This is what I do Sam. I'm good at this.'

'I know you are.' He shakes his head. 'But this is too hard. I'm trying to look after you.'

'I don't need looking after. I need a team that is completely committed. Are you saying you won't help?' I stick out my chin like I couldn't care less, but I know it won't be possible without Sam.

He sighs and puts his hands on the table, palms down. 'Of course not. Of course I'll help, if we vote to do it. But I think it's a mistake.'

We do not talk for much longer. Ruby asks some more questions about the specifics, about who should play which roles, about how the tasks would be divided. She sounds like her usual cautious self but this time I think she is not on my side. Greta and Uncle Syd have some other plans in train for a job of their own but these could be postponed for one week without detriment. By ten, everyone has said everything they need to and some have said more than they should. We have already invested more time in this than we had planned.

By the time my father calls for the vote we are tired after our busy weekend and early morning running around the university making everything ready. Nine arms go up to vote yes, some confident like me and Julius and Aunt Ava, some reluctant like Beau and Ruby. Only Sam votes no.

It's three o'clock in the morning and I cannot sleep. I have lain still on my front and back and tossed and turned, and the more I worry about the few hours remaining before dawn the more violent my movements become. In the kitchen I put the kettle on to boil and as I wait my eyes drop closed by themselves. This is infuriating. Bloody eyes. They couldn't manage this while I was horizontal? I hear footsteps in the hall and snap my head up: someone has seen the light.

'Della?' says Ruby. She pulls out a stool and sits at the servery, rubs her eye with her fist. Although we bought our dressing gowns separately they are nearly the same: a soft golden satin that drapes around us. It is the middle of the night, and her hair is perfect.

'Tea?' I say. I make Russian Caravan in a china pot the way she likes, and I lean against the cupboards as we sip.

'He might not be right, your brother,' she says eventually. 'There's a good chance you're right.'

'What's the risk—return ratio of "a good chance"? How do I add that up on Dad's blackboard?'

'That's the game, isn't it? That's where the courage comes in.'

Yesterday at the university and in the meeting, I wasn't thinking about the technical issues. Now it is all I think about. Changing mid-job from a short con which relies on paperwork with only one face-to-face to a long con with several meetings and three consistent personas is risky. It's almost never done. If I had known from the beginning it was to be a long con I would have done more research. I would know Daniel Metcalf back to front, better than he knows himself. But there is no time for that now.

'You're not even sure it's a good idea. You don't believe in it. I could see it on your face, when you voted.' I put my cup down and close my eyes and tap my head against the cupboard door. 'A Tasmanian tiger. For God's sake. What was I thinking?'

She says nothing. She waits. She looks at me with her Ruby eyes.

'He is not going to believe this,' I say. 'No one is going to believe this. I should have picked something more sensible, more reasonable.'

Ruby takes a slow sip of her tea. She spreads her hands and counts as she speaks, ticking off her fingers. 'A cream that melts away cellulite,' she says. 'A powder that goes in the fuel tank that means you hardly ever have to fill your car. Tablets you swallow that fill in your wrinkles from the inside. Plant juice from a remote village in Siberia that will stop ageing if you drink it every day. There are so many wonderful ideas out there.'

I nod. 'I know, I know.'

'And don't even mention the Hitler Diaries. I've never seen your father so depressed. It nearly killed him, not to have thought of that first. It was 1983, I'll never forget it. He wouldn't get out of his bathrobe for months. Those clever men made millions and they were only in jail for a few months. Worth it, I would have thought.'

'I guess.'

'You only have to read the papers to see what people will believe. Gods of every description. Angels. Ghosts. UFOs. Wives who would never cheat on their husbands. Mining company shares you can buy for ten cents that'll be worth two hundred dollars by the end of next week because a secret mine's going to be announced. Investment funds that pay twenty-seven per cent.'

'You're right. I know.'

'It's the Gods I really don't understand,' she says. 'If you fervently and absolutely believe in your own God, you must acknowledge that someone on the other side of the world believes in their God just as fervently. You can't both be right. Yet believers never have any doubt at all. They actually despise other people for feeling exactly the same as they do.'

'Someone has to decide what's true and what's not.'

'No, Della.' She leans across the counter and touches my hand, something she rarely does. 'I don't think so. Anyone who thinks they can make that decision for someone else is not to be trusted. And anyway, if there is someone who's so perfect, so right, all the time, that they get to decide what's true; well, it won't be you. It's not up to you to dictate who will believe what. It's your job to open a doorway. It's up to him if he walks through it.'

'I thought you were a sceptic,' I say. 'Apart from the slimming tea.'

'I am a sceptic. I'm just not a cynic. I don't think there's a human alive who doesn't believe in something that would be impossible to justify by logic alone, and sometimes people like us are actually the most susceptible to being taken. Possibilities are hard-wired into our brains. I've met people who believe in nothing, and you know what? I'd hate to be one of them. The most sour-faced, bitter, humourless people on earth. If it's a thousand-to-one shot that I'll lose weight because of drinking tea, I'll take the chance. Lottery tickets have longer odds and they're more expensive. Also, I like tea.'

To prove this she drains her cup and rinses it, leaves it on the edge of the sink. Back in my room I take off my gown, drape it on a hanger on the front of my cupboard and climb into bed. In the half light the gown could be Ruby, floating in space, watching over me.

I am leaning against my nondescript borrowed Toyota in the overnight car park at Wilsons Prom National Park and I can hardly keep my eyes open. It's Friday midday and I've slept around fifteen hours since Monday night. This morning I left home before dawn to drive for hours. I have already been to the ranger station and filled out the appropriate forms, given them Dr Ella Canfield's details for a camping permit and a fake emergency contact in case one of us falls off a cliff. This is compulsory for anyone staying overnight in the park and did not present any difficulty. I feel so securely Ella that this paperwork took no thought at all.

I'm wearing long khaki pants that I've stained with mud and olive oil, and a white T-shirt one size too small that Greta chose for me. I have a long-sleeved shirt over the top to keep the sun off my arms. A baseball cap and thick socks. My glasses of course, although if I had known at the beginning this job would be a long con I would never have started wearing them. Heavy hiking boots, bought just before the shops closed last night and roughed up with dirt and scratched with stones from the driveway around midnight. The clothes are all new. Somehow I had always pictured that my biggest ever job would take place in a ballroom at the Ritz, with me in a crushed velvet evening gown the colour of sapphires, and involve a minor member of European royalty who looked like Cary Grant. After this job these clothes are going straight to the Salvos. I have a rucksack for me and one for Daniel, also new, dirtied up. If he doesn't arrive soon I'll curl up on the back seat and have a kip.

Just when I think he's not coming, the BMW pulls into the park next to mine. He gets out and stretches like a cat, arms over his head, triceps flush against his ears. He's dressed for camping too, but he's made no attempt to artificially age his outfit. He looks like a model from an adventure store catalogue.

'So,' he says. 'When I finish this, will I get a merit badge?'

'You'll get a merit blister. It's ten kays walk in, steep, with a full pack. Are you sure you're up to it? I can't carry you out when you've had enough.'

This is silly, of course. He'd be half my weight again and looks like an athlete.

'That won't be necessary.' He raises one eyebrow. 'Though I'd like to see you try.'

Before I lift my own pack on to my shoulders I need to fit his. I have packed it as heavily as I can, with the bigger tent and sleeping bag and more than half of the food, because of course it's my own stamina that concerns me. I am not accustomed to a long walk over hills with heavy weight. Daniel has brought a small bag of clothes and personal items that fits neatly on top of his pack. When he has swung the pack up like it weighs nothing and it is resting on his shoulders, I need to adjust it so that the weight is carried by the frame instead of his spine. My brain is full to bursting with everything I've learned about camping from the staff at the adventure store and advice I've found on the internet. I am so busy thinking about which straps to pull and where the pack will sit that before I realise it I am standing directly in front of Daniel Metcalf, whose arms are raised, with my arms around his chest so I can reach the straps at the back.

My first instinct is to back away. This astonishes me. It's so foolish. This is what I should be encouraging, this accidental touching. Intimacy creates a sense of obligation so there'll be no doubt of my getting that cheque. Yet I cannot bring myself to do it. It's a sensation of being repelled, as if Daniel Metcalf has a force field. I keep my eyes on the pack, my mind on the job. The most important things here, more important than competence, are confidence and speed. Procedural memory is easy to obtain with a little time and focus, and convincing someone that you have any particular skill is more process than outcome. As I pull each strap and adjust the pack I curse once or twice, at people who don't look after equipment, at the design of the pack. I act like I know what I'm doing, even when I don't. On no account do I look up at Daniel's face.

Eventually we are done. I lift my own pack on to my knees and then around to my shoulders, as I was taught in the shop. The weight hits me like a falling piano. If I can carry this for ten kilometres without dropping dead, I'll have earned the money.

'And whose did you say this was? The pack?' Daniel says, as we head down the path.

This is the kind of thing that can get you into trouble. I can't confess that the pack is new, bought from an adventure store at the Mall. I am an outdoor person apparently, and I don't have much money. It fits that my friends are outdoor people so it is more likely

I would borrow a pack than buy one. But this is a man's pack, a tall man's pack at that. If I have borrowed it from a friend of mine, it reveals I have a tall, broad male friend whom I know well enough to hit up for expensive gear. This is counterproductive to fostering a feeling of intimacy, or impending intimacy, in the mark. This is also an example of why I am perpetually exhausted. Every simple thing is a calculation.

'I borrowed it. From a friend of my brother's. He's an idiot.'

'Because he trusted you with his pack?'

'Of course not. I'm absolutely trustworthy. My brother's friend is a little geeky, but fine. It's my brother who's the idiot.'

'Ah.'

Where possible, the rule says, stay close to the truth.

The first hour is hot and we don't speak much. Mostly he just looks around; he's new to all this outdoor business. He asks the occasional question about evolutionary biology in general. Nothing I can't handle. The life of Darwin, a bit about the theory. I tell him little factoids, like Darwin waited for twenty-one years before publishing *On the Origin of Species* because, although he believed in his theory, he did not have enough proof to satisfy himself. If not for the pressure of Wallace's imminent publication of the same theory, Darwin might never have gone to print. Darwin believed, but he knew the difference between belief and science.

Sometimes when I was a child I wished I had gone to school instead of being taught at home by Ruby. On Monday, when I saw those students in the food hall, I even wished I had gone to university. I know that this is just an abstraction, the idea of an intellectual life rather than the reality of seeking knowledge. In my career I have learned more about a wider range of subjects than any graduate. I speak enough French and Mandarin to get by, I can play competition tennis and golf, and crew a yacht competently. I have a better-than-working knowledge of the law and banking and financial planning, could pass as a geriatric nurse and I can back a semi-trailer around a corner although I don't have a licence. Ancient history and philosophy, my father's specialities, I know backwards. I have read many of the classics but only those my father favours, where helpless people are oppressed by the wealthy and powerful— Dickens, Gorky, Solzhenitsyn.

As we walk I think of those books and Daniel's inherited wealth and I'm happy I loaded up his pack with the heavy things.

The bush is odd here. This part of the park was burnt out by fires and the hills around the track are an eerie desecrated moonscape with black trunks stuck in the ground like angry spears. Along the edges of the trunks and the forks of the branches are flashes of new growth, iridescent green, and sprinkled along the black ground are long tufts of leaves, each cradling a perfect white native orchid. Once I almost stop to admire the scenery, then I realise I have seen this so many times that I barely notice anymore. In this section the path is wide and gravelled, and apart from the first steep hill where I thought my boots might slip, I saunter with just the right amount of nonchalance. I'm keeping up, and I'm not labouring. That's what matters.

By the end of the first hour, things aren't looking so good. I've already stopped for water twice, telling Daniel I'm concerned for him, stressing the importance of keeping up his fluids. He nods, but he doesn't seem as red in the face as I'm sure I am. I can't find the breath to speak. It must be over forty degrees.

Finally there is a clearing at the top of the hill, where we'll stop for lunch: two chicken schnitzel and mayo rolls I bought on the way. We take off our packs and sit on a flat platform in the clearing. Without the weight I feel I could float. The air is thin and fine. We are alone, except for an older couple on the other side of the clearing. Perhaps they are in their mid-sixties. They are fussing around a stand of native trees on the opposite side of the clearing, bird-watching with a borrowed pair of opera glasses. I can't see the opera glasses from here, but I know what they look like. Burgundy enamel, gold trim and a squat little handle.

It must have been a tremendous effort for the two of them to get this far, in this heat at their age. It would have taken them hours. I'm very impressed and humbled that they would go to such an effort. I hope there are no ill effects.

We eat our rolls and after a while the old couple wander over. They nod and smile. We nod and smile, and make room. They sit. The man takes a thermos and a plastic container of biscuits from a worn backpack and pours his wife a tumbler of tea. He is gentlemanly towards her, adding milk, checking it's hot enough, insisting she take a biscuit. I know what they will say, the substance of it, because I wrote their lines myself. They will make it their own; it is up to them how they will begin and the precise words they will choose. But the conversation will come from pages of eye-witness accounts I uncovered in my research, real interviews of people who have seen the animal around here, so this is not actually lying. It is just putting other people's words in their mouths. Ruby was right: who am I to say what should be believed?

'Biscuit?' says Uncle Syd, holding the container in front of me and Daniel. 'The wife makes them herself.'

'This is the life. Thanks,' says Daniel.

'Nice day for it,' I say.

'Beautiful, beautiful,' says Uncle Syd. 'Wonder what the poor people are doing today, heh?' He is wearing a ghastly plaid shirt I've never seen before, the same brown colour as the nearest tree. The fraying sleeves are pushed up to his elbows. He holds up his hands as he nibbles a biscuit, like a surgeon who has just scrubbed.

'Ooh, there,' says Ava, and she points to a shrub down the hill and reaches for the opera glasses. 'In that tree. Oh. The small branch. Near the top. It's got a blue head. It's. It's. Oh. It's gone. Never mind.'

Uncle Syd laughs. 'We're like fishermen, us twitchers, aren't we? Always on about the one that got away.'

'Spotted much so far?' says Daniel.

'Always, always,' says Syd. 'There are short-tailed shearwaters here, if you keep your eyes open.'

'I wouldn't know a short-tailed shearwater from a vulture,' says Daniel.

'It's only practice. Young fellow like you, nothing wrong with your eyes. Pays to be observant, sometimes.' Uncle Syd jumps a little, then looks around to check that no one can overhear him. 'Never know what you'll see around here, if you keep your eyes open.'

A little awkward, I think. Too fast, too forced. Still, Daniel does not seem to notice. He gives me a sideways glance.

'Simon!' Ava smiles. She looks tired. Her face seems more lined than usual. She's wearing baggy shorts and a white cotton blouse and sandshoes instead of her usual floral house dress, but has kept her striped hand-knitted bed socks. She pats Uncle Syd on the shoulder. 'Never mind my husband. He lets his imagination run away with him sometimes.'

Syd stretches his arms behind him and leans back. 'Quite right dear.'

I look at Daniel, and he looks at me. I scan the horizon. I speak slowly, for country people. 'Lots of bush out there. Miles of it,' I say. 'Never know what's hiding.'

'Not wrong there,' says Syd.

'Simon,' says Ava.

'Actually that's why we're here,' I say. 'We're researchers, from the university.'

'You don't say.' Syd raises an eyebrow.

'Simon. Drink your tea.'

'We're looking for people to chat with,' I say. 'About strange animals.'

'We didn't see nothing,' says Ava. 'You're wasting your time.'

'Too right,' says Syd. 'Long time ago and that. No sense dragging it all up again. Upsetting everyone.'

This is better. Nothing succeeds like reluctance. Aunt Ava is doing fine—she looks convincing, like she really doesn't want to speak. Her cheeks are rounded and red as if they were rouged. Her eyes are faded.

'My wife. She hasn't been well,' says Syd.

'I'm sorry to hear that,' I say, blinking. It's too hot. I shouldn't have made them come.

'You'd be doing us a real favour,' says Daniel, 'even if you told us what you didn't see.'

'I told you, we didn't see nothing.' Ava burps the biscuit container closed.

'And how far away were you, when you didn't see it?' I say.

'It was too long ago. We don't remember a thing,' says Ava.

'Oh Aggie, come on love. We didn't do anything wrong,' Syd says. 'I remember it like it was yesterday. It was 1979. Early November, the first week. I remember we stopped at the mailbox on the highway to post little Emmy's birthday card and it was her fourth. Her birthday's the seventh, so we would have posted the card a few days before. Emmy's our niece. Kids of her own now, of course.'

'We told all this to that newspaper man. No good came of it. They made us out to be a pair of loonies. Everyone had a big chuckle about it down the pub.' Ava wipes the back of her neck with a white handkerchief. I mustn't keep them too long. Ruby would have coped better but Daniel had already seen her in the Zoology Department.

'These young people won't laugh Aggie. They're scientists. From the university.'

She sips her tea, scratches the paper-fine skin on her neck. 'We'd come down here, to the park, for a drive. It was something we did on a Sunday. I'd pack sandwiches and a thermos of tea. Condensed milk in a tube. People don't seem to do that anymore, just go for a drive.'

'Everyone rushes these days,' Daniel says.

'Me and Aggie, we could never leave the farm for a proper holiday. But we always took a couple of hours, Sunday afternoon.'

'We weren't going very fast. Simon's a very careful driver, aren't you Simon? Especially in the park. Animals and that. Easy to run over one and then where would you be? We wouldn't have been going more than twenty-five mile an hour, I'd say. Wouldn't you say, Simon? It just walked straight across the road, right in front of us. Casual, like.'

Daniel seems entranced. He sits forward, hands on his knees. 'Can you describe it?'

'I remember saying to Simon at the time, that thing's taller than Blackie at the front, but its hind legs were real skinny and wasted like. Blackie was our Labrador. Cream coloured. That's why we called him Blackie. Bit of a joke,' says Ava. 'Anyway, it walked real peculiar like. Hopped, almost. I remember saying to Simon at the time, Simon, is that a dog or a kangaroo? But the tail didn't look like a dog's. Kinda fat at the behind end, pointy at the tip. Then we saw the stripes. I've lived round here me whole life and I never seen one of them before. So when we got home, I said to Simon best we call up the paper.'

'That Goldsmith, the newspaper fella. Pretended to be so interested on the phone. Even came out here to take a picture of us, and Blackie. Nearly died when we saw the write-up. Took the mickey out of us good and proper. You'd think we'd seen a flying thingamabob. Couldn't show me face down the pub for a fortnight.' Syd picks up the thermos and goes to pour another cup, but it is empty.

'Are you going to catch it?' says Ava. 'The poor little beastie.'

'We'd like to try,' I say. 'If it's still alive out there it would be our responsibility to keep it safe. To make sure nothing happened to it.'

'Oh it's still alive all right. We ain't the only ones who've seen it. Other folk have spoke to me on the quiet. I know it's there.'

'So do I,' says Daniel. 'So do I.'

It is hard for me to remember that I am normally level headed, cool, collected. I have never worked on a job with as many swings in emotion as this one. Just as I was convinced last night that Sam was right, that I will never pull it off, now I know I will. I know it. The look on Daniel's face tells me. He did see something, when he was a child here in the park. He has kept it close all these years. He wants to give me the money, he is dying to. It will take a disaster of monumental proportions to stop me getting that cheque.

Uncle Syd and Aunt Ava leave then, after packing up their backpack and making country goodbyes and shaking hands and easing to their feet. They pick their way towards the path. They wave. I have known them my whole life. As they go I have a brief image of them silhouetted against the sky.

'You didn't ask for their details,' says Daniel.

'Sorry?'

'Their names and address. Shouldn't you have asked, so you can find them again if you need more information?'

I squint into the sun, and then I swing my legs violently and kick up dirt. '*If*, Daniel. *If* this was a proper interview. *If* I ever get the bloody funding for a proper interview, I'd ask proper questions. How long they've lived in the area. Had they ever seen a photo of a Tasmanian tiger? Can they draw me a picture of what they saw? Had they been drinking? I'd bring a digital recorder so it's all on record. But there're already dozens of reports like that, and it isn't enough. If anyone's going to believe me, I need a whole lot more.'

'I've told you. If everything goes according to plan, you'll get the money.'

'Well.' I sniff. 'I'm not counting my chickens.'

'There are enough strange things down here to justify more research, surely. Like that old couple. They seemed convincing to me.'

'Over thirty years ago. A lonely country road. Two people, tired from a week's hard work on the farm. Perhaps the light was fading. This is precisely the kind of eyewitness testimony that counts for nothing in biology circles.'

'They've lived here, probably, for their whole lives. They know all the animals. They obviously saw something.'

I stand and hoist my pack over my shoulders. 'If I had a dollar for every time a well-regarded local citizen witnessed a rare, endangered or impossible animal, or for that matter, saw a ghost, UFO or politician outside of election time, I could fund my own research and I wouldn't need grants from people like you.'

He raises his eyebrows. 'People like me?'

'Yes.' I pick up the rubbish from the lunch and stand close to him. I lean in to put it a side pocket of his pack, but my fingers touch only the canvas. 'Outdoorsmen,' I say.

From then on things get better, and they get worse. The next four or five kilometres of the track thread through heavy rainforest, which is good: it's cooler here and the air smells sweet. There is a gentle rustling in the trees and I hear the sound of birds and it's much easier to think quickly without the sun beating down on my skull. It also slopes very steeply, downhill, and is rocky and slippery underfoot. This is bad. I can feel my thighs quivering already and I don't want to think about the pain I'll be in tomorrow. We are single file now, and I insist Daniel walks in front so I can limp or grimace in privacy.

'You're my responsibility,' I tell him when he protests. 'There'll be no damaged millionaires on my watch.'

Occasionally he turns and offers his hand to help me over rocks or steep drops, which I tell myself is common courtesy and not any doubts about my superior hiking credentials. I do not take his hand.

Apart from these times, for paces and paces what I do is watch the back of his head. I watch the way his shoulders tense and flex through his shirt, his forearms as they swing by his side. It is somewhat compelling, the sight of him, merely because this part of the trail is boring and there is nothing else to look at but trees trees trees. When we pass other hikers he stops. He is one of those odd people who chats idly with strangers, asks them how far we have come and how far we have yet to go. Sometimes he slows and stretches his neck to his shoulder on each side. Every so often he opens and closes his hands into fists and I wonder if the pack is too tight or not the right size and if it's cutting off the circulation to his arms, but even if it is I don't know how to fix it.

Single file makes conversation difficult. This is good. If we were chatting he might ask me the names of trees, or which birds are making which calls. These are things I ought to know; I think I do know some of them, but there is no sense risking a wrong answer if I can avoid it.

When we dip out of the trees the walk is pleasant enough, I'll admit. Not for this park the endless kilometres of tedium and forest trails that lead nowhere. The Prom is studded with views, with rocks and creeks to delight the most reluctant hiker. At one point we stop in a shady glen near a waterfall that forms a small creek. The water makes a tinkling sound. Daniel takes off his pack and kneels by the water, scoops some in his cupped palm and holds it to his lips.

'Wait. I'm not sure you're supposed to drink that water,' I say. 'It might be polluted.'

'Here? It's the Garden of Eden. This water's crystal clear.'

'You can't tell from just looking at it. Things aren't always as they appear.'

'Thank goodness for that. Otherwise the world would be very

dull.' He drinks, then wipes his wet hand down his neck and through his hair. 'Beautiful,' he says. 'Come on. You try it. Have faith.'

It does look beautiful. I imagine the taste: it would be cool and fresh, pure like nectar against my dry mouth. I reach around to my pack and pull out my water bottle, take a swallow. It is warm and flat. It tastes like plastic.

The last part of the track is a meandering boardwalk, blessedly flat. After almost four hours we walk out upon a perfect beach of white sand so pure it shimmers, and a perfect bay, an impossible arc of blue water meeting blue sky. There are no other humans in sight.

'Wow,' I say, then catch myself. 'No matter how many times I see that view it never fails to dazzle me.'

We walk the length of the beach. It is mid-afternoon now and these strange clothes are sticky against my skin and the pack is heavy on my hips. I look up the beach at the scrub where, if everything has gone according to plan, Anders and Beau are watching. I see no sign, no movement in the trees or peeking eyes. Daniel has not seen either of them before, but it's best to keep some faces unused. We do not know when they might come in handy.

Sweat has stuck my hair to the back of my neck and my T-shirt clings along the length of my spine. I'd like to swim in cool clear water, feel my tired legs floating and taste salt on my lips. If I thought it would be possible to bend and straighten my legs I'd walk to the water's edge to trail my fingers in the foam. I catch a glimpse of Daniel's face and am not surprised to see desire etched there. He's also looking at the water.

This is peaceful, this Crusoe-like stroll. I am almost enjoying myself until we stand on the edge of the creek that we must cross to reach the campsite nestled on the other side. I stop dead. I could cry.

On Tuesday night I pored over the tide table, even swallowed my pride and asked Sam for help, but clearly neither of us could decipher the times or location or phases of the moon. It is not ankle deep, as I had envisaged. It is much deeper than that. The water is clear and I can see the sand and stones on the bottom but I know by the waves the water is not to be trusted. It is a metre deep, maybe more.

'Well.' Daniel turns to me. 'What now?'

'This is a minor problem. When I was at Harvard researching I walked all day to a skunk research site, then I had to wade a raging river carrying my tent over my head. Alone. In the dark. If I remember right, it was raining. That was fairly hard. The only challenge here is not getting the packs wet. Wet clothes and wet food are no fun.'

He squats down, balanced despite the weight of his pack, and flicks his fingers in the water. He doesn't look at me. 'We'll have to take our pants off,' he says.

I can see the sign to the campground just across the creek. It must be thirty or forty metres away. I am almost there. He is right. We must get across the creek and if I don't take off my pants they will be soaked and sticky with salt water and I only brought one pair suitable for walking because I was concerned about the weight of the pack.

I have never had to take my pants off on a job before. What would my father say? And Ruby? I dread to think. My family has a proud tradition of gentlemen and lady con artists that goes back generations. They were called artists for a reason. Their job was to cast a spell on the unwary and the undisciplined. It's bad enough that I'm wearing these clothes, stained and smeared with mud and sweat. Wading half-naked across a stream in my underpants is neither elegant nor sophisticated. It is not likely to cast any spell other than making my dignity disappear before my eyes. Who would give money to someone not wearing pants? Except maybe the guy who smells of urine on the footpath in Swanston Street.

'Afraid so,' I say. I keep my voice light and cheerful, and somehow refrain from taking off this bloody pack and tossing it in the creek. I see movement. On the beach on the other side there are other people milling around, setting up tents. A circle is forming of ten or a dozen hikers, young men and women, passing around paper cups, toasting and laughing. An audience for my pants-down humiliation. Terrific.

'I don't know much about the great outdoors, I'm afraid,' Daniel says. 'You'd better show me how it's done.' His eyes are wide and round, his face is straight. He looks like a small boy asking if Santa Claus is real. Show him how it's done, he says. Like he can't take his pants off unless someone shows him.

'Right. Of course.' We're both adults here. I just need to be mature about this. Cool. Aloof. 'Right,' I say.

For heaven's sake. My hands go to the fly of my pants. I undo the top button. Then I do it up again. Then I scratch the side of my head. 'Why don't I go first?' I say. 'I'm the professional. I can judge the depth for you. Make sure you don't get into trouble.' My hands go to my fly again. This time I'm doing it. Just do it. Any minute now.

'Actually,' he says in a slow drawl, and I look up. 'I'm taller. I could pick my way across and find a path for you. It's up to you of course, but maybe it'd make more sense for me to go first.'

I realise I've been holding my breath when it comes out in a whoosh. 'Right again. It would make more sense for you to go first. Good thinking. Well done. Great. Thanks.'

He walks along the creek a short way and picks up a long stick from the shadow of a tree. Then in an instant he has unlaced his boots and taken them off, and then stripped his socks—I had not thought of this. If not for his offer I would have dropped my pants to have them trap my ankles and then I would have fallen face first in the sand. His pants are down before I can turn my head. I catch a glimpse of moulded thighs above shapely knees. Tartan boxers. What a stereotypical establishment choice. How bourgeois. How boring. Studying all this biology has taught me one thing: this Daniel Metcalf is certainly a product of his environment.

From the corner of my eye I see him unhook the buckle of his pack, swing his pants over one shoulder and, hiking boots in one hand, wade into the creek. I take another tiny peek to watch him walk across, purely to make sure he is not at risk of drowning. If he drowns now, there's a fair chance I won't see any money at all. He is using the stick to prod the creek bed ahead of him, to find where it is shallowest. The water is half-way up the back of his tanned legs.

He pauses in the middle and turns his head to look back at me; I avert my eyes just in time and pay careful attention to a rock at my feet. Then I take another quick glance, for safety purposes only, because I genuinely don't want any harm to come to him and after all I am responsible for his wellbeing and I need to make sure the water doesn't reach as high as his bottom which I can clearly see under the boxers because they are quite revealing and I can see the muscles of his bottom tensing as he walks and the line where it meets his thighs. Clearly he exercises regularly, whatever exercise rich people do. Personal training, or polo.

His wading has attracted the attention of the campers on the other side too. They are standing, plastic cups in hand, cheering and toasting his progress.

He is on the other side now, legs wet and shining in the sun. He bends his arm at the elbow and rests his forehead to his fist, miming a he-man pose for the campers, who laugh and clap. 'Right,' he yells back at me. 'Your go.'

'Right,' I say. 'I'm on my way.' I hop on one leg for a moment but I cannot balance, so I sit on the sand, ungainly, unattractive. I take off my boots and peel off my socks and my feet do not look like my own: they are white and sock-marked and there is no polish on the nails. Ruby was insistent that scientists do not wear polish on their toenails. I fold the socks carefully inside the boots. Then I fold the laces in, to make it neat, and struggle to my feet.

'And don't forget to unbuckle your pack. You don't want the weight of it to drag you to the bottom, if you fall.'

I freeze for a moment and stare at him. He shrugs. 'I saw it on Discovery Channel. "Minutes from Death", it was called. But of course I don't need to tell you about hiking safety.'

I snort. 'Of course not.'

He gestures to a section of the creek near where he crossed. 'I think it's shallower here,' he says. 'You'll get across without your pack getting wet.'

'Good,' I say. 'Now turn your head.'

'What?'

'Turn. Your. Head. This is not Men's Gallery. In fact, turn right around and face the other way.'

'You're shy,' he says. It's not a question. I can see from here he's frowning, like he doesn't understand.

'I'm shy for a normal person. I'm extroverted for a scientist. Of course, an extroverted scientist is one who looks at *your* shoes when speaking to you. Now turn around.'

He laughs, but he does it. The circle of campers guess what's happening and laugh too. Some ostentatiously turn their backs, others peer at me more closely now they know it's forbidden.

The sooner this is over, the sooner my dignity can begin to

repair. I might check the first-aid kit. There's Stingose for stings, and burn cream for burns. Dignipatch, perhaps, for my wounded pride. One more deep breath, and my trousers slip off in a quick movement. I stretch my shirt down to cover my undies, a pointless attempt that only makes me feel even less graceful. At the first step into the creek I almost jump out again. The water is fiercely cold, something Daniel failed to mention. He was right about the shallowest way across, though. I am shorter than him but the water doesn't reach the bottom of my pack.

'Going all right?' he calls.

'Just don't turn around.'

The cold water brings all my consciousness to the skin of my thighs. It tickles. Finally the sides of the creek begin to slope upwards. I dig my toes into the sand for better purchase and haul my legs out. The drag of the water makes walking hard. On the other side of the creek I shake my feet and water sprays off them like diamonds.

'Can I turn around now?' he says.

'No.'

I stand directly behind him so I can't be seen and rest one hand on his shoulder.

'Single file, and don't look back. Off you go,' I say.

He grunts and walks along the beach a little way. I can see the circle of campers more clearly now. I was right: they're backpackers, northern Europeans by the look of them, a mix of handsome girls and boys, some just back from a swim, some dozing under broad hats and others drinking. It must be nice not to work all the time, not to spend every moment thinking about this job or the next one or honing skills for the one after that. As we pass them, we nod and they wolf whistle us both, offer us wine and a towel. We decline.

★

Julius and Greta are kneeling in a small clearing in front of four bright blue tents. This campground is a flat ledge in the side of a hill; the pit toilet is at the top and the creek is barely visible through the scrub at the bottom. The clearing they have selected for the tents is at far end of the campground and except for Julius and Greta it is deserted. There are no other tents or people in sight.

The trees around the clearing are gums, tall and clean like the masts of a ship, with smaller scrub beneath them. The effect is a protected terrace that is at once cosy and exposed. The tents are huddled in a half circle around a long-fallen tree that is the right height for sitting on or resting a lamp. The tents are chest height, taut fabric made igloo-shaped by flexible plastic poles threaded through sleeves in the nylon. We practised in the backyard at home but they never seemed to work the same way twice so we decided it was best for Julius and Greta to hike in earlier. They could take their time and put up the tents without Daniel watching, in case things didn't go as smoothly as we'd hoped. Julius and Greta look hot and ruffled. I dread to think how long this has taken them.

There was also too much equipment for them to carry, so Beau and Anders walked in earlier this morning as well with the rest of the gear, everything that we could scrounge or steal or buy in the last few days. This was a thankless job for our poor packhorses.

The equipment is spread around the campsite in piles, looking real; not like a stage set. Much of the equipment was borrowed from the Zoology Department store room and looks convincingly abused by decades of students: surplus night vision goggles that might have been antique when originally acquired by the Third Reich; dinky wooden frames of various sizes—I assume to make casts of tracks; another set of frames with mesh of varying sizes that stack one on top of the other, with the largest mesh on top; plastic toolboxes filled with zip-lock bags, gloves, brushes, labels and trowels; a leather pouch of what looked like old dentist's picks; one pre-Cambrian SLR camera with the film compartment held closed by a rubber band; old field guides of tracks and scats with stained covers and dog-eared pages. Julius and Greta turn around as we approach.

'Well,' says Greta. She is dressed conservatively this time: neck to wrist to ankle, her hair in an unflattering high ponytail that stretches the skin of her eyes and will probably give her a headache by sundown. No makeup. It's not until I see her and feel a flood of relief that I realise I was worried about this. She looks us up and down; we are still dripping in our underpants. 'You go girl.'

'Ella had an overwhelming desire to get naked, so we stopped for a quick skinny-dip,' Daniel says. 'The water was so cold I'm now a soprano.'

'The creek was up and we didn't want to get our packs wet,' I say. 'There was no skinny-dipping involved. We were clothed, except our trousers. That's all.'

'Mr Daniel Metcalf sir,' Julius says. He also looks perfectly crumpled and student-like, which must hurt. He has borrowed clothes from Sam which were already pre-creased and pre-stained. He rushes forward and helps Daniel off with his pack. 'On behalf of my colleague and myself may I mention what a pleasure it is to see you again.'

While Daniel is distracted I whisper to Greta about the campers on the beach.

'We've spoken to them already,' says Greta. 'They arrived an hour ago. They're German backpackers, very friendly. They've brought in wine in plastic bags. Lots of wine. They've already asked us down for a few drinks. I've told them we're working. They're just here to relax and swim. They won't disturb us.'

Wine in plastic bags sounds like a good idea. Shame I didn't think of it, but it doesn't really matter since all the bottles were in Daniel's pack. I turn my head. Legs now dry, Daniel is stepping into his trousers.

I suppose if I looked at it objectively, he would be attractive. If he wasn't, as Beau would have it, a battery hen. A mark. Greta gives me a smirk. My face feels hot; I pray I'm not blushing. I'm glad the backpackers won't give us any trouble. I am feeling quite disturbed enough as it is.

I do not come from a family of savers. We are grasshoppers, not ants; we do not put something aside for a rainy day. You might get hit by a bus tomorrow, my father often says, so all of us revel in our surpluses now without heed for the future. But now I must ration. I know only as much science as I could acquire with no formal training in four days in a library. It must last the whole weekend.

'Dr Canfield,' Julius says. 'We have walked quite a long way today and set up the camp. As keen as I am to begin work, I fear missing some small but crucial detail through fatigue.'

'It wasn't that far Joshua,' I say. 'You're used to this.'

'It's almost dark,' Greta says.

'It isn't,' I say. 'There's hours yet.'

'By the time we unpack all our equipment it will be,' Greta says.

'I'll help,' says Daniel. 'It's no trouble.'

I make a show of looking at the sky, at my watch, then I regard my feckless subordinates. 'All right. I'm tired and sweaty from the walk too. Let's just relax this afternoon. We'll start work bright and early tomorrow.'

Julius and Greta rejoice at this, as though I am usually a hard taskmaster and free time is unexpected. Daniel frowns.

'Not on my account,' he says. 'I don't want to disturb you. I want to see you in action.'

'There's plenty of time for that tomorrow,' I say. 'For now, let's unpack, have a swim, a nice dinner. Relax.'

We change and walk down to the sea. At the last moment I wear my dirty T-shirt over the top of my swimmers—if anyone asks I will say I burn easily. I go first, with Greta, to keep her eyes front. Daniel and Julius follow. The backpackers nod and wave as we pass. The sea here is not like the bay back in Melbourne, which is a dull grey like Soviet milk. Here it is almost alive, sometimes green and sometimes blue, deep, and quiet. The sand is white, spread like sugar, so fine it squeaks under our feet. Greta and Julius wade only up to their ankles before squealing like children.

'Bloody hell,' says Greta. 'I'm not going in there. That water must be straight from Antarctica.'

'I too have gone far enough. I am African. We are hot-climate people.' Julius nods at the backpackers. 'Only Scandinavians or Germanic peoples would swim in this water.'

'You don't know what you're missing,' Daniel says, and he runs, splashing, until the water is deep enough for a shallow dive. He comes up shaking his hair, gleaming like an otter, and dives under again.

I glare at Julius and Greta, they glare back at me. 'Go on,' I say. 'Dive in.'

'You dive in,' they say together.

'I'm the supervisor of this expedition,' I say. 'It would look very weird if we three hardened campers were scared of a little cold water while Mr Toorak was swimming. Dive in.'

Greta squats a little and dips her elbow in the water. 'Not even for a quarter of a million dollars. I'd get hypothermia.'

'And I'd freeze my balls off. Greta's right. That current's straight from Mawson Base,' says Julius. 'Anyway boss, it's your project.'

'Right,' I say. 'Thanks. Thanks very much.'

I wade out further and I will not call out or even squeal but my face is away from them and they cannot see me grit my teeth. Finally the water is over my shoulders and it feels warmer now that I am all under, and now I am glad I have done this. I will sleep better tonight cleansed of the sweat and dirt of the walk, I tell myself. My tired muscles will feel better. Then I look up and see Daniel, floating on his back, lazily kicking. I look back and see Greta and Julius, shivering and complaining.

All at once I know why I do not like to touch him, why I have not been flirting with him as I normally would. There is something wrong with him, something I should have seen before. Daniel Metcalf is lying.

It is morning now and I have thought about Daniel Metcalf most of the night with an intensity bordering on obsession. I have turned everything over in my head. The night was long and cold. Sleeping bags make your legs feel pinned and your arms trapped. The tent was a thin membrane hardly sufficient to block out the world. It is difficult to imagine that people do this on purpose. Camping is like a celebration of poverty designed for people nostalgic for the Great Depression.

I must figure this out, I must. I won't be made the fall girl if this operation goes south. I have leafed through the pages of my memory for everything he has said, every expression I have seen on his face. There are times his face becomes set, determined, in response to some inner thought, but these are rare. At these times he rolls his shoulders and rubs them, like the weight on them is more than he can bear. Other times his face is soft: he is an innocent and this is all a lark. *Surely we'll have to take our pants off.* Sweet as a schoolboy. Mostly he is cynical, sarcastic, wry.

Yet he did not turn around when I told him not to. Did he not want to see me in my underpants? Perhaps he does not find me attractive? Nah. Perhaps he is gay? That would explain this feeling that he is lying. No; I know this is not true. Even if I missed this, it is not a mistake that Greta would make.

I should have realised earlier that something was not right. My father said it first when I told him that Daniel had asked me a technical question in our first interview. *It's a rare millionaire who will reveal his ignorance on any topic.* And here he is, our rare millionaire. He swims in freezing water without hesitation when we three professional con artists shiver in our bathers. He carries a heavy pack for ten steep kilometres, not only without complaint, but with solicitous care. He offers me his hand to climb over rocks and considers my welfare at all times but is also sarcastic and cynical. There is clearly something wrong.

I have known many millionaires and there are two types. The first are those who have made their own money, whether by hard work or luck or talent. These are a varied mix of people and their behaviour cannot be predicted. The second group are those, like Daniel Metcalf, who received their money without a drop of sweat from their brow and are proceeding, quickly or slowly, to lose it. And they do not behave like this, that much I know. They were born to wealth; they know no other life and they consider those who are not wealthy to be somehow flawed. They do not have his flippant air.

But the most telling thing was this: the twenty-five thousand dollar cheque he offered me and said I could keep unless I wanted to try for the quarter of a million. *You can keep it, if you like. Or you can hand it back to me.*

I cannot believe I fell for this old trick, one my father taught me when I was not ten years old. Sharp gamblers use it often, allowing their mark to win the first few hands convincingly when the pot is small. My father would have used it in a slightly different fashion: perhaps he sold a mark a hundred shares and offered to buy them back for double the price in just a few weeks. The mark pockets a large profit on a small investment. Then Dad would sell the mark ten thousand shares under the same arrangement and when the time came to buy them back he would have disappeared. This is a variation on what we call 'bait and switch'.

The conclusion is simple. Either Daniel has no money or he is trying to con me. But con me out of what? He is no longer just another good-looking mark. Now I find Daniel Metcalf very, very interesting.

Today the three of us run through the science stuff we have practised all week. I am alert, engaged. I watch Daniel Metcalf's every action, mark his every word. When I look at him my pulse races. He is an eagle after all, not a chicken. I cannot confess this to Julius and Greta, whom I have dragged here. I have no evidence and I am culpable.

Now I see all the things I neglected to do, like obtain a recent estimate of the Metcalf wealth. I took the Metcalf name as all I needed to know, like any foolish mark, when Daniel could be a gambler or an addict or could have spent the fortune a thousand ways. He has a fine house and expensive car and clothes but I of all people should know that these things count for nothing. I did not ask for any proof that he could pay the money he has promised. My father has a friend in the city, a financial journalist, who keeps up with things like this yet I never asked him.

The science itself progresses well. Despite Sam's fears, this is not as difficult as it sounds. One must exude confidence, that is all. As you must if you're being anyone, even yourself. All movements must be sure and dextrous. There can be no hesitation. The work itself is of less consequence than its appearance. Daniel Metcalf will have no idea if we are doing these things correctly.

We do not wander far from camp. This is not the research project itself after all, just a small taste of what we will do when we are properly funded. We pass stands of impenetrable rainforest, tall open forests, woodlands, ancient Aboriginal middens. We find likely spots, some just off the main track, some at the bottom of the hill near the creek.

Daniel stands back and patiently observes us working. Julius and Greta squat on a path or kneel on squares of foam rubber as they measure and photograph tracks and collect droppings, a skill we practised with the help of a ranger in the closest national park to our home. In real life, even finding the tracks was harder than I expected: the walking trails are mostly small rocks and hard to distinguish from the bush itself, the forest floor overlain with leaves. Sometimes I think I am pointing at nothing and sometimes I fear I am diligently measuring my own boot-print, but I do it with such authority that anyone would believe.

Yet after a few hours I begin to see things I could not see before. The smallest pad print set in dust along a dry creek bed, the finest scratches near the base of a scraggly eucalypt. It takes surprisingly little practice to make these things come alive. As I kneel to pick up small white bones I would not even have noticed last week, I instinctively hold my breath so they do not gust away. Once I find a tooth from some kind of animal lying in a pile of dead leaves and peeled bark. It is white and pure and smooth like porcelain and if I did not know it was only an old tooth I would have thought it remarkable. In the palm of my hand it could be an oddly shaped jewel.

'Look at that,' Daniel says. 'That might be a tooth from a Tasmanian tiger. You never know.'

He is right. You never know. I had never thought of science as gambling before but now I see it is a roulette wheel. It is two-up. Gambling is, as they say, a tax on people who do not understand probability theory, but now I see that winning is not the point. The point is that divine moment when the coin hovers in mid-air or the silver ball speeds around the outside of the wheel or just the merest hint of bone is visible above the ground. In that shining moment before anything is decided, everything is possible.

I could have managed this, if I had gone to school and then to university. This might have been my career. Science, at least this kind of science, is more like a country craft; it is a manual skill, a dextrous one, where the clever hands of clever people make a story from bits of bone and photos of tracks and scratches on trees. Like making a quilt from squares of coloured fabric.

I feel light, energised, focused. Julius and Greta work in unison as if they had laboured together for months, as though they were in the Olympic synchronised evidence-collecting team. They show Daniel how to gauge the weight of an animal by how far the tracks sink into wet sand, how to make a plaster cast of a small paw print, how to place a ruler near a burrow so a photo shows its size. They are professionals and I am grateful as I watch them work. I also say a silent prayer for libraries and librarians. Perhaps I will make a small donation to the library nearest our home if I ever get my hands on the cheque.

And it is working. He is buying it. I am pleased, and something more. The thrill of this contest is making my skin feel alive and every sense is alert. I sometimes stand at the back and watch Daniel watching Greta and Julius and he frowns in concentration and asks sensible questions, and I wonder over every one. This is like playing chess with my father. I cannot help but smile. Julius jumps into the silences to insert little-known biology facts he has cribbed from textbooks.

'Did you know, Mr Daniel, that biologists do not call their field work sites digs? This is a common misconception caused by the seepage of archaeological terms into popular culture. Neither living animals nor fossils are found in a single, manageable site like a small buried village that can be roped off and excavated. Either they roamed free over a considerable distance, or they belong in a single geological stratum and can be found over miles of terrain,' he says.

'Is that so, Joshua?' says Daniel. He is endlessly polite, annoyingly courteous, only slightly sarcastic. *Is that so, Joshua?* could mean he is genuinely interested, or he disagrees, or he realises that Julius is talking half-digested rubbish. Or he could be thinking of something else entirely. I try to match each possibility to the expression on his face, without being caught observing him. Which turns out, even with my years of practice at reading faces, to be an impossible task.

At noon we stop for a light lunch and as we sit under the shade of a stand of trees, he asks me how we would spend the money. His money. I smile and it crosses my mind to tell him the truth: some new furniture, fix the gutters, a small fund to cushion the old age of my father and Ruby and Ava and Syd.

Instead I smile ethereally like I am glimpsing heaven through a shining portal, and say all the things I have rehearsed. I tell him about the army of researchers, and the command tent with a map and coloured pins: pink to show the location of sightings, and blue to show the traps I would spread through the park. I tell him about the pheromones, the special blend I intend to develop from marsupial species genetically closest to the tiger, and how I'd spray them on a dead chicken. This would be the perfect temptation for a carnivore like the tiger but repugnant to herbivores like wombats or wallabies.

I kneel down, pick up a stick and draw patterns in the dirt that represent a long tube attached to a square. I keep talking as I wave the stick across the ground. This is the camouflaged wire trap I'd build. It has a trick hatch leading to a long tunnel *here* then finally a holding cage *here*. This hatch wouldn't catch smaller animals like rodents or possums. I'd place the bait carefully in the kind of habitat that tigers were known to prefer when they were observed in Tasmania. I'd choose spots far away from tracks and campsites. The whole area would be surrounded by a network of movement-sensitive night vision video cameras. By the end even I am enthusiastic. Daniel looks positively transported.

'Sounds irresistible.'

'But this is where researchers have gone wrong in the past: I'd spray everything with a fine mist of diluted tea tree oil to cover any human scent. The tiger was famous for its sense of smell.'

'You've got it all worked out.' Daniel kneels to get a better look at my trap drawing.

I sigh and shake my head; part hopelessness, part yearning. 'I've had years to think about it.'

I tell him more, on a roll in both fiction and reality. 'I'd also have a couple of researchers set up a stand in the main street of town, asking locals if they had ever seen an animal they couldn't identify and recording each interview for posterity.'

'And I would like to see some money put aside for DNA testing,' says Julius. He is just off the track, peering to look at small white fragments scattered at the base of a tree. 'DNA technology is the key to the identity of all animals and will prove the future of our work, I'm sure. Some things are in our genes.'

Daniel walks over to look at Julius's pieces of bone. I walk behind him, he does not look back. As Julius points out the bone fragments and speculates about the kind of animals they might have come from, Daniel idly picks up some small stones from the edge of the path and begins arranging them in groups and piles. I watch his long fingers, the nails clipped short. His hands are larger than I would have expected, the knuckles angular and defined and dusted with fine hairs. As he turns his hand I see the scar on his palm, fine and even as though an artist had drawn it in white enamel. His wrists pivot by the most ingenious mechanism every time he turns his hand to the side. It takes me a moment to look down at my own hand and realise it moves the same way. I had never noticed before.

I look at Daniel again. It is tiredness and stress, I know, but for a moment I cannot look away: the way he casually sorts the stones by some means unknowable to me—perhaps by size or shape, or is it colour?—suddenly seems the most interesting thing I have ever seen.

Before long it's almost evening and time to head back to camp. Julius goes ahead with Daniel. Greta holds me back by my arm until they are out of sight.

'What the hell do you think you're doing?' She lifts her sunglasses and squints at me, although her tight hair makes it difficult for her to close her eyes.

'Nothing. I'm not doing anything.' This is true, but it's what we planned. My role is mainly to supervise my students. Daniel has been trying to assist, fetching things from the camp sometimes: different lenses for the camera Greta hadn't realised she would need, the right size of envelope to hold the samples. I walk with him to different sites, show him the correct forceps, which horsehair brush is best, or at least those that feel the best to me. We breathe the air, we walk on the beach. Everything is going according to plan. I cannot think what she means.

'Exactly,' she says. 'You're doing nothing. You're just standing back and watching him with this strange smile on your face.'

I shake my arm free of hers. 'Greta. Don't.'

'"Don't"? Is that all you can say, "Don't"? We've all put a lot of work into this, Della. Hours and hours. I am dressed like an Amish man and this hairstyle hurts my brain. I am not pretty. I hate not being pretty. I'm looking like this, as directed, so as to not take the focus off you.'

'Yes,' I say, and I try to walk around her. 'Thanks for that.'

She holds me by the shoulders and moves us behind a tree. 'Della. I have dirt under my fingernails. If you don't close this deal I will undo these buttons and cut these trousers into short shorts and let my hair down and I will close it for you. I swear to you Della I will.'

I look down at my clothes. They are fine. Adequate. If I dressed as Gypsy Rose Lee, Greta would think I was in a burka. 'What do you suggest I do?' I say. 'Club him over the head and drag him back to my cave? That'll make me look like a serious researcher.'

'Don't be ridiculous,' she says. 'You know exactly what to do. First, listen to him. Uncle Laurence taught us that. Rule number fourteen B or whatever. It's the listening, not the speaking, that draws them in. Then lead him down the path until he takes over, until he thinks it was all his idea. Then scurry away like a delicate little flower who doesn't want to unfairly influence his decision because of your so-called ethics.'

She is right about the listening. That is what wins someone over, although it isn't as easy as it sounds. Agreeing with every lame political opinion or implausible religious view. And never appearing bored, no matter what idiocy comes out of their mouths.

'We're doing well enough with the science,' I tell her. 'I won't need to do anything else.'

She grunts and pulls at her ponytail. 'Closing something this size is half logic and half emotion, you know that. OK, the logic half is going well. But you *have* to look after the emotion. You have to make sure he's gagging to give it to you. And the money as well. Stop him thinking with his brain. Get him thinking with something else.'

'It's not that easy.' I sound pathetic. Whiney.

I don't feel the physical reluctance to touch him that I felt earlier. Now I still want to keep my distance until I work out what's going on. But my intuition about Daniel makes it all the more important that I engage his feelings, throw him off balance. In a closer contest he might make a mistake. I know Greta is right. This cannot be avoided any longer.

'Of course it's that easy.' Greta snorts. 'It always has been before. But I'll admit it doesn't help that you're dressed like that.'

She stands in front of me and closes one eye like she's judging Best in Show. Then she pulls my T-shirt down at the front and tucks it in tighter, and she pushes up my breasts so more cleavage is exposed. Then she stares, and freezes.

'What?' I say.

She looks like she's about to faint and peeks down my top. 'Thick straps, mesh. No shape. Beige. Don't tell me you're wearing a sports bra. What in God's name were you thinking?'

'It's hiking, Greta. Camping. I'm like a method actor. It's about characterisation.'

'It's about stupidity, that what it's about. Wait here,' and she stomps back to the camp, returning with a bundle clasped tight in her hand. 'Here,' she says, handing it to me. 'It's clean.'

I can feel the lace. I look down—it's fire-engine red. I'm not moving.

'It's French. Push-up. Come on, Nanna. Put it on.'

'We're camping, not pole dancing,' I say.

'Put. It. On.'

There's nothing for it. I duck behind a tree, strip off and change bras. I hand Greta the sports bra. She hesitates before touching it.

'Thanks,' she says. 'I'll treasure it always.' She rolls it into a ball and shoves it in her pocket, then she tightens the belt of my shorts and kneels so she can fold up each leg higher. I hold on to her shoulder to steady myself.

She stands again, and frowns. 'Hold still,' she says, and takes a tube of lip gloss from her pocket. She holds my chin and applies it. It wouldn't be my choice, I can see from the tube. Too shiny. Then she stands back and admires her handiwork.

'That's better. I'm beginning to think Sam was right. You're not yourself on this job. There's some reason you're not playing this right. You're chilling.'

'All right, all right. But how do you expect me to do anything with you two around? In dirty hiking clothes? In tents? I do better work with champagne and soft music.'

'You have stars. You have wine. You have everything you need. After dinner Julius and I will wander down to our German hiking friends for a few quiet drinks. You'll have the whole camp to yourselves for at least a couple of hours. Long enough to lead him on, not long enough to get yourself into trouble. We'll be back to rescue you if things go too far. Just do it, Della. We're all counting on you.'

We walk back up the track and stop when the camp is just in sight, then Greta holds me still by the arm again.

'Are you going to ask him about the tiger? About the time that he saw it, when he was a kid?' she says.

I shake my head. 'There's no way I can know about that. It'd give the game away. I'll try and encourage him to tell me. That's all I can do.'

In the camp, Julius is kneeling by the camp stove, cooking sausages and instant pasta. He and Daniel are talking, laughing, but I can't hear what they're saying. Then Daniel walks back to his pack, lying beside the tent. His back is to us. He feels around for a moment and brings out a clean T-shirt, then he whips his shirt off in one smooth movement. We can see the flat plain of his back, the brown muscles as they slide over his shoulder blades, the shadow in the channel of his spine.

'Oh, and Della, remember,' Greta says. 'If you really don't want to do this, that's fine. I'll be more than happy to step in for you.'

It is done, just as Greta said it would be. We have eaten a simple camping dinner and the cleaning up, such as it is, is finished. Greta and Julius have retired to the backpackers' camp on the beach. No doubt Julius will make new friends and tell them all about the pitfalls of carrying water from a well. Greta will have shed her Amish exterior and be surrounded by a legion of tipsy German admirers.

It is dark and Daniel and I are alone. Aside from the occasional cheering in the distance that may be part of a drinking game or a welcome for a late-comer, we might be the only people alive on earth. Daniel lies on his side on a rug in front of the lamp, a plastic tumbler of red wine in his hand. I also have a tumbler of wine, but no possessions: no keys or handbag, purse or mobile or lipstick. It has taken me some time to realise that the incredible lightness I feel is in part due to this lack; the absence of things that couldn't weigh more than a few hundred grams but that no modern woman would consider being without.

There is no wind. I can smell the sea and a lemon-scented gum not far down the hill above the creek. I have drunk more wine than is sensible and even as I register this I take another swig. The horizon tilts slightly when I turn my head. I can delay no longer. It is time to begin.

'The scar,' I say. 'On your hand.'

He holds his hand out straight with the palm toward me. Perhaps this gesture is meant to show me the scar, or perhaps it is a stop sign. But it is too late. I cannot stop.

'How did it happen?' I say.

He rubs the scar with the thumb of his other hand, as if he has been derelict and it is a stain he could scrub away with enough effort. 'It's painful to think of,' he says. 'I don't talk about it often.'

I say nothing. I make space for his words to come.

All at once his face looks gaunt, his eyes hollow. 'I was on a bus in the city. It was just a normal day. Then this bomb-squad cop jumps on board. One thing leads to another, and the bus driver gets shot so I take over the steering. Then it turns out that there's a bomb planted on the bus, and we can't slow down below fifty miles per hour or it will explode and kill us all. I have to drive and drive. Until eventually we get to the airport where we can go around in circles and if the bomb goes off no one will die but us. It was horrific.'

'That sounds vaguely familiar.'

'When we finally get everyone off the bus, me and the bomb squad guy get kidnapped and forced into an abandoned railway car, which explodes. That was the first time I kissed another man.'

'That must have been very traumatic for you.'

'It was. That's why I always drive. Me and public transport—it's not good.' He shudders. 'After all this time I still can't bear to get on a bus or train.'

'Just as well you have a nice new BMW.'

'Lucky, isn't it?' he says, sniffing and wiping his eyes on his sleeve. 'But emotional scars take a long time to heal. I still can't see Sandra Bullock on the cover of *Who Weekly* without sobbing.'

'And where did the scar come from exactly?'

'Oh, this? I did it when I got home. Broken wine glass in the sink.'

I stretch out on my back for a moment, hands behind my head, looking at the stars. 'And are you always this flippant? Or just with me?'

'And are you always this serious? Or just with me?'

'I'm serious because life is serious. I have responsibilities.'

He puts his hands behind his head too. He is mimicking me. 'Not now you don't,' he says. 'Now there's just the sea and the stars.'

'My work is serious, I mean. I do serious work.'

'It's just a job, Ella. It doesn't define you.'

I have no idea how to reply to such a ludicrous statement. What does he think defines us, if not our work? I'd like to tell him that he's never had to work a day in his life. That he can joke around all he likes: he's never had to worry about money or if all the deadlocks on the front door are bolted properly or if he can pull off one great big deal to buy a bit of pride. He can spend money where he chooses, give it to whomever he likes.

I bite my tongue because telling him all this will not help me seduce him and find out what he is hiding, and also because I remember just in time that his father is dead and so is his mother. Then I want to tell him that he has it easy because his father is dead and he doesn't have the weight of history and expectations and tradition on him and he has no Thursday-night meetings to report to and can do what he likes because no one is watching, but I don't say this. Perhaps, from the perspective of someone whose parents are dead, it might come across as a little insensitive.

'Tell me something serious,' I say. I wriggle a little, cross my legs, lean forward. Sitting on the ground is uncomfortable. It didn't mention that in my research on camping. 'Tell me something serious, something you have never told anyone else, and I'll tell you something flippant.'

'A challenge,' he says. 'OK. Something serious.' He pauses for a while, then, 'How's this? When I was eleven I was madly in love. Andrea Garida. She was an older woman. She was thirteen.'

'A friend from school?'

'No, no. There were only boys at my school. She was a friend of my sister's.'

'Did you propose? Is this story about your elopement?'

'A little sensitivity, please. My heart was broken. Andrea had this tiny button nose with freckles, and a little gap between her front teeth. That gap drove me crazy.'

'Sounds like a perfect match. What happened?'

'My mother had a pendant in her jewellery box that she never wore. She always had a lot of jewellery, rings, necklaces, earrings. This one pendant wasn't even a pretty colour. It was clear, like glass. Like a big piece of glass. I thought Mum'd never miss it. I gave it to Andrea.'

'And?'

'Andrea was thrilled. She let me kiss her and I thought I'd died and gone to heaven. At home, things weren't so good.'

'Your parents didn't think that it was a fair trade, the pendant for a kiss?'

'By the time the police were called and the staff were questioned and the security people had been to check all the locks, I was frantic.

I think I wet the bed. By the time I confessed I'd seriously considered running away to join the circus. Andrea's parents were very understanding. Andrea, not so much. She didn't want to hand it back. My mother bought her something more reasonable from a department store to make it up to her, but she never spoke to me again.'

'Ouch.'

'You know, when my mother died, most of the jewellery went to my sisters. I only kept a few things, for sentimental reasons. I kept that necklace. The house, well, you've been there. It's not exactly me. It doesn't really seem like mine, but upstairs I have a study that belongs to me. I keep everything that's important there. I keep the necklace to remind myself that stuff like jewels and money aren't that important.'

'Still, it was your mother's necklace. Weren't your parents mad?'

'Not overly. They thought I was being generous, and after all I was pretty upset. I was the baby of the family, got away with murder. If they had thought I was stealing, then lying about it, they might have been a little cross.'

'They thought stealing and lying were bad things?'

He laughs. 'Well aren't they?'

'It depends,' I say, and I know this is dangerous territory, but perhaps he will reveal something. 'Robin Hood is always the hero of the movie. The sexy, courageous one. The Sheriff of Nottingham was always the villain, plus he was ugly. Of course Marion preferred Robin. And Robin was just a thief and a liar with good PR, so I guess everything is relative.'

'I guess it is.' He smiles and narrows his eyes. 'I didn't realise you were so fond of liars. Sexy and courageous indeed.'

This is almost a confession. I almost have him. 'It's nothing to do with me. It's a fictionalised historical fact.'

For a moment I think he's going to take it further, but instead he says, 'Now you. Something flippant.'

This seemed a good idea at the time, this stupid game of swapping confidences. But now I can't think of anything flippant, true or invented. 'Um. I still have all my teddy bears from when I was little, in my bedroom,' I say.

'Boring,' he says. 'Neurotic, not flippant.'

'Once I went through the twelve items or less lane with thirteen items. And I didn't even care.'

'You rebel.'

'You're right. I'm nowhere near as good at flippant as you are.'

'True. King of flippant, me.'

I'm quiet for a moment, and then I say: 'I suppose you'd become pretty good at being flippant, over the years. After the first few girls said they liked you but really just wanted the necklace.'

He drains his glass, bends his head forward and rubs the back of his neck with one hand. Then he tilts his head the other way and looks up at the sky. 'You mustn't think the girls who like me are cheap,' he says finally. 'It's not always just a necklace. Sometimes they want a holiday. A European car. And they don't just *like* me. They love me, usually at first sight.'

All at once I see Daniel Metcalf as a young man, with women like Greta hovering and complimenting and touching his arm and fluttering their eyes. He did not have a family like mine to provide solid ground beneath his feet. He would not have known who to trust.

'An occupational hazard, I guess,' I say.

'Interesting, since I don't have an occupation. What's amazing,' he says, 'is how they never know who I am. "Really," they say. "You're wealthy? I had no idea!" They love me just for who I am.'

'You'll be pleased to know,' I say, 'that I know exactly who you are. I see you as a big fat cheque book, with legs.'

He laughs. 'That's refreshing, at least,' he says. 'You might be the only woman I've ever met who's admitted that.'

I was right all along, my reticence, the way I did not overtly flirt with him. Women do that to him all the time. Now I know how to proceed. I must be aloof, not touch him, not behave as Greta has said. I think back over all I have read, things that I now know about evolutionary theory. I clear my throat a little and lean back on my elbows, hang my head backwards.

'Look at the stars,' I say. 'Aren't they magnificent? I've often wondered what early man thought of the stars. *Homo habilis. Homo erectus*. The stars seem amazing to us, and we know what they are.'

Daniel pours more wine for himself, and for me. 'Perhaps they thought the stars were the children of the sun and moon. Or the souls of long-dead warriors.' He takes a sip. 'Maybe they are. Maybe they were right and we are wrong.'

'It must be a comfort, to believe in things like that. That those who've passed are watching over you.'

The wine is tingly on my lips. I should not have drunk so much. My lips are probably stained red. Drinking red wine: this is an amateur's mistake. When working, you should only drink white wine or champagne or pale spirits. There is nothing more unconvincing than discoloured teeth. And even then the drinking should not be real. Take a tiny sip, tip a little in a pot plant when no one is looking.

'If people knew more about the history of science,' I say, 'they wouldn't be so judgmental about other people's wacky ideas. Science has had some pretty wacky ideas too.' My head suddenly seems too heavy for my neck to support. I stretch out on one side on the blanket, rest my head in my hand.

'Wacky? What's wacky about science, other than your project of course? All those serious geniuses doing serious genius stuff.'

'Oh there're plenty of oddball theories. Plenty. Ontogeny recapitulates phylogeny, for a start.'

He raises one eyebrow. 'Is that even English? What is that?'

'It's English all right. It was a full-on scientific theory in the mid-eighteen hundreds. It means that the development of an embryo goes through the same stages as the evolutionary history of the species. "Ontogeny" means the growth and development of an individual. "Recapitulates" means repeats. "Phylogeny" means the evolutionary history of a species.'

'Thanks for explaining.' He laughs. 'No, thanks. It's much clearer now. Students must queue to get into your lectures.'

'Look,' I put down my tumbler, digging it into the sand so the wine will not spill. 'See right here, on your neck?'

This was intended to be an example of the fascinating nature of biology, but instead I stretch out my hand and smooth the short waves of his hair behind his ear. This is wrong, badly wrong. It means I am not different from all the other girls who wanted necklaces and stuff. His hair is coarser than mine, and straighter. It has only a slight kink in the end that wraps around my finger. I hold my breath, I don't dare swallow. But he doesn't speak or move away. He stills and looks right into my eyes.

I have to focus. Although taking advice from Beau is a habit I hope never to develop, I try to picture Daniel as a chicken. His hair could be soft brown feathers. Now I feel like touching it again, to feel if it is soft or wiry through my fingers. This positive visualisation was a stupid idea. He is certainly no type of bird. Perhaps if I thought of him as a crocodile.

Somehow I am sitting closer to where his head is resting. Then, unbelievably, I touch his skin. I run my middle and third fingers slowly around the curve of him a few inches under his jaw, starting in the fine hair of the nape near the bones of his spine and finishing in the soft space above his collar bone. Then again, then again: my fingertips sear three imaginary lines into his skin. At the end of my final sweep the pads of my fingers stop and linger as though they were waiting to feel the pulse of blood in the base of his throat. He shuts his eyes. He does not move or seem to breathe. I can only feel the movement of my fingers and the warmth of the blanket underneath my legs.

'Here,' I say. 'When you were an embryo, you had pharyngeal arches right here on your neck.' This is a terrible mistake. I have found my very own self-destruct button.

'When I was an embryo. That's quite a while ago. I can hardly remember. What are pharyngeal arches?' he says.

'Gill slits.' My hand feels cold now that it is back in my lap. Bereft. 'As you grew, they moved. The top one became your lower jaw and bits of your ear.'

As I speak my hand moves again: this time, my thumb runs along the edge of his jaw, pausing at the tip of his chin. Then I brush the back of my fingers behind his ear.

'But they were never actually gills,' I say. 'You could never breathe water. And they weren't there because humans are descended from fish. Because we aren't. Descended from fish, I mean.'

If he is going to pull away, make an excuse, reach for the wine, he will do it now.

'I could not breathe water. And the gills slits were there not because we come from fish,' he says, and he opens his eyes.

The memory of the texture of his skin imprints on me. It is rougher than it should be, as though he worked outdoors instead of doing nothing for a living.

'Right. And here.'

I move closer. I am almost behind him now and I cannot see his face, which is probably just as well. I lift the edge of his shirt where it lies on the top of his jeans. His lower back is exposed. He will feel this now—the night is warm but there is a cool breeze. He will feel the night air on this bare triangle of skin. In one movement I lay my palm flat on the small of his back, and here I am not slow and rhythmic like a finger tracing the curve of a throat. I am firm. His back feels hot compared with the air and my hand; I start a little. My fingers reach around his hip, indenting, digging a little into his side. His back is smooth and I wish my palm could stay there forever. If he moved, my hand could stay there. I feel a sudden desire to scratch the surface of him with my nails and hook my fingers to pinch his flesh. I would like to hold him still. I would make him cry my name.

'Here is your coccyx, this flat bone at the bottom of your spine,' I say, low into his ear. 'It's also called the tailbone because when you were an embryo, your tail was here.'

He takes a deep breath, then releases it. 'I had a tail?' he says.

I am breathing in sympathy with his rhythm. The only place we are touching is here, my hand in the small of his back. A wave of lethargy overtakes me and I cannot keep my body upright any longer so I lie down and I am stretched out flat in the space behind him; a mirror, an echo.

'Yes, you had a tail. Right here,' I say. 'But that's got nothing to do with primitive ancestors. It's not because we evolved from something with a tail. It's about our basic body blueprint, the similarities we share with all vertebrates. We're all animals you know. All connected.'

'Right,' he says. 'Tail not about ancestors. Got it.'

The wine, the smell of him, the way the small hairs on his neck move with my breath. My face is tingling. Any moment now he will pivot around on his side and face me and perhaps our roles will reverse. Perhaps he will put his hand on the small of my back, fingers facing down my spine, and his fingers will move the smallest distance and slide under the waistband of my trousers, force their way under the elastic of my pants.

There is a loud shout from down on the beach and the backpackers begin singing a drinking song. I shake my head. I have been touching him, which was the opposite of my intentions. Concentrate, I tell myself. Drink some water. I blink a few times and spin away from him, sit up, crawl back to other side of the rug where I started.

'So they thought that humans duplicated the different stages of our evolutionary development while in the womb. That human embryos are first fish, then salamanders and tortoises and chickens before they become people. It's a great theory. It's a shame it's not true. It sounds true. We should all carry it around with us, the weight of our past, the remnants of what we used to be.'

'When you put it like that I don't like it. It seems like a terrible burden. Carrying around everything you've ever been,' he says. His voice seems muffled by the dark.

'I guess you're right,' I say. 'Everyone is entitled to a fresh start.'

'What do you want, really?' he says.

I look right into his eyes, square and true. 'Relax,' I say. 'You're safe with me. I only want the cheque.'

He opens his mouth to speak, and we both start at a noise coming as if from miles away, a scuffling on the rocks, murmured voices. Greta and Julius walking up the path toward the tents. Then I see them standing near the edge of the clearing, highlighted by the moon and each holding a torch. They were noisy on their approach, dragging their feet, talking loudly to give us fair warning. Greta is as pale as I have ever seen her. Julius looks ill.

'Hope we're not interrupting anything,' Greta says. 'We know we wanted the night off, to chill out for a while. But when we got to the beach the German backpackers invited us over for a few drinks.'

'We were just talking,' I say. 'Pull up some rug. Did you have fun?'

'A most convivial social gathering,' says Julius. 'They were very interested in my stories about Africa especially that time I was walking under a baobab tree and a cheetah almost jumped on my head, and I of course wanted very much to discuss the wildlife especially the wild boars in the Black Forest outside Düsseldorf.'

Greta and Julius are not themselves. They are speaking with an enforced naturalness but their eyes are darting and Julius is biting his lip. Greta flares her nostrils at me, and bites her cheek. I sit up straighter. I am beginning to have a bad feeling about this.

'Oh, and Ella,' says Greta. 'We have a surprise for you. The Germans had already picked up a solo hiker late in the afternoon who'd been having some trouble getting across the creek. Then they had dinner with their new guest and they'd already knocked back three plastic bags of wine by the time we arrived. You'll never guess who it was.'

Greta takes one step aside and buries her face in her hand. It is dark, but in the glow of our kerosene lamp I can make out a figure swaying behind her on the path. Julius steps aside also and shuts his eyes and drags his fingers across his forehead like he feels a migraine coming on. Standing behind them, looking bleary-eyed and damp-haired, wearing a faded blue tracksuit and runners and carrying a hard-shell suitcase, is Timothy.

Now it's my turn to shut my eyes. Tight. Perhaps I will never open them again. Perhaps this is some kind of dream. Yes. When I open them he will be gone.

I open them. He is not gone. He is standing there on my path in my national park in the middle of my sting wearing a tracksuit and looking like an inmate from a mental institution on day release. He holds his suitcase in his arms and it must be heavy. He jostles it and as he changes the angle it begins to drip, no doubt saturated with water from the creek. Drip. Drip. It is the loudest sound I have ever heard in my entire life.

'Hello, er, Ella,' Timothy says. 'Dear. My clothes. They're a bit wet.'

I am already tipsy. When I see Timothy standing between Julius and Greta I feel all the blood drain from my body, so the only thing

I can logically do is drain all the wine from my glass in sympathy. I cannot summon up my usual frustrated anger. I don't even feel like hitting anything. I can do nothing but stare, as though a Neanderthal had walked out of the bush instead of a Timothy. Daniel stares too but he recovers quicker. He rolls away from me and to his feet, dusts himself off and walks over to Timothy.

'Imagine our surprise.' Greta looks slightly frightened, probably of me. 'We were just sitting down for a quiet evening of wine out of plastic bags and German drinking songs.'

'Not me,' said Julius. 'I have resolved never to drink alcohol. It would be disrespectful when my mother and fifteen brothers and sisters must walk so many miles to the well.'

'They were just about to serve up the bratwurst when—you'll never guess,' says Greta. 'One of the Germans—he wasn't actually one of the Germans, we know that now—who was asleep against a tree with a sombrero on his head, woke up. And lo and behold, it was…'

'Such a coincidence, like an act of God,' Julius says. 'This same very good friend of yours, Mister Timothy, whom both Glenda and myself had met in your company at the Zoology Department Christmas party, was right there. Like us also not German and no longer asleep.'

'He didn't know us, at first,' says Greta. 'He'd already had a few wines I'd say. We reminded him of our names so that now *he knows our names*, and told him what we were doing here. So now *he knows what we are doing here*. We told him you were working and perhaps it wasn't a great idea to disturb you but he insisted. He had made some new friends down there, among the backpackers. He was getting by on remarkably little German.'

'Those Germans are great people. Great. What a tradition of hospitality to their fellow travellers,' says Timothy, rubbing his hand over his chin. 'Every time I said *ja* they poured me another drink. I'd never have got across the creek at all without them. I fell in, I think, once. Or twice.'

The three of them are looking at me with hopeful eyes but still I cannot speak. I quit. They can bury me where I fall. I cannot think of one rule of my father's that would be suitable for this situation. Oh no. My father. And Sam. Oh God. I hope I am struck by a meteorite before we leave so I never have to explain this to them. Sam will be intolerable. He won't say I told you so, but he won't have to. It'll be in his eyes. And then he'll rail and rant when I tell him we didn't get the money. Then when I tell him that Timothy showed up dripping wet in the middle of the forest, he will laugh so hard he will drop dead of an aneurism. Best case scenario.

'In retrospect,' continues Timothy, 'I probably should have brought a rucksack instead of my suitcase. I just thought the little wheels would come in handy.'

Greta breaks the painful, chirping cicada-filled silence that follows by saying, 'Tim. How on earth could the little wheels come in handy?'

'Wheels, er Glenda,' says Timothy, his forehead creasing with solemnity, 'are one of the most crucial discoveries in human history. They are very, very handy.'

Now. The earth can open up and swallow me now.

'I wanted to come down yesterday and meet you in the car park. Walk in with you. That was my intention since…er…Sam mentioned where you were going,' says Timothy. 'He never imagined I'd actually drive down here, I expect.'

'Sam is my brother the idiot,' I say to Daniel.

'Right,' he says.

'There must be something wrong with my GPS. It's a shame there's no warranty. I got lost. And when I was talking on the phone, I must've missed the turnoff,' said Timothy. 'But I didn't let that stop me. If my girlfriend is going out in the wilds, braving the, er, wilderness with nothing but her assistants for, ah, assistance, well, my place is to help. No creek too wide. No mountain too high.'

'Such a surprise,' says Julius. 'Although we had met Mr Timothy before as I detailed previously, until right now we didn't even realise that Dr Ella had a boyfriend.'

'We kept it hush hush,' says Timothy.

I'd like to hush hush him, by shoving that suitcase in his mouth. Hang on. I must be feeling better. I feel the urge to hurt Timothy returning.

'Especially not such a handsome boyfriend.' Greta's eyes gleam: a plan is forming in her pulled-tight brain. She loops one arm through Timothy's and he almost drops the suitcase. 'What did you say you did for a living?'

'Retail. Wholesale. You know, trade,' says Timothy. 'It's not as exciting as it sounds.'

'Indeed,' says Daniel. 'Well…'

'Tim,' say Greta and Julius together.

'Well, Timmy. You made it,' says Daniel. 'I'm Daniel. Pull up some blanket. Any boyfriend of Ella's is a boyfriend of mine. Would you like some wine?'

'*Ja*,' says Timothy. 'Oh, you're Daniel? She's…er…told me so much about you.'

'It's all lies.' Daniel produces extra tumblers from the rucksack near the closest tent and pours for the three of them. '*Prost.*'

Timothy takes his tumbler in both hands and swallows half in one gulp. Then finally after all this talk he seems to notice me, still sprawled in front of the camp stove. 'Hello, dear,' he says. He leans over and kisses me on the cheek. I fight the urge to smack him. 'Are you having fun?'

'Yes. Yes, thanks.' I fill my own tumbler and take another mouthful. 'Timothy. Were your parents siblings? I'm working. What the hell are you doing here?'

'Dear, sweet, er, Ella. Do you know my BlackBerry doesn't work out here? What would happen if someone called about a shipment? Or Mum tries to get hold of me, to ask if I'll be home for dinner? There's no reception. At all. It's as if we went back to the eighties in a DeLorean.' Timothy takes my hand between his own two, like he was making a Della hand sandwich. 'I need to talk to you, dear Ella.'

'I think we are like the fourth and fifth wheels on a tricycle,' says Julius. 'Or possibly a scooter. A scooter that has three wheels.'

'We should go to our tents,' says Greta.

'Nonsense,' says Daniel, pouring them all more wine. 'Don't go to your tents. Especially not you, Glenda. Not with your claustrophobia. It might bring on an attack.'

'Quite,' says Greta. She deliberately moves further away from Timothy.

'Besides,' says Daniel. 'We're all friends here. We have no secrets from one another, do we Timmy old man? I'm sure you don't want us to go.'

'Of course not, of course not,' Timothy drains his wine and holds his tumbler out for more. 'It's just that, well, Ella and I...' He looks from side to side to see that no one is eavesdropping out here in the middle of nowhere, then drops his voice to a whisper barely loud enough to be heard back in town. 'There are things we need to discuss. Something I need to ask her. Very important.' Timothy taps his finger against the side of his nose and looks meaningfully at Daniel.

'That sounds serious.' Daniel nods gravely. 'Better have some more wine.'

'Don't mind if I do,' says Timothy. Finally everyone sits. Julius and Greta look like patients in a dentist's waitingroom listening to muffled screams from behind a closed door, while Daniel lounges completely at ease. Timothy sits next to Daniel. The leaning tower of Timothy.

'What is it you want to ask her?' says Daniel. 'In my experience, with a serious kind of girl like Ella it's best to have your ideas clear before you start. Can't be making it up as you go along.'

'I'm with you. Been thinking of nothing else on the drive down,' says Timothy.

'I'm two metres away,' I say. 'I can hear every word you're saying.'

'She's the kind of girl who needs a plan,' says Daniel.

'And I,' says Timothy, 'I have a plan. We could get married in May. Just a small ceremony. Then she could give up this...science business and work with me. Live at home with us: me, and Mum and Dad and my sisters. They'd love to have her.'

'Nothing wrong with my hearing,' I say.

'Any girl would be proud,' says Daniel.

'Any girl at all,' says Greta. 'No sense rushing into anything. Plenty of fish in the sea.'

'So you're prepared. You have a ring,' says Daniel.

'Not on me, no. But I can get a ring. Wholesale. Mind you, I have some concerns,' says Timothy. 'There are some points I'd need to be reassured about. Look before you leap, you know.'

'Absolutely,' says Daniel. 'It'd be best to resolve them before the wedding, I'd say.'

'"Concerns?"' I say. 'What do you mean "concerns"? Do you want to marry me or not?'

'She's got a bit of a temper, I'm afraid.' Timothy sighs. 'I don't. I'm a peace-loving man.'

'I must admit I like a girl with a temper,' says Daniel. 'It makes things more entertaining.'

'You only think it's entertaining because you've never had your nose squeezed nearly off your face. Or had your ears pulled. I bet she's never pulled your ears when she's wearing her pyjamas.'

'That's sadly true,' says Daniel. 'But it's definitely something I'd like to try.'

'I only have a temper because things infuriate me. If everyone would just fall into line I wouldn't have a temper. And there's nothing wrong with your nose. It's recovered just fine. It's poking into other people's business as well as it ever did.'

'Perhaps we should discuss this in the morning,' says Greta. 'I'm sure Daniel doesn't need to hear all about this.'

'Oh yes Daniel does,' he says. 'Daniel wouldn't miss this for the world.'

'Because relationships aren't just about compatibility, are they?' says Timothy. 'Sure, it's important to find someone who puts the lid back on the toothpaste and who doesn't take your phone recharger out of the wall when they want to recharge their own phone and your phone is not yet fully charged but instead finds herself another socket because it's terribly bad for batteries to be continually charged half-way. I sell phones, too, did I mention that? If you ever. No? If you're sure. Anyway. I'm not downplaying the importance of like-mindedness and shared values.'

'I would never do that,' says Greta. 'Values are very important. I'd definitely find another socket.'

'But what's even more important than sockets is the look in her eye. In both eyes, I mean in both persons' eyes. Four eyes in total.' Timothy staggers to his knees and peers, squinting, into my eyes like he is an optometrist updating my prescription.

'Why are you kneeling?' I say. 'Stop peering and stop kneeling.'

'It might only be a small business now, but imagine hundreds of shops Australia-wide,' says Timothy. 'And then we could expand. A chain of pawnbrokers. Short term loans at staggering interest rates with no collateral. And sex toys. We could mail-order sex toys throughout the world. Porn's out, though. The internet killed porn distribution. The seventies, that was the golden age of porn. These days it's all amateurs, over the net, no professionalism anymore. But other than porn, the sky's the limit. There's one proviso. It must be built on a stable foundation, and that stable foundation is a man and a woman working hand in glove together the way my parents did. How is a couple supposed to get through the next forty or fifty years without that look in their four eyes?'

'How indeed?' says Daniel. 'Well said, and what a fascinating empire you are building Timmy. How can I buy shares, and would you like some more wine?'

'*Ja*. And you don't, do you Della?' Timothy is on one knee now. He leans over and takes my hand again.

'He means "Ella",' says Julius. 'This is a further example of why I do not indulge in the evils of alcohol. It makes you forget even the name of your own girlfriend.'

'I've known you since you were five years old and I don't think I've ever seen it,' Timothy says. 'The look, I mean. Tell me the truth, Ella.'

'Nothing like the truth, Ella,' says Daniel. 'If the truth fits, wear it.'

'Exactly! Couldn't have said it better myself,' says Timothy. 'Ella, I have eyes too. And there are mirrors in my house, you know. Three: bathroom, behind the bedroom door and over the hall table. That doesn't even count the one in the sun visor of my car, the one with the slidey door and its own little light. So I've seen my eyes, on more than one occasion. Keep that in mind before you answer.'

'Have you had a blow to the head?' I say.

'I've been trying for weeks to ask you this. It's a simple enough question. It's not rocket surgery,' says Timothy. 'Are you in love with me?'

'Take your time,' says Greta.

'Don't rush it,' says Daniel. 'Think before you answer.'

'Timothy, I hardly think this is the place,' I say.

'Nonsense Ella. Timmy has asked a fair question. The least you can do is answer it. Here...let me see your eyes.' Daniel leans across and takes my chin in his hand and tilts my face up. 'What d'ya reckon, Timmy? I can't see anything myself.'

'What do you two expect? My pupils to actually take the shape of hearts?' I brush sand from my legs and do my best to avoid his eyes. 'All right, all right. No. I'm not in love with you Timothy. Satisfied?'

'Very,' says Greta.

'So I suppose that marrying me is out of the question?'

'Completely.'

'Despite the romantic nature of this gesture?' Timothy says. 'Despite the fact that I have driven for hours with only intermittent satellite support and hiked down the track carrying quite a heavy suitcase and fell over twice and saw a snake on the path and had to pee behind a tree and nearly drowned in the creek before the German backpackers saved me?'

'You're certainly romantic, Timmy,' says Daniel. 'I'll say that for you. If I was a girl I'd jump at the chance.'

'Perhaps I should have asked her father first. Should I have asked her father first?'

'In my country yes,' says Julius. 'And you would need to offer goats.'

'What would my father do with a goat?' I say.

'Not one goat, heavens no.' Julius laughs. 'You are not a one-goat bride.'

'Thank you, Joshua.'

'Certainly you are worthy of one entire goat, and some change from a smaller goat,' says Julius. 'Say one and one third goats, roughly.'

I squint at him. I know where he sleeps. I can kill him later.

'So you never loved me. You were just using me. For sex,' says Timothy.

'Let's stop right there.' I struggle to my feet, swaying mildly.

'We're just getting to the good bit,' says Daniel.

'I'm going to thump you both in a minute.'

'See? Temper,' says Timothy.

'You're right,' says Daniel.

'Cover your ears and nose,' says Timothy.

'Shut up, shut up, the lot of you.' I brace myself against the sand, which seems to be tilting under my feet. 'You. Timothy. No, I will not marry you.' I take a deep breath to calm myself, and stop the bushes spinning. I think for a moment I will kick him in the crotch, but then I look at his face. 'But, Timothy. I will forever treasure the memories of the time we spent together. I will tuck them away in a secret place near my heart and I will throw away the key so no one will ever find it, including myself.'

'A secret place,' says Timothy. 'Like a container? Or a storage unit?'

'Exactly. Now you, Joshua. One more story about wells or goats, I'm calling immigration and having your student visa cancelled. I mean it. You'll be sleeping in the hut with your thirteen brothers and sisters before you can say border security.'

'Yes, Dr Canfield ma'am. Not one more word of goats or wells or even cheetahs will pass my lips.' He mimes zipping his mouth closed.

'Good. Now Glenda. Stop looking at Timothy like that. For God's sake woman, I'm not even cold in the grave. There's a whole Oktoberfest of German backpackers just down the track for your recreational pleasure.'

'I feel so ashamed,' she says. 'It's this hairstyle. It's cutting off the blood flow to my brain.'

'And you, Daniel Metcalf.'

He stands in front of me. His lips are pressed together but his eyes are laughing. 'Yes Dr Canfield. Ma'am,' he says.

'You, you,' I begin, but the puff has gone from my anger and there is nothing more I can say. Also the wine seems to have unhooked my arms at the shoulder joints. Just then Timothy struggles to his feet and gives me a clumsy embrace.

'There there Ella,' he says. 'Please, don't look so glum. Really. Don't give it another thought. Unfair of me to put you in this position. It's really not as bad as all that. I'm feeling better already. I'm very fond of you, of course, but I'll recover. Never mind. Chin up. You know what they say: better late is the better part of valour.' He presses one arm around my shoulders, and winks at Greta.

The night continues on for about another bottle and a half. Greta grows increasingly giggly. Timothy explains how his father has never understood him, pledges his undying friendship for me, his genuine fondness and manlove for Daniel and Julius and drapes his jacket over Greta's shoulders when he notices she is shivering. Daniel offers to share his tent with Timothy tonight, unless Greta would rather sleep outside under the stars on account of her claustrophobia, an offer she declines as her therapy is progressing well. Daniel seems exceptionally jocular, even joining Timothy in a painful rendition of 'Summer Nights' with Daniel in falsetto as Olivia Newton-John and Timothy as John Travolta.

Only I am quiet. Sitting still, by the lamp, I hope my face is in shadow and that they cannot see me. I wonder if my father or Ruby was ever in this situation when they were younger, when they were pulling grand stings, living the high life by their wits. I bet they never sat around in the bush hours from civilisation surrounded by drunken lunatics singing songs from the great musicals of the seventies, a decade apparently not distinguished only by the glory of its porn industry.

When we were children we would sit home and wait for Dad and Ruby to return and we would hear only the peaks of their success, not the depths of their struggle. This job is curdling before my eyes. I doubt I will ever see this money and what is worse I cannot seem to stop looking at Daniel. His smallest movement, each tiny gesture. Yet he seems so far away and so does the money. They both seem further with every chorus.

Here is something serious: Ruby, who says I have no memory of my mother, is wrong. I do have one memory. I have never told this to anyone, especially not to anyone who might be able to disprove it, like my father or Sam. I am in a dark quiet room. I am sitting on a soft surface and I fight to balance and not to topple. My hands are gripping thin bars of wood through which my arms will fit but not my head or my body. I shake them but I cannot make them budge. I reach one hand down and pick up something big and soft—a teddy bear? There is a crack of light and I see her face appear. This part shames me: I do not remember her face. Of all the thousands of faces I have seen and memorised over the years, hers is perhaps the only one I cannot recall. Hers, and sometimes my own.

Although I cannot remember her face, I know the sight of her fills me with joy and comfort and peace. I drop the bear and let go of the bar and stretch my arms out—this will make her come closer,

I know. All that matters now is being picked up, held by her. But she does not come closer and she does not pick me up. After a time I drop my arms. I grizzle a little from frustration, which seems always to have been part of my character. At this the light disappears and so does the face. That is all I remember.

And here is something flippant: I feel a desperate desire to sneak out of the tent while everyone is asleep. I wouldn't even undo the zip. I would take a pen knife and make a jagged cut in the back of the tent, the side facing the bush. I would hold the knife in both hands and start high and pull it down with my whole weight. In the dead of night I would move silently down the path, past the sleeping Germans, wade the creek and climb the path again by the light of the moon or my torch. Or perhaps I would not climb—I might swim around the headland until I found a spot to land and then I would drag myself ashore. This country of mine has always been a place where people have dragged themselves ashore and begun new lives. I would carry nothing. My new life would not be so exhausting and frustrating as this one.

When this thought first occurred to me it seemed flippant. It certainly does not show a respectful attitude—to my family, to Daniel or even to the tent. But now that I have thought it out in all its detail, this also seems serious. Of course, I do not do it.

The water is still but not still enough and I cannot see my reflection. My arms move across it like ripples in sand. I'm aware I have a certain level of vanity, having been brought up by Ruby, but now that it is morning and I am swimming I realise I have forgotten to bring a mirror.

I woke early, if I slept at all. I changed into my bathers inside the tent and crept down here as the dark was just lifting. There was no sound from our camp, and no sign of life other than Timothy's feet sticking out from Daniel's tent. There was no sound from the Germans' camp as I passed either: most of them had slept in sleeping bags straight on the sand, others only on bedrolls and some against the trees where they were leaning last night. When I first waded into the sea the tree-tops seemed the same colour as the sky but now they are not. They are back-lit. The water seems over-salty; it holds me up. Here I can barely feel the throb of my stiff thighs or the crick in my neck from sleeping on the ground. The air and the water are both cold but I barely feel them. I tilt my face towards the sky. I am floating.

There is a movement on the path; someone is walking down here, bare-chested, carrying a towel. I do not have to look to know that it is Daniel. The water is covering me up to my chin. He strides in from the sand and is beside me in a few easy strokes.

'If I knew scientists were this much fun I'd have started hanging around universities a lot sooner,' he says. He sculls his hands backwards and forwards, pushing them against the water as if they were webbed.

'How dare you not be hung over,' I say. 'It isn't right.'

'You don't look too shabby yourself.'

'One voice I can possibly manage. As soon as the birds start or the Germans wake up, I'm in trouble. I feel like there's an angry dwarf sitting on my shoulders and squeezing my ears between his knees. Are the others coming down?'

'Not yet. Joshua will be OK. Glenda and Timmy...well, I wouldn't want to be in their heads this morning.' He raises one eyebrow, thinks for a moment. 'Or ever, really.'

I can feel the current his hands make. Small waves jostle my shoulders.

'I'm not sure what you had planned to do today,' he says. 'How much work you intended?'

The water has formed small beads on his shoulders and some have nestled in the divot at the base of his throat. I think about what my father would do now. What rule could I rely upon if a person from one life intruded into another, destroying my dignity, transforming me from a seductive femme fatale to an angry flirt worth one and a third goats?

There's always the option of murdering Timothy, and possibly Sam for telling him where I was, and burying them in the apple orchard. The thought gives me some comfort.

'I had things planned,' I say. His eyes are cool. His mouth is straight. I can read no expression here. I swallow and pray for inspiration. 'But after our behaviour last night I'm beginning to think I'd be wasting my time.'

This is a final roll of the dice, to give him an opportunity to say *No no, not at all. I'm even more interested in your kooky project now that I've met your deranged ex-boyfriend and my cheque book is right here down the front of my swimmers. Do you have a pen? And don't worry about your fears: I'm not lying. I'm rolling in money and in any case, I really fancy you.*

But as soon as I speak I know I have made a mistake. There is no going back from here.

He stretches out on his back for a moment, toes towards the sky, then twists upright again in one quick movement. 'You're right,' he says finally. 'You'd be wasting your time.'

For the rest of the morning I carry with me a feeling of calm unlike anything I remember. We have not convinced Daniel we are professional safe hands. This has not been a cheap expedition: there is the cost of everyone's time, but that's just a start. Hundreds of dollars of camping equipment, clothing, books and the rest.

No one will hold me personally accountable. We all agreed to take the risk. Yet I feel it. I should, in fact, feel worse. But now I no longer have to worry about what Daniel is lying about. Now it is out of my hands and I am free of the worry.

All morning Timothy buzzes around me like a fly. He makes tea and delivers my breakfast. He washes the dishes afterwards. He keeps saying, over and over, *I hope I haven't messed up your research* and *there's no need to mention this to anybody else, is there?* He gives me desperate looks, and tries to pull me aside for a private chat, but I want the next time we speak to be dignified, on my side at least. I know I cannot manage this yet. I also suspect he only wants to speak with me to circumvent what is coming to him. When we get back he'll have to face not just me, but my father and Sam as well. Not that Sam is blameless, the moron.

Daniel and I pack our belongings. We will walk out first, as per the original plan. Beau and Anders are waiting on the beach in a reversal of Friday's operation, and will come to the campsite when they see us leave. Timothy will stay and carry equipment too: his penance for stuffing up this sting. He is sheepish when I tell him there will be more for him to carry than his own suitcase. He volunteers to do whatever he can to help.

Daniel and I hoist our packs and are half-way down the beach before I hear a panting behind me. I turn: it is Timothy, running on bare feet over the sand. When he reaches us he leans over, hands on his knees, unable to speak. He must have chased us all the way from the camp. Daniel raises his eyebrows at me and keeps walking. He'll wait for me a little further on, he says. I wait until Daniel is out of earshot, then I turn to Timothy.

'Well,' I say. 'Is there something you want?'

'Yes. Yes there is. I know you have to do this,' he says eventually, his face red and blotchy. 'I know it's your job, and all that. But I don't think you should. I don't think it's fair.'

I make my hands into fists and restrain myself from raining them

153

down on his empty skull like it was a bongo. What I have to put up with is unbelievable.

'So, Timothy. You don't like the way I make my living. Since when?'

'Well. Since last night.'

I poke my finger at his chest and almost break the skin. 'You, Timothy, are an utter, utter bastard. And you've got a lot of nerve. First you bust in here, uninvited, and mess everything up. And now you're lecturing me on what I should and shouldn't do. If Daniel wasn't just down the beach watching us I'd dig a hole in the sand and put you in it, face first. Your fat head would feed the crabs for days.'

'Listen Della. This hasn't been much fun for me either, you know. I've never proposed before. To anyone. And I had to sleep in a tent. Or half in a tent. And my feet are very itchy because they were sticking out of the tent all night and they're covered in mosquito bites. I've scratched them so hard I'm bleeding. And I've already said I'm sorry about coming here, to the park. I wasn't thinking straight. I can't undo it. But that doesn't change the facts.' He tucks his shirt into his shorts and straightens his collar, and nods his head up the beach at Daniel. 'He's a good guy, Della. He doesn't deserve this.'

'You know better than anybody that there are two kinds of people who always deserve it: the rich and the greedy.'

'You don't really believe that.'

'I'll tell you a secret: that's the only thing I do believe. What's this all about, Timothy? You've never minded my job before. In fact I seem to remember that you've even helped us once or twice. And been paid for it. And last night you didn't seem to mind at all.'

'It's different. Knowing you were a grifter, that your whole family was. That's one thing. But meeting someone who's about to get ripped off. Drinking wine with them. Singing "Summer Nights". That's another matter entirely.'

'Well, well Timothy. Maybe singing a duet with Daniel Metcalf has turned your pretty head. Maybe *you've* fallen in love with him. Perhaps I should leave you two alone for a bit of privacy.'

He snorts. 'Don't be ridiculous. Even if I wasn't one hundred per cent hetero, he's not my type.'

I am about to yell at him again when I see Daniel further down the beach. He has taken his pack off and is sitting in the sand, looking out upon the water. I come closer to Timothy and lower my voice to a growl. 'You, Timothy, are a hypocrite. What about all the people you rip off?'

'That shows how little you know. I don't rip anyone off. For a start, my customers receive excellent value for money. Excellent. Where else can you buy a mobile phone worth hundreds of dollars for ninety-nine ninety-five? Customer satisfaction is what separates me from my competitors.'

'And what about the people you steal the phones from? They're not quite so fortunate, are they?'

'But Della, I don't steal from people.' He speaks slowly, and wags his annoying head in my face. 'I steal from *companies*, and companies, by definition, are not people. Most of the time they don't even notice that the stuff is missing. And if they weren't so stupid, if they put in some decent systems, nothing would go missing at all.'

'Oh, you are the master of self-justification. The master. Who do you think owns those companies? Fish? Those companies are owned by people, you gormless idiot. The stock that goes missing straight into your warehouse is owned by someone. And then you go ahead and blame them—the victim—for your own theft. You are incredible.'

'Everything OK back there? Not having a lovers' tiff, are you?' Daniel calls out.

'No, no,' Timothy says. 'We're discussing business strategy, that's all. Issues of, ah, stock sourcing and supplier management.'

'Just one more minute.' I wave at Daniel and attempt a smile. 'And we're ex-lovers. Don't forget the ex part.'

'It's not right,' Timothy says, his voice low again. 'I'm just saying.'

I take a deep breath. 'Well I'd certainly hate to disturb your delicate conscience Timothy. That would be the last thing I'd want to do. I'll put your mind at rest. Thanks to your interference last night, Daniel Metcalf isn't going to give us any money. Not one dollar. We did not behave in a professional enough manner to convince him to part with a piggybank of five cent pieces, much less a quarter of a mill. So you can sleep soundly tonight. No one is taking any money off anyone.'

Timothy frowns. 'Della. I've seen him looking at you all morning. I'm very good at telling when you've got your customer hooked. It might not be right, but it's a done deal. Relax. You'll get your money.'

The walk out seems shorter even though my legs are tired. Return journeys always are. I am thirsty and hold my water bottle in my hand so I can sip as we walk. When we reach the waterfall that he was so enthusiastic about on Friday, Daniel steps over it and keeps going. He doesn't speak much, except when necessary and even when we pass other walkers he delivers a grim nod rather than his usual chat.

I am thinking furiously. I go round and round the events of the last few days, and keep coming back to the same irrational point. Even if I have failed, I need to know what Daniel is hiding. I must know. Who is he, exactly? I have almost ruled out the idea that he isn't wealthy. I'm sure he has always had money, and that he has it still. There is a confidence that comes from wealth, a bullet-proofing against minor fears and worries. He has it, a scatheless surface, undented.

I cannot stand it. I am the one who is supposed to be hiding something, not him. I cannot let him get away without discovering it. I need to shake him up, jolt him into revealing something. I could feign a fall, or pretend to twist my ankle. I could stumble against him, unbalance my water bottle so it drenches my T-shirt. Greta would approve, but I cannot imagine this would work. I am watching him walk in front of me and I just want him to stop. Timothy might think I'm still in with a chance, but at the moment I wouldn't give two cents for his judgment. For once in my life I can think of nothing to say and nothing to do.

By lunchtime we are back in the car park. We take off our packs. I stretch my calves against the car, rub my tired shoulders. Just let this be over and done with, as quickly as possible. I keep my face turned away. Chances are I will never see him again.

'Well,' I say. 'Sorry to have wasted your weekend.'

'I wouldn't say that,' he says.

All at once I feel ashamed of myself. I must give it one more try. I know my father would never have quit, and certainly Ruby would have fought and fought not to let a mark escape. Whether Daniel is lying to me or not; whether he has money or not, my family's opinion of me is at stake. Get a grip, Della. I straighten myself slightly and turn to face him.

'Look, Daniel. I hope you didn't think…last night…'

I can see the tendons in his neck, arched and stiff. 'You hope I didn't think what last night?'

I take a deep breath and let it out slowly. 'I hope you didn't think there was…there is… anything…unprofessional…between us. We'd both had a bit too much wine. That's all.'

Daniel leans back against the car and folds his arms. 'Nothing unprofessional, did you say? Too much wine?'

I attempt a smile and swing my arms in a carefree fashion. 'Exactly. Wine, stars, moonlight et cetera et cetera. I was in a relationship at the time. Apparently. In the dying seconds of a relationship, I'll grant you, but I didn't know that yet. At that precise moment I was explaining the gill business I was happily… well, perhaps not happily, but certainly…ah…committed. So there could have been nothing going on. And I'm here on a professional basis. Representing the university. Which is a venerable institution. Though I understand we won't get the money.' I feel my shoulders drop as I finish speaking. There. I've done it.

Daniel looks up, as if he has only just noticed I am here. He folds his arms. 'Right. Professional basis.'

'Exactly.'

'So, if we can put aside the issue of the money for a moment. What you're really saying is,' Daniel rubs one hand over his chin, bristles crackling, 'you don't fancy me.'

'Well. Well.' I smooth the front of my trousers, then hold my hands clenched in front as though I am praying. 'Well, I'm sure this is no reflection on you. I'm sure there are many, many women who do, as you say, fancy you.'

'But?'

'But I don't.'

'Does this have anything to do with Timmy? Perhaps you're not quite over him. Perhaps you need more time.'

'That's not it. Timothy and I…we didn't have…it's got nothing to do with time.'

'Right. Just so we're clear. No fancying. None whatsoever. Take it or leave it.'

'Indeed. Leave it.'

'Is this a general thing? Does this lack of fancying cover all younger sons of families who give away money for scientific research? Or does it just apply to me?'

I frown. 'I didn't realise this was such a difficult concept. I'll try to make it very clear so you can understand. I don't fancy one hundred per cent of sons of families who give away money for scientific research, with a sample size of one.'

'So, if you were to look up "fancying" in the Ella Dictionary, the definition would be: verb meaning to desire to shag, not to be used in relation to Daniel Metcalf.'

'Quite.'

'So if I was to, say, stand quite close to you,' Daniel is in front of me now, bare centimetres of air between us. 'It wouldn't disturb you in the slightest.'

I swallow, raise my chin. This is possibly the most stupid idea I have had in decades. Why did I begin this in an isolated car park, miles from anywhere, with no one else around? I should have picked a place that held a fair chance of interruption. So that when I put an end to this, it doesn't look as though I wanted him to stop. Although of course I do. I mean, I will. I will want this to stop. I manage a small snort of derision.

'Of course not. I work on a busy campus, students everywhere. In an office, with other people. I take trains. Elevators. Physical proximity with people I do not fancy does not affect me.'

'I see.' He raises one eyebrow. 'And if I were to touch the side of your face, like this.' He smooths the hair from my forehead, then runs the back of his hand down the side of my face, slowly, softly, then along the line of my jaw to hold my chin, his thumb nudging my lower lip down. He tilts his head forward, almost whispering. 'You'd feel nothing.'

For some reason, I have trouble coaxing air into my lungs. It's the hike, up from the beach. All this physical exertion. 'Like a brother,' I say.

'A brother. I see. And your wrists. They're so delicate, aren't they?' His hands are on my shoulders now, inching their way down my arms, until they reach my wrists which he crosses one over the other. He pins them. 'See? I can hold the two of them in one hand. This is probably something that a brother would do. It feels very pure, doesn't it? Neighbourly, almost.'

I cannot move my hands, my wrists are manacled tight in his grasp. 'Just because I don't fancy you. Doesn't mean. I will tolerate. Being manhandled.'

'No, no, of course,' he says. 'But it wouldn't make your heart pound, would it? It wouldn't make your blood pressure go up.'

He steps backwards until he is leaning back against the car again and he pulls me with him, pulls me closer by my helpless wrists. I feel dazed and dumb and stupid and know that I must stop this and I would welcome even Timothy to appear but I cannot stop because I do not have the strength. I am touching him now. My thighs are pressed against his. The strength of him, the size. Would it be the worst thing in the world if I leaned against him? Surely just this touch of flesh through fabric would not be too far. His mouth is near my ear: I can feel his breath, his whispers against my face.

'Because it would be terrible if you let yourself go, wouldn't it? If you let yourself fall,' he says. 'Especially onto a big fat cheque book with legs.'

He releases my wrists then but they stay crossed where they are, and I am already leaning against him and I can't seem to pull away. For a long moment he does not hold me. We are fully clothed in a public place. My car is right behind me, just metres away. I could reach it in seconds, unlock the doors, be behind the wheel, moving, before he could blink. There are people at the ranger station down the road, lots of them, milling around. Ranging. Or I could cry out. I could make some kind of sound, any sound. Even though I can't see anyone the bush is thick just over the hill. If I cried out someone might come.

But I don't do any of those things. I stay still, eyes down. Then his hands find my waist, roll my body a little so that I slide closer. He bends his leg toward me.

'I'm sorry you don't fancy me,' he says, soft, into my ear. 'I'm sure you don't like this at all. Just tell me to stop any time.'

His hands are on my hips now, rocking them from side to side with small, ceaseless movements; my knees spread open slightly, one on each side of his leg. The inside of my thigh is soft through the thin fabric, his thigh is harder and fits between my legs. He arches his knee forward. He keeps rocking me. Now I feel the brush of his lips on my neck, now the breath from his open mouth is on my throat. It is gentle but somehow it makes me imagine the nip of his teeth. I clutch at his shirt, knead it with my fingers, feel his taut stomach through the cloth, his knee thrusting forward, the rocking motion spreading heat through the core of me, his fingers pinching the delicate flesh on my hip bone in a way that will leave faint bruises I know I will touch absent-mindedly for days.

'Isn't it funny how my leg fits right there? If you were naked, I could spread your legs and touch you with my hand. I'd like to see you naked, Ella,' he says. 'I'm not hearing you say stop. Perhaps you're a bit distracted. Just say stop, Ella.'

I am collapsing against him, magnetically drawn. I can smell him; he seems a different Daniel, no longer joking but sharp, fierce. I can feel him breathing me. I can't bear to see his face so I bury my open mouth in his neck. In one rushed movement he pulls up my T-shirt from where it sits tucked into my trousers and now all I can feel are two broad hands, one splayed on the skin of my back, fingers under my bra strap, tracing the dip of my spine and the other forced down the back of my pants, kneading the top of my bottom, scratching it lightly. This is a public place. Someone could drive up at any moment. This thought should calm me down but instead makes me feel more urgent. I reach my arms around his neck to pull him closer but already there is no space between us. Now I am the one holding him. He is the one pinned, folded against me with my arms around his neck.

'It's all right, Ella,' he says. 'Just tell me to stop. If you don't want me, just tell me to stop.'

His knee is hard but not hard enough, his fingers are close but not close enough yet he keeps rocking me, backwards and forwards now, more deliberately, the hand down my pants angling me against him. Why doesn't he lean over and open the car door? Hurry, hurry. All he would have to do is stretch back one arm, open the door and we could fall along the length of the back seat and he could fuck me. I am grinding, grinding, as best I can but it is futile. I need more than this. My mouth opens and it closes and between pants I make a low moan into his throat that is close to a plea.

'It's up to you Ella. It's all up to you.' he says. 'Stop or go. Tell me what you want.'

I struggle against him, release one hand and inch it down across his stomach and I find him, hard, through the fabric of his trousers. At first I only trace the outline with the tips of my fingers but then I roll my palm against it and scratch my nails frantically against the straining fabric. I could speak. I could just open my mouth and speak. I moan again into his throat but as soon as he hears it, before I can say a word, it is over. He pushes away from the car, adjusts me on my feet away from him, and walks to the other side of the boot. He leans forward on the car, on his arms, his fingers threaded together, his knuckles bone-white.

'Sorry. I'm sure you understand, being a scientist. I had to test my supposition,' he says. 'Glad to see you don't fancy me. Makes me feel much better. I might have felt rejected otherwise.'

And all I can do is stand there like a fool; rub my wrists with alternating hands, feel my hips, cross my arms. Everywhere his hands have touched is burnt. I seem to have no blood in my legs. I am shaking. I need to sit down but the best I can do is lean on the opposite side of the car from him and I know it's not far enough away.

'You're angry,' I say, after a while when the urge to weep has passed.

Daniel rolls his eyes and smiles in his old teasing way, one side of his mouth lifting. 'I'd like to pull you over my knee and give you a good spanking but that's got nothing to do with anger.'

I don't smile back. 'For God's sake,' I say. 'This isn't funny.'

'You're right. It's not funny,' he says.

He walks toward me and for a moment I think he's going to touch me again and I don't know which direction to run. But I don't run and he doesn't touch me. He steps around me as if I have a force field and he opens the back door, takes his stuff out of his pack and throws it on the back seat then slams the door shut. The pack topples into the dirt. He sits behind the wheel and starts the engine, then opens the window on my side.

'The mistake I made,' he says. 'Was at the very beginning of this conversation. I said, if you remember, "if we can put aside the issue of the money for a moment". That's where I went wrong, isn't it Ella? You'll never be able to look at me without thinking about the money.'

He waits, as if he expects me to speak. I can't speak.

'So let's get it out of the way. I need to shower, and there are some things I have to do this evening. Come to the house late tomorrow afternoon. I'll have your cheque.'

'I thought you said. This morning. You said that doing any

more research was a waste of my time.'

'I meant that I had already decided to give it to you.'

He starts the car and drives off, and I step away before a cloud of gravel swallows me whole. I watch him career out of the car park too fast, almost skidding, and join the main road with only a cursory slowing in case of traffic. It takes a long time for him to disappear over the horizon. I am left standing here alone, hands limp by my sides, with two stained backpacks and my borrowed car.

My home should be my castle, my haven. Usually, after two gruelling days in the forest with a barrel o' monkeys, I would have anticipated a little recognition. A banner across the door, perhaps. Minions throwing streamers. Today I do not feel like that. I don't think I have ever been so glad to see Cumberland Street but what I want is to creep in quietly, unseen.

I park the car in the drive and sit behind the wheel as if I am glued, as if I lack the energy even to open the door. I have no memory of the drive except the ten minutes when I filled up outside Kooweerup—I am thankful the car knew the way home. I have not eaten since a hurried breakfast of muesli bars and fruit juice at the camp. Unfastening the seatbelt requires an act of will. I move each leg individually out of the car and pivot my weight up. As I stand I feel my knees will give way and I fear I will be forced to crawl to the front door. I leave the pack on the back seat. It can wait till tomorrow. At this moment I can barely lift myself.

Ten people live and work in this house but there is no one here when I arrive and for that I am grateful. I undo the locks, sneak in. I can't even make it all the way up the stairs: I sit on the landing for a while and rest my head. When we were children, we would slide down this banister backwards on our stomachs, like small monorail cars. My father laughed, and said it was kind of us to polish the wood. He had Uncle Syd saw off the large carved pine cones at the bottom and reattach them with a screw, so they could be removed when we were playing and we wouldn't hurt ourselves. Sitting here, looking at the banister, I can see the grain of the wood. It is noticeably worn.

When my legs can move again, I choose the big bathroom on the first floor where the ornate mirrors are smaller and will show less of my body. It feels bruised all over. I close the bathroom door, turn the key in the lock and run water into the large claw-foot bath that stands in the middle of the room. I remove my clothes like a snake shedding skin and stand in the steam. The bathroom is tiled in lilac, antique and cold against my back as I lean against the wall.

The muscles in my shoulders and calves are tired and my head hurts and my thighs ache when I squat to sit. Every inch of me feels dirty: between my toes, the folds of my elbows, underneath my nails. My hair is like straw from swimming in the sea and the backs of my arms are sunburnt. I fill the bath with bubbles from a crystal bottle that belongs to Ruby and soon everything except me smells like strawberries. The bubbles cascade down the sides of the bath and puddle on the floor and I could not care less. I lie in the hot water until the pads of my fingers are as shrivelled on the outside as the rest of me feels on the inside.

I am sitting on the edge of the bed in my satin dressing gown, hair up in a towel. There is a knock at the door. Answering seems too much effort: I am staring out the window over the tops of the trees and they are absorbing all my attention. I don't answer the door, but it opens anyway. Four of them: my father and Ruby, and Sam and Beau, all crowded into my little room.

'Well?' says Beau.

'Well what?' I do not turn my head.

'Della,' says Sam.

'What happened?' says Beau. 'Did you get the money?'

I'd like to tell them that I'm in the middle of a chess game, but I don't know who my opponent is. That I feel excited and exhausted and confused. That part of me wishes this whole job had gone according to plan and was done, and the other half of me has never felt so alive. I don't tell them any of this.

'He said to come around tomorrow night,' I say. 'He said I could pick up the cheque.'

'My dear girl,' my father says, and he sits beside me on the bed and puts his arm around me. 'Felicitations.'

'This must be your biggest score ever,' says Beau. 'Is this your biggest score ever?'

'You actually did it. You crazy woman, I can't believe it,' says Sam. 'Don't tell me you managed to make a cast of a footprint. Paw print. Whatever. You can't even change a washer. You might have broken a nail.'

'Did you picture him as a chicken?' says Beau. 'I bet that helped.'

'We need champagne. Champagne and caviar. I have one bottle of '85 Krug that I have been saving for a very special occasion. Ruby, where is that bottle? And five glasses. Not the flutes, too stern. Too utilitarian. Let's have the wide ones, the ones shaped like Marie Antoinette's breasts. We'll have champagne, and then you must tell us, Della,' says my father. 'Tell us everything that occurred.'

There is certainly much to say. At the very least I should be threatening Sam with evisceration over Timothy's visit; talking with my father about new furniture and maybe a new car. A holiday. How long has it been since we all had a holiday? This should be a celebration. We should all be having a good laugh.

'Uncle Syd and Aunt Ava,' I say. 'Are they all right? It was very hot. They walked a long way.'

'They're fine,' Ruby says. 'Kept their fluids up. Ava had a rest on the way back. They said it went well. They were full of admiration for your Mr Metcalf.'

'But how did you manage it,' says Sam, 'the science? You actually faked it well enough to fool him? Thank God for brainless men of privilege. You know this time, for once, I almost hope he finds out he's been taken. I'd love to see the look on his face.'

'You'll find, Samson, that often rich people never realise,' says my father. 'Even when it is absolutely obvious that they've been done like the proverbial, their pride is too great to acknowledge it. They'd rather keep believing in the most outrageous scheme than admit to themselves that they've been idiots. Master Metcalf will never allow himself to work out what's happened. Mark my words.'

'I wouldn't count on it,' I say.

'Hello hello. What have we here? Head of the Daniel Metcalf fan club?' Sam raises his eyebrows.

'Privilege and its arrogant cousin, noblesse oblige, are contagious Della. I hope you haven't become infected,' says my father.

'I don't know if Della wants to talk about it,' says Ruby.

'Of course she wants to talk about it,' says my father. 'This will be a Gilmore epic, a story that will grow in the telling. Della versus the Metcalfs, armed only with a slingshot. This is history in the making.'

'Della,' Ruby says. 'Have you hurt yourself?'

'Maybe she doesn't feel like champagne. She might feel like a beer. Do you want a beer, Della?' says Beau. 'There's some in the fridge. Imported. Timothy did me a good deal on a few cases.'

'Della?' says Ruby.

'Let's wait until the others get home,' I say. 'They might be late. They might stop at the pub on the way. Let's wait for them. And I want to sleep for about a week. And we should wait for me to get the cheque, before we celebrate.'

'He must really have the hots for you,' says Beau. 'Just as well you're so pretty.'

'Just as well,' I say.

'I think you are very tired, and perhaps slightly ill,' says my father. 'Too much sun I expect. Would you like me to tell you a story, before you take a nap? Your favourite from when you were little.'

'I don't know that I'm in the mood for Charles Ponzi right now, Dad.'

'Scintillating George Parker and the Brooklyn Bridge, then? You used to love the part where he sold Madison Square Garden.'

When I don't speak again, Ruby shuffles the three of them outside. They grumble, but they submit.

What is this, Sam says, *secret women's business?* My father says, *we'll see you later for a real celebration.* Ruby stays. She shuts the door behind them. She moves some of my teddy bears aside, sits on my cane chair.

'A very successful job,' she says.

'Yes,' I say.

'You're to be congratulated.'

'I guess so.'

'You don't seem very happy, that's all.'

'It was a hard couple of days. A hard couple of weeks. I'm tired.'

She leans back in the chair and smooths her skirt over her knees. Her nails are flawless as always. 'I've seen you during and after a lot of jobs, since you were a little girl. You're usually happy and excited. High on adrenaline, raving about the money and what you'll do with it. You're not acting like someone who's just pulled off their biggest-ever sting.'

I stretch toward her and pick up one of my teddy bears, then I shuffle across the bed to lean against the wall. I set him on my lap and brush my hands over his soft ears.

'I'm just trying to keep a lid on it. Follow Dad's rules.'

'"Dad's rules".' She gives a little smile. 'Della. I think your father is having an affair.'

I laugh out loud, I can't help it. 'You must be joking, Ruby. He's working on something big, that's all. He said so himself.'

'He's dressing better. He's dyed his hair—did you notice? And he went to the shops, by himself, and bought new underwear. What else could that possibly signify? Everyone knows that men who start to buy their own underwear are having affairs. He's not as young as he used to be, I know that. But at our age men are scarce commodities.'

'What do you mean, "at our age"? You're twenty years younger than him. He's lucky to have you.'

She nods then, and is quiet for a while. I close my eyes and almost fall asleep. When I open them, she is still here. Her face has turned pale and serious.

'Do you ever think that every family is like a country?' she says. 'With its own leadership and language and customs, just like a country has?'

I almost laugh at this as well—it is so unrelated to what I'm thinking. I shake my head. 'Honestly Ruby, no. I've never thought about it.'

'This family is a classic example. We have very strange habits. Like the way we only talk about the good times. As if ours is the only business in the world where no one has a bad day. That's your father's way.'

'It's understandable.' I don't try to hide my yawn. 'It keeps us motivated. Besides, there's been some wonderful times, in the past. I remember lots of them. Exciting, glamorous times.'

'"Exciting, glamorous times"?' She laughs: I have made a joke that isn't funny. 'There's been lots of awful times too, but you don't remember those. No one does.'

'Ruby. I'd really like to sleep now. Can we talk about this later?'

'There was that time when you were about six. There are some people, very dangerous people, who you should never try to con. Your father chose the wrong mark. Someone who was planning to extract his own form of justice. We just piled in the car and drove, you and Samson and him and me. We kept going for about six weeks until we were sure they wouldn't find us. We slept in the car, ate whatever we could scrounge. Snuck in the back of orchards to steal fruit. Fished, when we managed it.'

'I do remember that. It was a holiday. A driving holiday. It was an adventure.'

'Della. It was a flight of desperation. We thought our systems had failed, that this house had been compromised. We were trying to prevent your father from ending up in an unmarked grave,' she says. 'We didn't even have time to pack. We had to leave with the clothes we were wearing and some cash your father had hidden.'

Days of driving, sleeping stretched out along the back seat or under a tree on a picnic rug. 'I don't remember it that way.'

'He would never have wanted to frighten you. He only ever wanted what was best for you both. You were too young. You wouldn't have understood.'

'That's right,' I say. 'He's only ever wanted what was best for us. I had the best childhood in the world.'

'But that wasn't the only time we were in trouble. Once we couldn't even keep you both with us. We sent Samson to an old friend of your father's with a cattle property in New South Wales. You, we sent to a woman I went to school with. Down on the coast.'

'I remember that,' I say. 'She had two dogs—kelpies. I used to play with them. That was a holiday too.'

'That's not to mention the stings that didn't come off. The months we were all hungry and didn't have fuel for the cars. Beans. God, if I never eat another lima bean it'll be too soon. The times we were too hungry to sleep. Ava once took a job as a barmaid, to bring in some cash. Sydney went fruit picking. Your father was furious with them; to him, it was a betrayal. He thought if they just held their nerve another job would come along. They were thinking about putting food on the table. They had four kids.'

As she speaks I have a vision of standing next to Sam in the front yard, crying, watching Syd and Ava and the cousins drive away. Julius's face pressed against the back window of the car as he waved. Cumberland Street seemed sad as well, empty without them, hollow and echoey. And I remember the beans, or rather the feeling of sitting down at the table to see a plate of them, white and split from boiling, with some bitter green on the side. 'Dandelion,' I say. 'I hated the dandelion.'

'But you were hungry enough to eat it. And nettles, and boiled pigweed.'

'I'd forgotten.'

'That's because as soon as each meal was over we never mentioned it again. Your father only ever talks about the good times—the celebrations and the champagne. He had this game: he'd scoop a bean up with a fork, about to feed it to you, and then you'd ask him what kind of bean it was. "Oh, this?" he'd say. "This is roast pork-flavoured beans." And the next mouthful would be chocolate cake-flavoured beans. Or pancake-flavoured beans. You and Samson would laugh and laugh. You thought it was the best game in the world. He almost had you both believing you were eating anything but beans.'

I have a memory, now, at the far edge of my mind: me and Sam, smaller, laughing, waiting for the next crazy flavour Dad would make up. 'I remember.'

'And no one mentions the flow of things in and out of this house. None of you kids have ever asked why things just appear and disappear. One year your father buys antique tables and fine china and silverware. Jewels for us both, real emeralds, not the rubbish he peddles. Then the next year he sells them again. I walk through this house like it's haunted. I see the spaces on the walls that were once paintings. The silk Persian rug that was in the sittingroom? I loved that rug. Once we had no plates. No plates! We ate dinner off saucepan lids with the handles unscrewed. In this house, things come and they go.'

I don't remember eating off saucepan lids. The rug I do recall: turquoise and gold, with glittering tassels and pile soft as a kitten. She's right. Once day the rug was just gone. Why didn't I ask?

'Perhaps I did know. Or perhaps I didn't want to.'

'You've always idolised your father. Mention something often enough, especially to a child, and it becomes their whole world. Memories are very easy to manipulate Della, you know that.'

'So we had hard times. Everyone has hard times.'

'When you were small you wanted a puppy so badly. Your father said we couldn't, in case we had to leave in a hurry. You don't remember all the tears you cried over that. And you don't remember crying because you wanted to go to school. You used to sit and stare out your window, the way you were when we came in just now, watching all the neighbours' kids head off to school. I had to sew you a pretend uniform, you'd wear it every day. You'd sit at the kitchen table with your books piled in front of you, barely big enough to see over the top, and every day you'd beg me to make you and Julius a packed lunch in the morning. Then you'd run outside and eat it under the apple trees, talking to the air, pretending you were surrounded by other kids. You insisted on calling me Miss de Bois, instead of Ruby.'

I shake my head a little to wake up. 'Dad loves us and wants to protect us. Should I be upset about that? I wanted to go to school, big deal. Millions of kids who do go to school wish they didn't. It doesn't mean anything.'

Ruby is sitting there, dressed in a cashmere sweater, with diamonds in her ears, talking about lima beans. It's hard to feel sorry for her. 'Look, Ruby. I've had a very trying day and this is all ancient history.'

'Not so ancient. Just because you live in this house doesn't mean you know everything about your father's life, or about my life. In many ways, Della, you're still a child. You and the others. The only reason we've kept our head above water has been the money that you six kids bring in. And then there's your mother.'

The room becomes deathly still, as though she just smashed a glass or slapped me. I don't have to listen to this. I can just stand up and walk down the stairs. Or I can order her out and shut the door. It's my room.

'My mother,' I hear myself say. 'What about my mother?'

'I know you thought it was somehow disloyal to your father,' she says. 'That's why you never asked about her.'

'I'm tired Ruby. Can't we do this some other time?'

Ruby leans across and takes the bear out of my hands. She flattens the fur across his ears and straightens his tiny bow tie. 'She bought this bear for you, before she went away. It was always your favourite.'

'I don't want to hear this,' I say. 'Please stop.'

'She couldn't face it,' Ruby says. 'The idea of going inside again. That first time almost killed her.'

'Inside again,' I say.

'Prison.'

She waits awhile but I can't speak. There is nothing I can say.

'That first time was only eighteen months, but she could never stand enclosed spaces. She would have been out sooner if she had told the lawyer that she had two small children at home but you know your father. All his rules. We must leave no trail. But I'll tell you one thing. She must have been terrified of going back in, to leave you and Samson.'

'That doesn't make sense. If she was only in prison for eighteen months, why didn't she come back? Why isn't she here?'

'Your father was always so proud of his family tradition. He didn't understand how anyone would want to live any other kind of life. She couldn't run any more stings, pick any more marks. She couldn't bring herself to. Yet she didn't want to deprive you and Samson of this house, your cousins, where you belonged. She'd changed. She thought she was the one who was wrong. So she just left.'

I ask her how she knows this, but even as I move my mouth I have my answer.

'She did come back, when she was let out on parole. But I was already here.'

A woman, locked away from her husband and children for eighteen months. The isolation, the separation, the fear. The joy of rushing back to her home to see them when she was finally released.

Finding another woman in her place.

'You were already here,' I say.

'You mustn't blame your father, Della. Your mother was gone a long time. He couldn't visit her. That kind of thing involved paperwork and identity checks and he would never submit to that. And he never let you and Samson go. He thought it would be bad for your psychology, to see the inside of a prison. They don't call us confidence artists for nothing, do they? That's what it takes above all else. And he had work to do. In those days men didn't raise children themselves, and most of his stings required a partner.'

'I saw her. When she came back, I saw her.'

'No, you didn't. She only opened the door a sliver to look in on you. You were asleep.'

'I'm very tired, Ruby.' I lie down on my bed and rest my head on the pillow. 'I need to sleep now.'

'She wasn't angry at me. She was very sweet, very happy that I was here to look after you. She wasn't angry at your father either. She knew he was living the only way he knew how. She was the one who wouldn't play by the rules, she knew that. She just looked in on you both and packed some things and she left. The last I heard she took a flight to London. She had some family there: her parents, and a brother. He was a printer, I think. He had his own business. In Manchester. I heard she wasn't coming back.'

I can tell by the way her feet are planted on the floor and the grim line of her mouth that she has done what she was resolved to do. Why she has chosen right now to tell me this, I can only guess. All I do know is that they were things I did not want to hear. Not ever, but especially not now. But I have heard them and it is too late.

'Please Ruby. Please go away.'

She comes over and sits beside me, and she rests her palm against my forehead in a way that, although I don't remember, I feel that she has done before. As though I was a small child she was checking for a fever.

'Della, I love your father very much. I have from the first moment I saw him. He says this life of ours is the best life in the world. I don't disagree with him, but then I've known no other kind. The family I grew up in was just like this one; I first met your father on a job. But you have choices. Before you take this money from Daniel Metcalf you have to know that this is the life you want. The reality of it. Not the rose-coloured way you've always seen it.'

'You think the idea of going to prison has never occurred to me before? I'm a grown woman. I know the risks.'

'Knowing something in your head is different from feeling it in your gut. This is not about your father's rules. This job has downsides as well as the upsides. Sacrifices and risks as well as champagne and caviar. And yes, you might go to prison. You might have to take money from someone when you don't really want to.'

'Don't be ridiculous. I do want to take the money. I do. The people we take money from are rich, stupid, greedy or lazy. And they deserve to lose it. That's all.'

'What you choose to believe is up to you, Della. You don't have to listen to anybody. You have to make up your own mind.'

'Please. Ruby. I have responsibilities. I have to get the cheque. I have to.'

I shut my eyes and when I open them again she has gone. I am alone in my room, alone with the wardrobe that holds all my outfits, with the hidden cavity in the floor that holds all my passports. I look down at my hands, still wrinkled from the bath. They are not scientist's hands. They are not secretary's hands, or nurse's hands, or hippy's hands. Yet I am all these things. Perhaps I have my mother's hands but I have no way of knowing. When Ruby says I should make up my own mind, I can only wonder which mind that is.

I have slept until dark and the house is quiet and I am resolved.
I need to talk to Sam. I creep down the stairs and knock on his
door.

'Come,' he says. He is kneeling on the floor amid trays of
chemicals, washing cheques. Dad would kill him if he found out.
We are not supposed to do this in our rooms in case we spill solvents
on the carpet. There is a bathroom downstairs fitted out like a
darkroom with bottles of bleach and acetone and hydrochlorides,
especially for this. I shut the door behind me.

'Hey.' He looks up and takes off his gloves. 'You look better
after your sleep.'

'Save it. I didn't say anything in front of Dad but we came *that*
close to tanking on this, thanks to your big mouth.' I shove a pile
of clothes and books on to the floor and lie on his bed, hugging one
of his pillows to my stomach.

'Yeah. I heard. The others are back and Julius told me all about it. Look, Della. I'm sorry about that. I had no idea Timmy would try to find you, much less to propose. I know I teased you about it. But really, it's ridiculous.' He laughs then, a lot, and stops to wipe a tear from his eye. I don't laugh.

'Ridiculous, how?'

'That you would make a wife for him. For anybody. Imagine you in an apron, making dinner. Ironing a shirt. It's hilarious.'

'Wake up and smell the twenty-first century, Queen Victoria. He wanted to marry me, not make me his bonded slave.'

'Get you, Germaine. That's your sexism, not mine.' He stretches out his legs and folds his arms. 'I didn't say you'd be making *his* dinner or ironing his shirt. You can't even do those things for yourself. None of us can. You might be able to become anyone you want and speak however many languages but you couldn't live by yourself for two minutes. And I don't think your prospective husband planned to move in here to Cumberland Street and sleep in your single bed.'

'I could learn. People learn to do those things.'

'Why would you want to? Marriage, children, housework. Mortgages, for God's sake. Leave those things to other people. We'll never have to worry about them. We're the lucky ones. We'll just live happily for the rest of our lives right here in the bosom of the family. You and I, Della, will grow old together.'

I rest my face against the pillow. It smells of my brother and makes me remember the childhood we spent together, playing and fighting. I will never be alone as long as he's alive. So much of who I am and what I do is also part of him.

'You're right. Whatever Ruby says, I know you're right.'

'What does Ruby say?'

I smile at him. 'Never mind. But if you ever tell anyone where

I am in the middle of a job again, we won't have a chance to grow old together. Because I will kill you with my own two hands and hide your body where no one will find it.'

'Fair enough,' he says, and I know that is the closest I will get to an apology. Now is the perfect time to ask my favour. So I tell him.

I tell him everything I feel about Daniel, the thrill of this, the exhaustion. I tell him that this job seems like life and death to me and I can think about nothing else. I tell him everything except what happened in the car park.

'I want to know what's going on, Sam. I need to. Will you help?'

'As if you have to ask,' he says.

I dress with infinite care, as though for a wedding, as though for a funeral. I paint my toenails and fingernails afresh, I wax my legs. My hair is straightened and coaxed into a French twist. This dress is my favourite from my society-girl wardrobe: off the shoulder, tight waist, flare in the skirt. Emerald velvet. It is unsuitable but I will say I am on my way to another engagement.

I sit in my dressing gown on a brocade stool in front of the mirror and lower my eyes as though it was an altar, and as I hold the mascara wand I see my hand is shaking. Ruby brings me solemn tea with her head down, zips me up, says nothing. This has an air of ceremony. In a few hours, this job will be over. I will be home safe with the money and my father will be opening champagne. I am dressing for my memories of this final time I see him. I am dressing for Daniel Metcalf's memory of me.

I leave my room with plenty of time to spare. As I walk down the stairs I am aware of noise and movement: someone is in the shower and some of the bedroom doors are shut. I leave the house without speaking to anyone. I want this whole night to slow down so I can remember every moment.

I am conscious of walking down the hall, unfastening all the bolts on the front door and locking them again. On the way to the car I see a light flickering in the largest apple shed. There is movement down there, a dragging noise. For a moment I think I should ignore it and continue on my mission but instead I walk down the verge so the stones of the drive make no sound and do not scratch my patent leather heels. Through a chink in the door I see my father and Beau piling ropes and shovels and folding tarpaulins on to the back of a truck.

'Della, go away. This is a secret,' says Beau, when he sees me at the door. He positions himself in front of a large crate and spreads his arms.

'Oh well. I suppose the time has come,' my father says. 'It's all right, Beaufort. Come in, my dear, come in. And shut the door behind you.'

When I step into the light, Beau whistles long and slow. 'Hurly burly,' he says.

This is the cue for my father to say *what a girlie* and when he doesn't, I look up. He has paled, and his eyes are closed. He has almost collapsed back on the truck behind him and one hand has gone to his chest.

'Dad,' I say, and I step towards him.

He opens his eyes and gives me a flat smile. 'I'm fine, my dear,' he says. 'You startled me for a moment, dressed like that. You are the image of your mother.'

I swallow. He is not dressed for manual labour: he is pressed and preened for going out, an old-man version of me, yet it's clear he isn't taking the Mercedes. I walk across the shed to the back of the truck. I open boxes and peer under tarpaulins.

'Don't change the subject,' I say. 'Ropes, pulleys, picks, shovels. Are you two planning a little grave-robbing?'

'What an uncouth suggestion,' my father says.

'We're treasure hunting,' says Beau.

I scan both their faces but neither is laughing. 'Treasure hunting,' I say. 'Right.'

I think: how can I get this equipment off them and take it away, without them noticing?

I think: is it legally possible to get someone, two people in fact, committed to an institution against their will? Or maybe I could just lock them in here for a few weeks and slide food in under the door?

But more than anything else, to my shame I think: how can I be lifted out of here? Levitation? Cyclone? Act of God? How could something just swoop down out of the sky and carry me away? I feel I am standing on the tracks and I can see the lights of the freight train bearing down upon us all and I doubt I have the strength to save everyone. And then I think: I am a coward.

'No, dear. Don't sit. You'll crush your dress.' My father takes my arm and dusts my skirt, tugs the hem back into place.

'It's the greatest job in the whole world,' says Beau. 'It's going to make us millions and millions. We'll be famous.'

'Famous,' I say.

'Although notoriety is always something I have avoided,' my father says, 'this job will be so monumental as to be worth sacrificing my anonymity. One might almost say that this is the job for which I have been saving my identity. I confess I haven't felt so alive since I was a small boy, travelling in a horse and buggy with your grandfather selling Ol' Doc Grayson's Magical Elixir good for bursitis, thrombitis, arthritis and anything that ails you at country fairs. Those were the days, my dear.'

'We won't forget you Della,' says Beau. 'We'll save you some jewels.'

'How.' I am almost lost for words. 'How could this happen?'

'It was chance. Mere serendipity that led us to this. I was online, in a chatroom about early Victorian history. No particular reason, you see, just following my curiosity. I have found throughout my career that keeping an open mind and following a line of enquiry often leads to something remarkable. I remember in '65, when I first saw the emeralds. I knew nothing about jewellery as a young man. What young man does? Women's business, we thought it was.'

'Dad. What happened in the chatroom?'

'I'm just getting to that. That's how I met Marguerite McGuire and her brother.'

'It's her brother who has the tattoo,' says Beau.

'Of course, of course,' my father says. 'Who would be so bestial as to tattoo a little girl? It would be an intolerable scar on such a beautiful woman.'

'Is she a little girl? Or a beautiful woman?' I say.

'She was once a little girl, but now she's a beautiful woman. That's what happens to little girls,' says Beau.

'Dad. Perhaps you'd better start at the beginning.'

'The beginning?' He chuckles. 'The beginning was in Peru, where the pirate Benito Benita stole millions of dollars in gold and jewellery from a cathedral. The riches are beyond our imagination, Della. There was an entire altar made of silver, golden railings that ran the length of the aisle, bejewelled crowns that rested on the heads of statues of the saints.'

'Right. And this pirate stole it,' I say. 'What's the world coming to? Pirates have so little respect for the church these days.'

'He's not a modern-day pirate,' says Beau. 'He's dead. It was the 1790s. And it wasn't the church's gold originally. They stole it first, from the indigenous tribes. And then they killed them. The tribes, I mean.'

'We would never steal anything that hadn't already been stolen,' says my father. 'That would be theft.'

'Well. That's fair enough then,' I say.

His face is flushed with excitement, his eyes are shining. I realise that it has been a long time since I've seen him so happy. 'Oh our sympathies are with the pirate, no doubt. Poor Benito was set upon by the British Navy and he led them a merry dance, right along the southern coast of Australia. His ship began taking water. Imagine it, Della! Two majestic sailing ships in a terrific duel across raging seas! Benito knew he couldn't sail much further, that he was one or two days ahead of them at best. So he pulled in near Queenscliff. He buried the treasure in a cave and exploded the entrance with gunpowder. In 1798.'

'Queenscliff. Only a couple of hours' drive from here,' I say. 'Handy.'

'This is all historical fact, Della,' my father says. 'I have affirmed it from several sources. I've even got the journals from a very well-funded expedition from the 1930s that tried to uncover the treasure without success. The government doesn't want people to know, of course. Doesn't want them to descend upon Queenscliff, presumably, digging holes everywhere.'

Beau is pacing and wringing his hands like he has a fever. 'This kind of thing happens Della. It really does,' he says. 'I found out all about it on the internet. Back in 2007 some treasure hunters found five hundred million dollars of Spanish coins somewhere in the Atlantic Ocean. From the wreck of a galleon. It was half a million silver coins. It happens all the time.'

'All the time. And the tattoo?'

'Benito was caught and hanged, but not before he tattooed a

map of the location of the treasure on a cabin boy. That cabin boy grew up and moved to Tasmania.'

'Right,' I say. 'Tasmania.'

'Where he proceeded to tattoo his first-born son with the self-same tattoo. And down the line it went, until it reached our friend Mal McGuire. Now brother and sister are here raising funds for an expedition to uncover the treasure.'

I close my eyes but when I open them again we are all still here, in the shed. 'Funds. Dad, you don't have any funds.'

'This is not a fly-by-night expedition. There are substantial costs, for excavators, surveyors and equipment, sonar imaging. And the living expenses of the McGuires. They have no source of income while we're working on this. Hotel bills. A car, so they can visit the site. Everything requires capital.'

'You don't have any capital.'

'We can't just stroll up with our shovels. If the authorities caught wind, we'd be handing the entire treasure over without so much as a finder's fee, probably back to Peru. The Peruvian Government is not the rightful owner. I doubt we could even negotiate with them. Since none of us speaks Spanish.'

'Dad.'

'We needed council uniforms, vehicles with government insignia, the right kind of paperwork and surveyors' documents. You can't just start digging on public land without a cover. We must have complete control of the treasure before the press release. It's been a tremendous undertaking.'

'Dad.'

'They drove a sharp bargain, the McGuires. I wanted a fifty-fifty split but settled for forty per cent, considering it is their family legacy. I'm very sensitive to the importance of family tradition. And I confess, Marguerite is quite beguiling.'

'I bet she is.'

'And quite a negotiator. I daresay I would have settled for a third. But this kind of discussion is ducks and drakes anyhow. Our share will be many, many millions.'

'But Dad. You contributed the capital? Where did you get the money?'

'I don't want Ruby bothered with this. What is an asset, if not a tool to build future assets? A great return always involves great risk.'

This is no longer a game. Of all the rules my father has taught us, the most important is that we all vote on every job. We decide everything together. I take his arm, and his face looks as tired as I have ever seen it, like he could just lie down on the floor of the shed right now and sleep. 'You all thought my best days were behind me. Even you Della. But imagine the look in everyone's eyes when I unveil this. This risk is negligible. By the time Ruby hears of it, the title will be back safe in my hands. Don't worry my dear. I will look after everything.'

There are people who will lend money, yet they are not banks. They do not charge the official rate of interest. They don't require the same level of identification or security because they are confident in their ability to…ensure their interests are covered if the loan defaults. Their means are always unpleasant. That's how he raised the money. Cumberland Street.

I am sitting in my car around the corner from the Metcalf mansion. I am only slightly late. My father has become ill without anyone realising, not even me or Ruby. I should have noticed, instead of putting each little inconsistency down to age or mere absent-mindedness. I am culpable. It is partly my fault that things have gone so far awry. For now I have done as much as I can: a quick phone call to the people my father owes so I know the details of the loan and when it is to be repaid, and I have extracted as many details about the McGuires as I could. I have made some calls to check their identities but I fear they will be long gone from their hotel. I thought the hardest part would be stopping my father from keeping his appointment this evening, but he was confused about the time or the day and was happy to be convinced to stay home.

Beau I sent on an errand of surveillance to the McGuires' hotel. I'll deal with him tomorrow, when I'll call an emergency family meeting to find a way out of this.

I take a few moments to compose myself, remembering my role. Remembering everything about me. I have bought new glasses for tonight; they are more elegant and suit my dress. I had feared it would be difficult to concentrate after speaking with my father about his treasure but it has actually made it easier, made me more determined. I have made the right decision, I know. I am focused, the result of decades of practice, I suppose. Everything else in my mind fades toward the edges.

Daniel answers the door and he is, amazingly, dishevelled. He looks like he's just woken up. His face is dark with a three-day shadow. He is wearing a tracksuit and T-shirt. His feet are in thongs and his hair is real bed-head, not stylists'. It is only when I see this that I realise I half-expected him to be wearing a tuxedo. If this was an Audrey Hepburn movie, he would be. My dress is now even more inappropriate but I do not care.

He does not mention my dress and he does not greet me or smile. 'It's in here,' is all he says, and he turns his back on me at the door and walks up the hall to the room where I first met him less than two weeks ago.

I shut the front door behind me and follow, and I am reminded of our walk through the forest. Of watching him in front of me for all those thousands of paces, and of everything I thought about then. The clip of my heels is cushioned by the long runner. In the diningroom he sits down at the table where some paperwork is spread before him. He pushes an envelope across the table.

'Quarter of a million,' he says. 'As agreed.' Then he picks up his pen and continues working. I just stand there. My weight is even on my feet. My hands are folded. I have all night. Then I catch sight of movement out the window, a flash of white and bright orange in the corner of my eye. I look: this room faces the street, and at the end of the drive there is a white Telstra van parked across the driveway. A man wearing overalls and a fluorescent safety vest is placing traffic cones around the footpath, and signs that say: *Pedestrian detour. Men at work.* The back of the van is open.

I walk over to the window and peel back a curtain. There is no other movement in the street. 'Are you having trouble with your broadband?' I say.

Daniel looks up and shakes his head. 'Why?'

I peer out the window again. The workman is quite far away, but I know he will soon take a pneumatic drill out of the back of the van and there will be a god-awful noise. 'There's a guy out there about to dig up the footpath across your drive. How will you get your car out?'

Daniel comes over then, and looks out the window. 'Hell,' he says. 'I'll be right back.'

I follow him to the door of the diningroom and watch him down the hall, down the drive. It will take him some time to speak with Sam. There will be arguments, paperwork to dig out, a supervisor to phone. When Daniel is out of sight, I head upstairs.

Upstairs I have a study that belongs to me. I keep everything that's important there. I sprint. The staircase is a grand one, carved banisters, ornate gold rods along each rise holding the carpet in place. First I must find the room. The first floor landing leads to a wide corridor lined with paintings in intricate gold frames. There are closed doors off it on both sides, in both directions. Then I notice that all the doors have ornate, old-fashioned keys in the lock, except for one. The door without a key is opposite the top of the stairs and directly above the diningroom. I stop. Even if it was not missing its key, something about this room draws me. Generations of instinct, perhaps. I place my hand flat against the door. It is alive to my touch.

From my purse I take a leather manicure kit that has a token nail file and emery board and, underneath these, a hidden pocket filled with tools to pick a lock. This lock is basic: it takes just a moment for the door to open. I look from right to left. The corridor is quiet; all the other doors remain shut. The rug is slippery silk under my heels. The door swings under the smallest pressure of my hand.

I can see two long windows with shutters facing the drive and further back, the road. The shutters are open; dusk has fallen. There is a green-shaded lamp on a desk but it is only dim, not dark, and I don't need the light. There is no sound but my breathing.

This room is a study, but one quite unlike my father's. The walls are lined with books, but they are not dusty and randomly shoved in any spare space. There is order here, yet they are not all decorator-chosen leather like the prissy books downstairs. Many of them are ugly, with cracked boards and garish spines. These books have been lovingly selected, used often, placed back, dusted. I run my hands along some of the jackets.

Evolutionary Biology. Evolution. Forms of Becoming: The Evolutionary Biology of Development. Then on another shelf: *The Origin and Evolution of Mammals, The Last Tasmanian Tiger: the history and extinction of the Thylacine.* There are more, many more; dozens and maybe hundreds, by palaeontologists and biologists and wildlife scientists. In the centre of the room there is a glass case and inside this is an old book bound in green leather. The spine says, *On the Origin of Species.* Darwin. I know without knowing that this is a first edition. Along the long wall there are a series of certificates in frames. I only look at one. It says: *This is to certify that Daniel Solomon Metcalf was admitted to the award of Master of Science, Organismic and Evolutionary Biology. Harvard University Graduate School of Arts and Sciences.*

My breath catches. I need to sit down. If I don't sit down I'll fall down. I breathe deeply, steady myself. I sit staring at this room, thinking over everything he has said to me, and as I do I feel myself smiling. That sneaky, conniving man.

Then I realise the dull ringing sound I hear is not the blood in my ears but my mobile phone, the signal from Sam that Daniel is coming back. I did not notice the first few rings. I am seriously out of time.

I bolt from the study, swinging the door behind me. Down the stairs, three at a time, almost falling on my heels. Daniel is not in sight as I dart back to the diningroom, but as soon as I sit I can hear him in the hall. I have made it with seconds to spare. I still my breathing, calm my heart rate. Of all the things I was expecting. All my fears and hopes. He has been pretending to be someone else, right from the beginning. He is just like me.

'Sorry,' Daniel says, but he doesn't sound sorry at all. He sits back behind his desk. 'Some mix-up with the address. The bloke didn't know what he was doing.'

He is all business again. He scowls and passes me a white envelope. 'It's all there,' he says. 'Check it if you like.' He opens a folder and starts to read. I am dismissed.

'I believe you,' I say.

'Fine. Believe me. Now I have a lot of work to do. If you wouldn't mind showing yourself out.' And still he does not raise his head.

I smile. I cannot speak yet. The room around me seems to have faded from view. The window on my right side, the books, the antiques that were here a few moments ago have all disappeared. I can't even see the carpet anymore. The ceiling was above my head but it has also faded. There is only Daniel. I know what he looks like. I have never seen him before in my life.

Now I am a scientist, a real scientist, and I can see him as though I am looking down a microscope at a brilliant new discovery, something incredibly rare that I hadn't believed really existed. I see the way his hair is cut short and fine around his ear, then longer as it skims away from the side of his head. I see the texture of the skin of his neck, each cell, each velvety hair, the way the skin is tanned on his arms and the way it softens and pales in the cleft of his elbows and between his fingers. The diamond notch above his top lip that meets the base of his nose. It is as if my vision was poor before and has suddenly improved, as if all those peripheral objects have been robbing me of clarity and now that they are gone, I am seeing Daniel more clearly than I have ever seen anything before. For just an instant, I feel super-human.

The wind is picking up outside; there is a squeaking and a gentle thud as the shutters bump against the house. It makes the air in the room seem deadly still by comparison. It is quiet in here, too, yet I can hear the distant pealing of a car alarm from Toorak Road. By now, Sam will be on his way home to park the van back in the rear shed and remove the decal and hide the tools. I pick up the envelope and hold it between my palms. It is white and plain and sealed. I do not need to open it. I can feel the cheque pulsing inside. I fold it once and put it in my evening purse. Now it is clear what I am free to do. I wait.

After a while, he says, 'Is there something else?' He says it as though he is speaking to his pen.

'Yes,' I say.

He keeps writing, flicking pages. 'What, then? What do you want?'

'Where is it?'

He looks up then. 'I just gave it to you.'

'Not that,' I say. 'Your bedroom.'

He blinks slowly. 'My bedroom?'

'Yes,' I say. 'The room. With your bed in it. Where you sleep.'

'It's upstairs.'

I twist my arm behind my back but I can't reach the top of the zip. 'Do you mind?' I say, and I walk around the table and turn my back to him. I hold the bottom of my hair up with one hand.

'Do I mind what?'

'I can't reach. Just undo me, will you?'

'Ella,' he says. 'What is this?'

'It's a zip.'

'Yes. Thanks for that. I mean what are you doing?'

'So many questions. The cheque is in my purse, isn't it? So whatever I'm doing,' I say, 'it isn't about the money.'

I feel the zip move slowly down, just an inch or two, but his hands are on the fabric and the metal and he doesn't touch my skin.

'You did that very well,' I say as I walk towards the door. 'I could swear you've seen a zip before.'

Half-way up the first flight I pull the zip all the way down the back of my dress and step out of it. Now all I am wearing is my underwear: my best matching bra and briefs, gold satin and black lace, and my patent heels. When I'm almost at the top I look back over my shoulder and see my emerald dress lying there on the stairs like a molten green shadow still warm from my body. I take off the glasses and put them in my evening bag. Then I snap it closed with a click and leave that on the stairs next to my dress. I see Daniel too, looking up at me.

'What a lovely hall,' I say. 'Left or right?'

'Ella. You need to go. Now.'

'Soon,' I say. 'I bet it's left. Your bedroom.'

'It's right,' he says.

'One of these doors?' I run my hand along one as I walk, feel the metal keys colder than the wood. I walk slowly. I memorise each pace. 'I can open every one, but that will take longer.'

'It's the one at the end.' I can hear him following behind me. 'Ella. Stop. Ella, I don't want you to make a mistake.'

'How sweet of you to be concerned about me.' As I walk I take the pins from my hair and drop them on the carpet. The twist unrolls and my hair falls down my back. 'If you're worried, you can always sleep on the couch.'

At the end of the corridor I open the door. There is a large bed, king-sized, covered in a plain white cotton spread. I dawdle as though admiring the walls and art but I'm not noticing anything. My heart is thumping right through my chest. I sit on the end of the bed and rest back on my elbows. He leans in the doorway and folds his arms.

'You think I'm going to sleep on the couch? This is my room.'

'You're a big boy. You can make your own decisions. I'm just pointing out options.'

He walks towards me and at the foot of the bed he stops. He kneels and lifts my leg and rests it on his thigh as if he works in a shoe store. He is gentle. He holds my knee while he takes off each shoe and places it on the floor. Then he crawls to me and I fall back so as not to touch him. I am flat on the bed, arms outstretched. He holds himself still above me, his knees spread on each side of my thighs. The bed is smooth under my back and I sink into the bedspread. There is half a foot of air between us. I can see the contrast of us, how we are opposites. I lie here soft and pale and his muscles are hard and tensed, his skin is browner, his face is rougher. More than anything I'd like to run my nails along the edge of his jaw.

'Last chance,' he says. 'Point of no return.'

'I'll make a note,' I say. 'Do you have a pencil?'

He shuts his eyes for a moment and takes a deep breath and then shakes his head and under his breath he murmurs, 'Fuck,' with such vehemence that I know his control has snapped like a thread. He drops to one elbow beside me, forces his arm under me, winds the fingers of his other hand through my hair. I am prepared for a kiss like anger but instead when it comes he is tender at first and warm and sweet and nuzzles my ear and down my neck and then only slowly does the force increase and he kisses me until I am dizzy and if he doesn't touch me soon I'll go mad. I take one of his fingers in my mouth and bite it and kiss my way down the scar on his palm. He kisses my forehead and the tip of my nose then flips me on my front in one quick movement and I feel his hand on the back of my neck. He sits on the small of my back, not with his whole weight, I know. He unclips my bra.

'Hmmm,' he says, and he shifts off me but keeps his hand firm on my neck. Then he rips down my pants and I feel a hand brush soft over my bottom. 'While I'm here, that arse is irresistible,' he says, and I feel a short sharp slap that makes me cry out. It stings where his hand has marked me. I wriggle and kick my legs but it's no use. I'm pinned.

'That's for loading up my pack,' he says. 'You think I didn't notice? I'm not an Olympic weightlifter.'

'You'll be sorry you did that,' I say into the mattress. 'I'll get my revenge.'

'Take your best shot,' he says.

After a time I feel like I am watching from the ceiling, like I can see both of us in this big bed, limbs and hands and mouths moving. I am greedy and frustrated. I want more of him, faster, but he makes me wait. He is hard and finally he is inside me and he takes his weight on his elbows but I groan and pull him down upon me. He moves inside me, faster then slower, his jaw is tensed, I wrap my legs around his waist. We are joined and I am pressed on to the bed. I am grounded from below and from above and when I come I writhe hard, arch my back. I have nothing to fear. His body holds me in place.

I am awake and I reach for the wall but it is not there. This is not my bed. I am naked and alone and in a strange place where no one knows who I am. Don't panic. Just breathe. Where is the way out? How far is it? The room is dark except for a dull floor lamp beside the door and then all at once, I remember. Last night. Daniel.

I pull the sheet up and hold it to cover myself. My body has forgotten nothing. Every inch of it is alive and much of it is sore: already I can feel four fingerprint bruises at the top of my thigh, a purple love bite forming on one nipple. My hip aches from when I misjudged the edge of the bed altogether and fell on the floor, to be followed down by Daniel. He kissed the grazes from his stubble down my throat and across my stomach. I was also strangely moved and regretful. The sight of the wild scratches on his back almost brought me to tears, but he only laughed and said that he would soon heal.

It's not that we weren't gentle with each other. At times we were that as well. He slept with his mouth slightly open and when I held my hand in front of his face I could feel the movement of his breath on my palm. His eyelashes made an arc like small dark feathers above his cheeks.

As my eyes adjust to the light I notice the room for the first time. The walls are powder blue and so is the chair in the corner. The floor lamp has a bronze base and cream-fringed shade. The bed head and the rug are the colour of chocolate. There is a nest of small paintings clustered on the wall behind the chair. They are only six inches by twelve but there are many and the frames all match. I squint a little in the half-light and I can make out now that they are photographs in black and white, all of nature scenes. Oceans and rocks and trees and such, the kind of art that would be in the bedroom of a nature lover.

My underwear could be anywhere under the twist of sheets and my dress is still on the stairs so I grope until I find a shirt on the floor and pull that on. It is soft against my skin and warm, though it hasn't held him for some hours. Only then do I notice Daniel in the dark, sitting on the windowsill on the far side of the room. He is wearing his tracksuit pants, that's all. He's just sitting there, looking at me.

'I got up to make sure I locked the front door,' he says. 'Then I put my cheque book away in my study.'

I look down at my hands, spread on the sheet. One of my fingernails is broken.

'The study door wasn't locked,' he says. 'Which is strange. I always lock that door. The Telstra guy. The workman, who was about to dig up my drive. Who was he?'

I stand and turn to face him. 'He was my brother,' I say. My hands find each other behind my back, I widen my stance on the carpet.

Daniel runs his hand over his chin. 'From the first moment I saw you, in the hallway when your glasses fell,' he says, as though I'd asked a question. 'They were right there at my feet. I could see through the lens and there was no warping of the pattern of the carpet. When I picked them up there was no distortion at all, not like you'd expect when you look through someone else's glasses. The frames were thick but they were only glass. I had to wonder why such a distinguished scientist was wearing frames with plain glass in them.'

Those glasses. I blink. I wish I had them here now so I could smash them.

'Then I made some enquiries,' he says. 'You said you studied at

Harvard. If you had, I'd have heard of you. You're not the only one with contacts. I knew from the very beginning. At first it was like solving a riddle. To find out what you were up to. That's how it started.' He folds his arms. In this light, his face looks grey.

We are both crumpled by sleep, the marks of each other on our skin. Bare feet. I am wearing his shirt. I take a few paces to the left towards the door. I run my hand along the wall to look nonchalant, make my other hand into a fist to stop it shaking. Daniel steps into the room toward the right, to the foot of the bed. We are moving like this is a dance. A slow waltz without music.

'After that you didn't put a foot wrong,' he says. 'Everything was good, all the science, all the theory. Oh, one thing. You picked up a tooth without wearing gloves. You didn't know what kind of tooth it was. It was unidentified, but that would have contaminated the sample, you see? Teeth are the best source of DNA but you can't touch them with your hands. You would have fooled anyone who wasn't a scientist. But it was too late. I already suspected. And I did a little digging. I found out everything I needed to know.' He steps toward me. He is looking at me now. He is taller than me, and stronger. If he holds me and pins me down and doesn't let me go, he can hold me here until the police come. I will be trapped.

'I know why: the money. The how is harder to figure out. This has been quite an operation. You even met me at the university. And there's Glenda and Joshua. You can't be acting alone.'

He takes one more step towards me. 'Your name is Della, isn't it,' he says, and it's a statement, not a question. 'That's what Timmy called you at the camp. Della.'

His palms are open and he is stepping slowly, like he is trying to catch a skittish animal. I swing my arm suddenly and knock the lamp over. It is heavy and as it smashes to the floor the cord pulls from its socket. Daniel jumps back instinctively to avoid it. The room goes dark. I run for the door. Slam it shut behind me. Lock it with the key, still on the outside. I have one second to spare: Daniel has reached the door and is pulling and twisting the handle. He turns the light on; I see it flooding out underneath the door. He is at the door now, kicking it and banging it with the side of his fist. Then I hear a louder, duller smack. He is running at the door with his shoulder.

'Ella!' I can hear him yelling as I run down the stairs. 'For God's sake Ella don't do this.'

On the stairs I take off his shirt. I cannot bear it on my skin any longer. It is burning me. For a minute I stand there naked and shivering although it isn't cold. I pull my dress back on but can manage the zip only half-way. I leave his shirt on the stairs right where my dress was. The shoes and underwear I can do without. My purse, with my car keys, is still there where I left it and I press it under my arm. As I dress I still hear him, though it grows more muffled as I run for the door. 'Please. Ella. Don't. Don't do this. Just listen to me. Please.'

I leave the front door open. I run; there is no other thought but putting distance between me and him, reaching the car, Cumberland Street, safety, not turning back. Half-way down the path I hear yelling again. 'Ella. Ella, wait.' I look up and see him leaning out the open window. His chest is bare and I can see the line of his collar bone where I kissed it a few hours ago. I freeze then, right here on his garden path, the concrete cold under my feet. 'Ella!' he yells. We are both still.

'That's not my name,' I whisper, but he is too far away to hear me. 'That's not my name!' I yell this time, up at him, my fists clenched, my arms stiff and ready for anything.

He is leaning out of the window to reach a drain that runs down the side of the building. It cannot take his weight. This is awful. He must stop. He is leaning right out now, reaching for the drain with his feet. I feel stuck to the spot but I must move, I cannot stand there waiting for him to catch me and send me to prison. I hit my own leg with my fist and it gets the message. I run again, faster now, but I still cannot bring myself to turn the corner until I see him hit the ground. He tumbles a little, jumps into a flower bed but the fall is not enough to hurt him.

On the street I pick up speed. There is a sharp stabbing pain in my sole: I have stepped on something sharp but I cannot stop. For a moment I think I should leave the car so he will not connect it with me, but then I glance over my shoulder. He is gaining. I have no option, the car it is. I run as fast as I am able. I feel the dress tearing under the sleeve. I thrust my arms and move my legs. Any moment I expect to feel his breath on my neck, his hands on me.

At the driver's door I fumble with the keys. I almost drop them. *Come on, come on.* Then blessedly the key finds the lock and I'm in, the doors are fastened and the engine started. There is a loud noise at the window—I turn my head to see him banging on the side glass with his open hand. 'Ella,' I can hear him say. His face is pale and there is blood on his lip. 'Ella for God's sake open the door. I'm not going to hurt you.'

I pull away fast without turning on the lights. He jumps out of the way and in the rearview mirror I can see him chasing the car, arms pumping like a sprinter. When it's obvious he can't catch me he stops in the middle of the street and holds his arms out to each side. I turn the corner and he disappears but it is not until I am five suburbs away that I pull over. I switch off the ignition but my hands are shaking so I can barely remove the key. I take a few steps away from the car to be sick.

I drive for the rest of the night, and all the time I do not think of Daniel Metcalf. Instead, I think of Cumberland Street, how much I love it. My room, that has been my room for ever and will be my room for ever. I will never take it for granted again, never think my world is small or prescriptive. There are troubles, I know. My father has mortgaged the house and we will have to find money. But the equipment can be sold and some of the debt repaid, and all of us working together can make some cash. Perhaps my father can run another sting with the emeralds: they always work.

There is nothing we cannot fix if we stick together. I love it. I love the apple trees and living with my cousins and my aunt and uncle. The way Ruby looks after us all. My family. I am so lucky. My heart is full of them, and of the knowledge of how close I came tonight to losing everything. Still, Daniel has a description of me, and perhaps the licence plate of the car which will soon be reported stolen by the people who lent it to me. I will clean it quickly at home then abandon it in a street far away. The danger is not past but I will survive this. It is over.

It is just dawn as I drive up. Cumberland Street is long, but it is usually quiet, and even four blocks away I see lights outside our house. Cars, many cars. By the time I am three blocks away I can tell they are police cars. As I drive past I can see people huddled on the footpath in their pyjamas. They are strangers and sticky-beaks wanting to see what is going on. I didn't think I could feel worse, but somehow I do.

I park around the corner. This is wrong, I know. This is breaking the rules: if ever there was a time to go straight to the safe house it is now. But I cannot leave them. In the back of the car I find an old blanket and drape it around my shoulders to hide my evening dress. I can do nothing about my bare feet.

I stand at the back of the milling crowd, just listening, trying to blend in. No one knows anything. There are two blonde women in velour tracksuits and a man in pyjamas and a dressing gown, among other people. Perhaps they are our neighbours but I've never seen them before. I can hear them chattering among themselves, buzzing like bees. *What's going on? Who would have thought? In this very street. Under our very noses. Strange family, weren't they? Never saw hide nor hair of them.*

There are no police around and I sneak a peek up the drive: more cars, marked and unmarked, and the front door is open. There is no mistake. This is a catastrophe.

There is some rustling in the branches on my left, above the wall. I hear a soft sound and take a few steps back towards it. Someone is standing behind me and I hear a quiet voice in my ear.

'Get in the car and go.' Sam. And Beau is with him.

I turn to face him and he takes us both by the arms and drags us around the corner, behind the wall where the crowd can't see. Then he looks at me properly.

'Bloody hell.' He lifts the corner of the blanket and sees my face and dress and feet. 'What happened to you?'

'It doesn't matter,' I say. 'What's going on?'

'I was dead asleep and heard the banging on the door. I snuck downstairs and went through the trapdoor in the diningroom. I've been in the cellar on the far side for almost an hour listening to them talking in the lounge. It's Dad. They've got him.'

'I heard them too. I climbed out the window and onto the roof,' says Beau.

'It's that stupid treasure business,' I say, and I glare at Beau.

'It can't be,' he says. 'We've been so careful.'

'I don't know what that is,' says Sam. 'But it's nothing to do with treasure. It's the emeralds.'

'See?' says Beau. 'See?'

'You must be joking,' I say. 'He's done that emerald business a dozen times. He could do that in his sleep.'

'This time I think he must have. From what I've overheard and putting two and two together, this latest one with the antique earrings was a set-up from the beginning. Maybe the people he stung last time beefed about it, but anyway the marks were undercover cops out to trap him. He's been tailed here, looks like. Probably been following his every move and he didn't even pick them.'

His glorious career, all his adventures. Our captain, my inspiration. To meet his downfall in this ignominious way. Ill, no longer himself. Arrested. I look down at the footpath, at my bare feet. I feel like I am going to be sick again.

'He'll go to prison,' I say, and think of him in a small dark room, all alone: grey uniform, cement floor, stainless steel toilet in the corner.

'And that's not the worst of it,' says Sam. 'He's in the system now. They'll know where he lives and what he does. He won't be a ghost anymore. And Ruby's inside the house too, with the cops. Somehow she's been trapped as well.'

'Or she decided to stay with him,' I say.

'He stalled for quite a while when he heard the knocking. He's an old man, he can get away with it. Then it took ages to undo the locks so I'm pretty sure no one else is inside the house. Maybe Syd and Ava are behind the dummy wall in the downstairs bathroom. They'll stay there until the cops go. It looks like Julius got away. We can be thankful for that. Greta didn't come home last night at all but I texted her to stay where she is. Shame about Ruby. That's her career over, pretty much.' Sam bends his head forward and rubs the back of his neck. I haven't seen him look so sad since we were children. 'We were just waiting around for you,' he says. 'Now we'll scarper.'

I stand here in front of my family home, in a torn evening dress with cut and bloody bare feet. I have not slept or eaten and my skin is covered in Daniel's marks that I have never felt before and will never feel again. And now my father has been arrested. Surely my life can get no worse than this.

'At least you've got the cheque from Metcalf,' says Sam.

'Cheque?' I say. Then I remember. It's on the front seat of the car, still in my purse where I put it a million years ago.

'Della?' says Beau. 'Della, are you all right?'

'What was going on with him, Della? You searched his study? You got the cheque all right? Didn't you?'

'It's a bust,' I tell him. 'He was on to us from the beginning.'

'That's impossible,' says Sam.

'From the beginning,' I say, and I laugh. Inappropriately, almost hysterically. 'He's a scientist, if you can believe it. He's an evolutionary biologist himself. He was lying to us all along.'

Beau makes a long, slow whistle. 'You can't trust anybody these days,' he says.

'So,' says Sam, and he looks me up and down again, my crushed dress. He reaches out one hand and moves the sleeve down past my bare shoulder, then slowly places it back. Then he brushes my hair back behind my ear. 'What have you done, Della?' he says.

It is useless to explain. It makes no sense even to me. I say nothing.

'Are you saying you didn't get the cheque? You stayed half the night with him and you've come home without your bra, no shoes, and you didn't get the cheque. Is that what you're telling me?'

I cover my mouth with my hand.

'Did you get it?' he says. 'Or not?'

'It's in my purse.'

'Surely he'll cancel it,' says Beau. 'If he was on to us from the beginning, he'll cancel it. He might be a mark, but he's not stupid.'

'He's not a mark,' I say. 'He never was.'

'If he was planning to cancel it, why did he give it to you in the first place?' Sam says.

'I don't know. He did, that's all.'

'Della,' Sam grips me by the shoulders and gives me a small shake. 'Think. For God's sake, this is important. We're on the verge of losing everything, including Dad. Why did he give it to you?'

'I don't know,' I say again.

'You're lying.' He lets go of my arms and pushes me away.

'Some sick idea of a game, probably,' says Beau. 'As soon as the bank opens for business he'll be phoning and cancelling it. A waste of time to deposit it, I reckon.'

'Della.' Sam raises his voice, then looks around too late to make sure no one will notice. 'Will he cancel it? You've been the mechanic on this job, you're supposed to be able to read him. Will he cancel the cheque?'

'No,' I say finally. 'I don't think he will.'

'Then just deposit it. Put it in an express envelope. Or take it in yourself and ask for a fast clearance. Even if you're wrong, the bank can't catch you. The worst they can do is decline it. But for God's sake Della, deposit it. We need that money.'

I don't speak. I can't. My head is telling me that Sam is right. There is no logical reason not to cash that cheque. But still I don't reply.

'There's no risk and maybe it'll take Metcalf a while to cancel it. In fact, Della,' says Sam, 'Metcalf might have his own reasons for not cancelling it.'

With quarter of a million dollars, we could pay out whatever mortgage Dad has taken on the house. So we could still live here, together. It could buy him a new identity when he got out of prison. It would mean my life could keep going just as it has been.

'No,' I say.

Beau kicks the wall beside us. Sam runs his fingers through his hair.

'Della,' he says. 'You know enough about banking to know there is no risk in this. You go to the bank, you put the cheque in, you leave. Your ID is solid and anyway, they won't process it in front of you. Just deposit the cheque.'

'I can't,' I say.

Sam's face is white, his lips turn under, his eyes narrow. The muscles working in his throat show me the effort he is making to be calm. 'Della. I'm begging you. It doesn't just belong to you. We all worked on this. Don't be an idiot. Think of someone besides yourself. We've got everything to gain and you've got nothing to lose. Just cash the cheque. It can't hurt you.'

I shake my head. Sam is wrong. This time I feel I have a lot to lose. And it can hurt me.

The bunk is hard under my back. Or maybe it's that my shoulders are stiffer than usual tonight. In the last few weeks my arms have browned in the sun and grown strong. My hands are no longer manicured nails, soft skin. I look down at them: they are callused, the nails are peeling polish, broken and rough.

For weeks I have not been to a shop or a restaurant. I have not used a computer or read a newspaper. My work is never dull, though: sometimes I pick the fruit but just as often I tend the chickens, chase them when they escape into the garden. I hunt for their small brown eggs under bushes. The farm dogs want feeding, their bowls need cleaning. The Jervises do not send me far out on to the farm. I am still too soft or, more likely, untrusted. Instead I weed the kitchen vegetable patch and pod peas for Janice, the cook. On rainy days I stay inside and scrub pots or stew fruit. Right now there are only two others in the women's bunk house. They are country girls from Queensland, ready to embark on a city life, only in their teens. They are working their way around the country staying on farms before they go to university. It is a lark for them. They do not speak to me. I do not know if this is because the Jervises have warned them or because of the look in my eyes.

The first week of my exile I could do almost nothing but lie in this bunk. I'm sure the Jervises thought I was dying. My head throbbed. Under the thin blankets I shivered and sweated. I could not bear light. I lay with my head flat on the mattress and the pillow over my eyes. Every moment I ached to have him again. I could not bring myself to eat, especially not the toast and eggs so begrudgingly left outside my door. I know they were only feeding me to avoid the one thing that would be worse than having me on their farm: disposing of my body.

But over time it would appear to someone who doesn't know me that I have recovered, and now I fit in with everyone else. We all rise at five to start work when dawn breaks, two or three hours of chores before breakfast. It is tiring but there is more free time here than I would have imagined. By three or four the day is done. On Sundays, the others go to town to see a movie or drink at the pub and I am the only one who stays behind.

On these days I stay in the front room and watch hours of television. The satellite brings in hundreds of stations: dramas and comedies and tragedies, old and new. Frivolous, my father would call it. Superficial chewing gum for the intellect and Novocain for the spirit.

It does not feel like this to me. It feels like luxury, these hundreds of actors and writers and their loyal crew striving to entertain only me. I love Discovery Channel. It's like actually being an archaeologist or a herpetologist or a medical examiner, without any of the research or practice. And I cannot stop watching British comedy. The idea that I can sit on this lumpy old couch and be entertained, for nothing, at the touch of a button? In past centuries queens and empresses made do with lame jugglers or some fool singing a ditty or a performing monkey with scabies. I am immeasurably richer than they.

While living and working on the farm I have learned many things. I love strawberries and am greedy for them. Even the sight of them cheers me, the colour and the smell. Sometimes I just stand and eat them instead of collecting them in the bucket. I love not only the farm dogs, as I have always thought I would, but the cats too. Early mornings I like better than I expected. There is a quietness in the air and a sense that anything is possible. I like mashing potatoes. Earl Grey tea with lemon. Sitting in front of the fire and reading. The farmhouse has a stained-glass window in the kitchen that throws jewel-coloured patterns on the polished floor. If I were to ever have a home of my own, I'd like a window just like that.

I've discovered I don't like country music. It's so sad. Who needs that? And I don't like clutter. If I still had my own room I'd get rid of the wardrobes and buy a bigger one, then I'd put all my bears and nicknacks out of sight. In fact, I'd throw out all the bears except the one my mother gave me. I don't like cleaning the bathroom, although I'm fine with doing dishes. I don't mind the curl in my hair anymore. I wear it up in a plain ponytail, out of the way. It's been weeks since I tried to straighten it. I dress in old jeans and men's flannel shirts and it's remarkable but I don't mind that either.

And now I understand that there is more than one way to be alone. At Cumberland Street, even when I was in my room or in the shower, the house breathed with all of us. Here, even when we gather around the table at dinner time, I am always by myself.

The other girls are outside having a smoke before bed, talking about their plans, telling stories about their parents. They roll their own cigarettes on white papers with agile, stained fingers, then smoke them pinched between thumb and forefinger instead of resting between the tips of their stretched middle and ring. It is almost as if they do not judge whether an action is ladylike or not before they do it.

I am nearly asleep when there is a knock on the door. I know at once it is something important. Jervis can barely bring himself to speak and Mrs Jervis does not acknowledge me; she tiptoes and whispers when she sees me coming. Perhaps they think I am a murderer on the run. It must be some debt they owe my father, to tolerate my presence like this when their discomfort is so apparent.

'Come,' I say, and the door opens with a reluctance I can feel.

'This was in the mail today,' Jervis says. He drops an envelope on the end of my bunk and clears his throat. 'I don't want any more of these coming, do you hear? Upsets the wife.'

His face is twisted like a coil of rope. I would hate to disillusion him; clearly he thinks I'm powerful enough to control distant people who want to write to me, using only the power of my mind. I cannot resist.

'It's here,' I say. 'Great. Instructions for my next job. Who's gonna get iced and where I should put the body. Say, Jervis. You've got that empty field in the north-west corner, don't you? Can I borrow a shovel?'

His eyes and mouth grow wide and for an instant I think he's going to cry. Then he slams the door and I can hear him rush back down the hall. I can't help but laugh. These days even when things are serious I can't help being flippant.

The envelope says: Heloise McGregor, c/- Jervis. Then the address of the farm, written in a spidery hand.

Dear Hel,

You've been quiet lately but I know you can't help that. Your dad's
well and waiting his trial. He's had the best lawyers that money can
buy, paid by a friend who has stuck by us. If you can spare a day I'd
be glad to see you and tell you news. There are no hard feelings Hel.
Just so's you know. I'll be in the house every Friday at 2, until the
end of next month. It'll be safe, I promise.
R.

This is not the first note I've received. Once I even had a visitor, a
bikie with a grizzled grey beard, entrusted with a message. So I
already knew Ruby wasn't charged by the police, but she had been
identified and forced to give statements. This was punishment
enough. I also knew that my father was managing all right on
remand. He was using his enforced sabbatical to broaden his knowledge of Aristotelian philosophy and organise a chess competition
for the inmates. He was seeing doctors, following instructions like
a lamb.

So this is not news. I am glad that someone has provided a good
lawyer, but surprised. Lawyers are expensive. It's a miracle that one
of my father's ragbag collection of friends has cash to spare, and also
incredible that now he has been arrested they have not all shrunk
from him like he was contagious.

I also knew that my Uncle Syd and Aunt Ava had hidden behind
the false wall just as Sam assumed. It was built especially for them;
they are not of an age to climb over roofs or down into cellars. They
stayed there for almost thirty-six hours, sneaking out at night for
water and food, because the detectives were busy during the day
searching for evidence and a patrol was stationed outside for the first
night. After that, they packed their belongings and let themselves
out the front door. They have moved to North Queensland where

the climate suits them better. They have both pierced their ears and are working as travelling psychics, making more money than they have in years. The reports I've received say they are happy.

Julius has stayed in Melbourne and is renting a penthouse in the city. He is building his fortune, apparently, as a Russian online bride who only needs a few thousand to bribe an official for a visa and then a few thousand more for an air ticket to come here to Australia to be with her new beloved. I'm sure his Russian English is convincing. He has a real knack for patois.

Anders has moved to the country and started a cult. Only two followers so far, I'm told, but he has high hopes. I am pleased about this. For years we have known that religion is the best way to encourage people to hand over cash without hesitation, but we haven't capitalised on it until now. I can see Anders in robes and sandals, Christ-like, but not so wan. Good for him.

Greta has certainly landed on her feet. She has moved in with Timothy. A surprise, but the more I think of it the more it makes perfect sense. His family empire is booming and Timothy is dipping his toe in more legitimate pursuits. She would not have given him a second glance before but Greta knows a good business opportunity when she sees it.

Sam is in hiding, like me. It was decided that he and I were the most at risk from the law, being Dad's only children. I don't even know where he is. At times I want more than anything to speak with him, to know he is all right. But I know we have nothing to say to each other. Of the things that haunt me, the look on his face when we parted outside Cumberland Street that morning is one of the worst.

Only Beau is struggling outside the bosom of the family. When word of my father's arrest spread, the McGuire siblings unsurprisingly disappeared as though they had never existed, along with

Beau's hope of the treasure and all my father invested. Dad's probably still defending them. *Naturally they've disappeared, my dear,* he'll say. *What would you expect? That they stay around in the face of the police? Although they badly misjudged my character if they thought I would lead the authorities to them.* Beau is, I hear, also blind to the truth about the McGuires, who I know in my bones are husband and wife. Beau is leaving the family business and getting a proper job. This is for the best, I can see. Not everything is in your genes, and he's never really been cut out for it. He's planning to become a stockbroker.

'No hard feelings', Ruby says in her note. Maybe not from her. When my father is thinking clearly again he will know that he was the one who broke the rules, so he must accept the consequences. If any of us had broken his rules he would have expected that we take our punishment with our head high. He certainly expected this of my mother.

The rest of the family may be another matter. That day I left Sam standing on the footpath in front of Cumberland Street, he was beyond angry with me. And that was before he knew that the house was mortgaged and we needed Daniel's money more than he'd thought. I know none of the cousins are speaking to me either: I have received notes or messages from all of them expressing their horror of my betrayal. I understand all of this. I have stuck fast to my decision but if I were in their place and it was Greta or Sam who had done this, I would feel the same as they do.

I never imagined I would end up fighting with my family this way. And all because of this slip of paper I keep in its plain white envelope under my pillow when I sleep, and folded inside my bra when I work on the farm. This is not for sentimental reasons. There is nothing of his handwriting on the front, only the inside. It does not bear my name at all. I have opened it a number of times, and closed it again, and lifted the flap little by little so it doesn't tear, then resealed it.

I am happy that Ruby at least will see me. When I go back to Melbourne to meet her on Friday I will bring the envelope with me, but not for sentimental reasons. Just because I cannot bear to let it out of my sight.

If Ruby didn't know I was coming she would not recognise me. My jeans are impossibly stained and worn to shredded holes above one knee. Mrs Jervis found this old flannel shirt and singlet in her rag bag and before handing them to me she checked over every inch. She was looking for any marks that might be used to trace the clothes back to the farm if I was captured. I'm almost tempted to go into town and have her name and address tattooed on my skin, just to see the look on her face.

I sent away for these boots weeks ago, charged to the Jervises' account, because I had no shoes at all when I arrived. The emerald dress I arrived in has long since vanished. I cannot believe anyone would throw out something so beautiful, but the pictures of their daughter on the mantel show a woman twice my size so it cannot have gone to her. Somehow I cannot mourn for this one dress among everything I have lost. The Jervises have given me fifty dollars for my trip today. Very generous, considering they have had my labour for weeks now and paid me nothing. They are hoping I do not come back.

On the walk from the train station, I realise I have never travelled down Cumberland Street on foot before. The houses are very close together and surprisingly small, but neat. There can't be room for more than two or three people in each one. When I get to where our house should be, I stop. I've made a mistake. Lost my way, surely. This can't be where I've spent my entire life.

The real estate agent's board on the front looks out of place and is almost as big as the whole bunkroom back at the farm, but it isn't that. The sign shows a large picture, not of the house itself or any of the rooms inside. Instead it's a drawing of the block with the dimensions written in large type. *Calling all developers!* it says. *Once in a lifetime subdivision opportunity!* Again the repercussions of my decision are here in front of my face, in real estate agent-speak, in bold. Not just our family, but our entire house is to be destroyed without my lifting a finger to save it.

I walk down the drive. Everything is deserted, the house locked up, the windows tiny and dirty. The bars on them are so thick; I had never noticed. It was dark inside the house, I realise now. We always had the lights on even in the middle of the day. The paint is peeling. There are spiders' webs under the eaves and in the back corner the guttering has come away from the house. There is a dull stain where water from the roof has run down the timber.

Down the slope to the backyard I see the sheds half falling down. It looks like a tip and everywhere is the sweet decaying smell of rotten apples.

It is just two o'clock. I take the key from the small box hidden at the base of the third tree. The cellar door at the back of the house creaks as I pull it open. It is dark inside and dusty, but I find my way along the passage past my father's office. I touch the doorknob but know I could not bear to go inside, so instead I go up through the trapdoor. The curtains are all drawn and flecks of dust float through the air in the chinks of sunlight. These rooms are where I was born and raised and learned my craft. This is where all my memories live. I want to touch every surface, pick up every object and hold it in my hand. Each vase and trinket and cushion.

I think of the smallest things: the Chokitos that Uncle Syd would bring home for me when I was small. The way Ava would make my salad with mayonnaise instead of the vinaigrette everyone else preferred. Even Greta. Now I can only think of the games we played with our dolls, the way we would make cubbies by throwing a sheet over the dining chairs. I would climb the trees in the backyard with Anders and Beau and we would race to see who could reach the highest. The memories of Julius and Sam and Ruby and my father are more intense. I know that if I begin to think of them I will never stop. I will stand forever right here in the hall, covered in dust, unable to move.

And it is not just this house, and it is not just these people. I have suspected for some time and now it is certain: we are like the Tasmanian tiger itself. We are extinct. Those grand days of my father's are gone. Con artists are no longer glamorous and persuasive, with charming personalities and wits like lightning, travelling the world, courting trust. We were once beautiful, gracious. We made castles in the air, using nothing but our imaginations. Now we have been succeeded by spotty teenagers and organised crime lackeys, hacking or stealing identities or sending emails so unbelievable that it is only by dint of sheer volume that anyone is taken in at all. There is surely no skill in it. It is right that we should fade away. People will always strive to give away their money but the world has no room for us anymore.

All at once I see in a darkened corner my father's favourite chair. There is a shadow in it. Someone is sitting there. My knees almost fail beneath me: it is like the ghost of my father is here, watching me. I blink and take a step closer. It is not my father. It is Daniel.

My first thought when I see him is to run, like I did before. The front doors are locked from the outside but I could make it back down the trapdoor and perhaps through the trees, over the back fence. I am fitter than the last time. Wirier. These clothes are better suited for flight. But my arms feel heavy and my eyes feel wet and I just cannot run, not anymore. Last time I managed to escape, yet I still dream of him every night so what is the use? I cannot get away. It is pointless to try. I lean back against the wall and shut my eyes.

'Hello Della,' he says.

I shake my head. This is just as impossible as if it were my father's ghost, sitting there talking to me. I was so careful. I was always so careful.

'How did you find me?'

'"Hello Daniel",' he says. '"It's been too long. What have you been up to, since I locked you in your bedroom and ran out of your house in the middle of the night?"'

His body. Every cell, every hair. If I took half a dozen steps forward and stretched out my arms, I could touch him.

'I have your shoes in my car around the corner, and your underwear. If you're in a Cinderella kind of mood.'

He is resting his elbows on the armrests with his fingertips together, relaxed, but then he leans forward. 'God, you're so thin. I imagined seeing you a hundred times a day but in my mind you didn't look like this.'

I look down at my hands, my jeans. Work boots, for heaven's sake. He is imagining a woman in a green dress with black heels, another person from a long time ago. I sit opposite him, sink into the couch, cover my forehead with my hands.

'You can't have this address. No one has ever found us. There's no way you could have traced anything back here. I don't understand.'

'Details, I see. You want to talk about details,' he says. 'Fair enough. It was the forms. At the national park. The camping permit. I drove back down there. The rangers were very helpful when I explained who I was and what I wanted. They let me look at their records.'

'No.' I swallow, blink my eyes, try to stop shaking. 'I remember signing those forms. I used fake details. That's not a mistake I would make.'

'You didn't make a mistake. You used fake details all right,' he says. 'But Timmy didn't.'

'Timothy.'

'He used his real name, his real address. I went to his house. We had a long talk. Narrowly escaped buying a watch. Greta says hi, by the way, and if she ever sees you again she's going to make you sorry you were ever born. That's her name, isn't it? Your cousin. Greta, not Glenda.'

My neck feels weak. I'm not sure it will continue to support my head. Timothy. I can almost see him now, in the cramped ranger's office, scribbling his real details on that form in regulation block letters, tongue between his teeth. All my effort, all my hard work. All unravelled by Timothy.

'No sign of Julius, but I expect he had his laptop set up somewhere else. Flat out, probably.' Daniel crosses his arms and leans back in his chair. He has won. I have lost. 'If he's ever interested in becoming a scientist, the Zoology Department would be happy to have him. You tell him that.'

'You'll have to tell him yourself.' I pull the envelope out of my back pocket, smooth it between my fingers. 'Here. This is what you want. Take it.'

I reach out one arm and hand it to him. He shakes it, holds it to his ear like it might explode then he rips one end off the envelope and tips it upside down. Out tumbles a wave of confetti: the cheque is shredded into tiny pieces of paper as small as my fingers could tear. They drift onto his lap and the chair and the floor and make a white mosaic against the rug.

'That's not what I want.' He looks up. 'That's not why I tracked you down.'

'I didn't cash it.'

'And I didn't cancel it,' he says. 'So why all the little pieces?'

I pull at the flannel of my sleeve, try to smile. 'I've been on a farm. Wearing these. I thought I might weaken and make an emergency visit to a day spa or a dress shop. Call it insurance against future bad judgment.'

He scoops some of the little cheque pieces up in one hand and sprinkles them to the other. 'The whole point of this operation was to get this cheque, wasn't it? And now you don't want it?'

My legs won't be still now so I stand and walk over to the fireplace. The mantel is dusty. I trace my fingers along it.

'I thought you were fair game,' I say. 'I didn't realise you were pretending as well.'

He laughs, then. 'I'm glad I gave you that impression. That room was no end of trouble to set up.'

His words seem to drift on the still air of the room, floating like the dust motes. It takes a while for them to reach my consciousness. 'Set up? What do you mean "set up"?'

'You think you're the only one who can pretend? It's some bylaw? Della Gilmore is allowed to make things up, but the rest of us have to tell the truth?' He is sitting there in my father's chair like he has been busting to tell me all this. Like it's the greatest joke ever and he can barely keep from laughing. He's grinning now, like a kid, like a child who's jumped out from behind a door and yelled boo.

'You should have seen your face when I got back to the diningroom.'

Set up. 'How did you know I'd go up there?'

'I didn't. But I thought if I gave you the opportunity, you wouldn't be able to resist having a look around. You got me out of the way just before I disappeared on a long phone call.'

I shut my eyes, summon my memories, everything he said early that morning, everything I did. 'But what about the tooth? You said I made a mistake. That I should have picked up the tooth, the one I found in the park, wearing gloves. To preserve the DNA. How did you know about that?'

'I saw it on *CSI*.' He's still smiling. Dimples I had never noticed before appear in his cheeks. He stands, walks over to me near the fireplace and leans on it with one elbow. Mirror behaviour, like I was the mark and he was the artist. 'Don't think it was easy. I had to work fast. Those books were hell to round up in one day. Five or six separate shipments, by taxi from every store I could get on the phone. There was dust everywhere. The cleaners only left ten minutes before you arrived.'

I shake my head. 'No. You went to Harvard. I saw your degrees.'

'That was the easiest bit. I hired a freelance designer, but in retrospect I could have managed myself. Next time, maybe.'

I close my mouth, shake my head. I feel like my father loading shovels onto a truck.

'I had to rent that copy of *Origin of Species*. It was exorbitant, let me tell you. From friends of the family, but that didn't help. I had to wear white gloves the whole time and sign away my first born if it was damaged. For a while I didn't think they'd take the risk.'

I took a deep breath. 'But you convinced them.'

'Ah. Yes. You see, I had an argument no one can resist. I told them it was an affair of the heart.'

The single bed in my attic room is small for two people. Often Daniel's feet hang over the end and once I hit my head on the wall. We make love slowly, languid but relentless, without the desperate urgency of the first time. Like we have time for all things now. After a while, we sneak down to the kitchen and find the preserves in the pantry, big jars of peaches and apricots laid down by Ruby and Ava. I open one; the lid gives way with squelch. We sit on the kitchen bench, me in my dressing gown, him in his shirt and undies. We eat peach halves with our fingers and drip the juices in the sink. I tell him stories about the house, show him this and that. If I tell him, there will be someone else who remembers it. Even when the house is gone. Mostly I talk and he listens, but there is still one thing I need to know.

'Did you really see a Tasmanian tiger when you were a boy?'

He kisses the palm of my hand. 'I thought you must have known about that.'

'Well did you?'

'Does it matter?'

'Tell me what happened,' I say. 'Tell me the truth.'

He talks for a long time, as if to show me he has nothing left to hide. After a while the sun goes down and I light a dozen candles in holders and we move to the sittingroom floor so the light can't be seen from outside. I don't interrupt.

He holds my hand and tells me a story about a little boy whose classmates called him Dunny, who was the last picked in every team. A boy who wheezed if he walked too quickly and carried his grey inhaler in the top pocket of his shirt always, sucking on it when he was anxious or shy like a prescription thumb-replacement.

By day he was quiet, evasive at school or tucked in a corner of his room alone, reading or playing with his Action Man toys. After dark he couldn't step on the floor of his room. He moved to the bed by a complicated process of leaps from the hallway to a chair, then to a pile of cushions positioned carefully on the floor so the monsters underneath couldn't grab his ankles. He dreamed of falling, drowning, being eaten by crocodiles, devoured by monsters. He woke with hair sweat-damp, heart hot and racing.

Then one day his father looked up from his desk and saw his son before him—wan, craven, pudgy—and knew action was required. Camping, Daniel told me, was like a secret tonic for manhood brewed by generations of Metcalfs. Confronting the dark built courage; erecting a tent, dexterity with mallet and peg; walking through the bush, muscles that would eventually replace the baby fat that clung so stubbornly.

The weekend Arnold Metcalf chose was cold; winter had come early to Wilsons Promontory. When they reached the campsite, scarcely fifty metres from the car, they found a few patches of tired earth separated by struggling grass and a prison-grey toilet block.

Arnold paused. *No*, he said. *Trimmed grass? Bloody toilet block?* He slipped his thumbs under the straps of his pack and kept walking. On to the far track, deeper into the forest, past the signs that said *No camping beyond this sign* and *Camp only in designated bays*.

Eventually Arnold chose to camp in a small damp clearing barely large enough for a tent, a few metres off a rough track. The ground was thick with dead leaves and shrubs, overhung with shadows. Danny watched his father put up the tent and imagined a carpet of black spiders waiting to jump on his defenceless ankles.

It was very late. Danny should still have been snuggled up asleep in his Tom and Jerry pyjamas, exhausted from the long walk and intense sulking. It was freezing outside. Dark. *Put it out of your mind*, he thought. *Go back to sleep.* If only he hadn't drunk that can of warm lemonade with the cold baked beans they had had for dinner.

The pressure from Danny's bladder was becoming extreme. Arnold was deep asleep. A long, low whistle came from one nostril, and a small slurp. Danny was frightened to wake his father now. There was no option. He would have to go outside under a tree. In the dark.

Danny edged out of his sleeping bag, slipped on his sandshoes and crawled to the door of the tent. Lifted the flap and peered outside. Nothing. The moon was deep beneath the clouds and the trees he had seen all afternoon had lost their shape in the inky black—a spreading dark that could conceal anything. An escaped criminal, perhaps. Or a dingo. If he were a dingo, under a tree is exactly the spot he'd wait for a small unsuspecting boy to take out his penis at dingo-jaw height. He crawled back and sat on the sleeping bag again. He lay down, shut his eyes. Then in a blind surge, he bolted for the tent flap and lurched into the blackness on hands and knees. The dark was complete and threatening. The night pressed in on him, hiding things.

He was uncertain of his direction; he inched forward with sounds around him on all sides. A dank smell from the trees, a rustling of leaves. Eventually he sensed space around him, enough to stand, and there he stopped, pulled down his pyjama pants a little and aimed into the blackness. The relief he felt almost weakened his knees. As if in reward for his courage, the clouds parted the instant he finished, sending a shaft of light down on the track just as Danny straightened his pants and turned to go.

Then he heard a noise almost directly behind him in the bush. A snuffling sound, something disturbing the fallen leaves and scrub. Not a little noise, like a snake or a spider or a mouse. A big noise.

Danny froze. It was a dragon, the last one in existence, breathing fire, waiting to eat him alive. It was a wild pig, tusks dripping blood. An axe murderer, hockey-masked and chuckling, coming to separate his body from his head.

Danny's heart beat faster and his brain seemed to function a long way above his body and screamed to him to run, shrieking, as quickly as he could back to the tent. But he didn't. Against all his better judgment, all his character, all his experience, Danny slowly turned his head and looked.

In the dark, through the bush, he could see a pair of luminous eyes glowing. Satanic eyes, staring straight at him. He sank to his knees and as he cowered there, frozen, out of the bush walked a monster. It might have been a wild dog, but it wasn't. It might have been a giant wolf but it wasn't that either. It was like no animal Danny had ever seen or ever imagined. Longer nose-to-tail than

Danny was tall. Heavy, with a head disproportionally huge; a sense of bulk looming much, much too close. Strong crouching limbs that seemed tensed to spring. The stripes on its hindquarters warning, like a hornet or a venomous snake. It hissed, a kind of low growling menace. Its eyes, pale and malevolent, bored straight into Danny's.

They stood and stared at each other, Danny and the monster. Neither so much as blinking. For a minimum of two minutes and a maximum of a lifetime, Danny was rooted to the spot. Eyes bugged, perspiration dribbling down his back. Two minutes. All the nights he'd been frightened, all the times he'd begged *please, Daddy, let me sleep with the light on*. And now, he was standing, body paralysed, mind utterly vacant, in front of a monster.

They might have stood there all night, staring at each other, but at a sound—a branch falling, a possum scrabbling up a tree—the monster turned its head. It opened its mouth impossibly wide as if its jaws were unhinged, as if it was about to pounce and tear out Danny's throat. Then it yawned and stretched its stiff tail. A dirty musk smell hit Danny like a fist to the bridge of the nose, and he vomited on the path. When Daniel looked up, the monster was gone.

'You don't seem much like a whiney brat now,' I say. The candles have burned low. I have pulled a throw rug from the couch and wrapped it around us. 'A bit, but not a lot.'

'Somehow my walnut-sized brain figured that seeing a monster was the worst thing that could ever happen to me,' he says. 'Somehow from that moment I knew I could get through anything.'

I had thought the whole idea of Tasmanian tigers was too impossible to believe. And yet he did believe it. It was me he didn't believe. 'Ruby was right,' I say.

'Ruby was right about what?'

'Why didn't you ask, "Who's Ruby?"'

'Ruby and I are old friends. I should phone her, actually. I promised I'd let her know how things went,' he says. 'Don't look so surprised Della. Once I had this address it was easy to track the owner of the house, find your dad in prison, find Ruby. How else did I know you'd be here today?'

He's had the best lawyers that money can buy, paid by a friend who has stuck by us. Of course.

'You've seen him,' I say. 'Dad.'

'My chess has improved out of sight but I keep getting Plato and Socrates confused,' Daniel says. 'He's tearing his hair out.'

'Is he still angry with me?'

'He's not even angry with himself. He's planning a whole new career when he gets out. He's going to become a fraud prevention consultant. He's got lectures with banks and police forces all lined up. They're recommending him for early parole on account of his willingness to reform.'

'Reform,' I say. 'That'll be the day.'

'And you, Della? What are you going to do now?'

And right then I know. Now, for the first time in my life, there is no sting I have to practise for, no obligation to fulfil, no work to organise. I am free. There is something I want to do. Something I have wanted to do my whole life, but I've only just realised it now.

This is what I know. Her name, of course, and her age. When I was small, I remember Ava once wore a dress I had never seen before to a cocktail party in the city: sapphire blue, kimono-style, with embroidered gold dragonflies and flowing sleeves. When I told her how beautiful it was, she said, 'It was your mother's.' I know my hair must come from her. I know my father met her when she was just seventeen, the daughter of an antique-dealer friend of his, my grandfather MacRobertson, who knew more about ageing timber and gluing Edwardian legs on to modern tables than he ought. I've seen her name on the flyleaf of books and once, when I was about twelve and playing hide and seek with Sam and my cousins, I found a small glass jar at the back of the pantry. The contents, brown and evil-looking, were not fit for pigs but a faded piece of cardboard attached to the neck with string said *Apple, sultana and cinnamon chutney Marla September 1977*. Once I heard someone say she had played lacrosse as a girl. She has a brother who is a printer in Manchester. When she left us, she was younger than I am now.

On the way to the airport we stop and pick up Ruby. She is staying in a motel deep in the suburbs, on the way to the prison. For a moment I wonder where she has found the money for that, but I look at Daniel and decide not to ask. She seems the same, in a dusty pink woollen suit. Chanel. I jump out to open the door for her and she smiles and hugs me a little gingerly. Either I am thinner than I thought or it pains her to touch these revolting clothes. She slides into the back seat of Daniel's BMW with an easy, familiar motion.

'I've been so concerned for you. So has your father. Lord, you look a mess.' Then she says, 'Hello Daniel dear,' and she leans forward and kisses his cheek.

'Ruby,' he says. 'I hope Larry's well.'

'Della. You can't go in those clothes,' says Ruby, as she cranes her neck from the back seat. 'You can't arrive in London looking like a scarecrow. Let me buy you a dress, something with a defined waist. Something that suits you. And for God's sake, no pastels. Something dressy you can wear if you find her. I mean when. When you find her.'

We are in the terminal, Daniel, Ruby and me. It's chaos here. We have had coffee and reheated lasagne and have walked around the shops while waiting. Around us are excited people: pale-faced teenagers with backpacks and crying parents; a group of Asian tourists and their guide who holds a flag over his head and blows a whistle from time to time; a bored-looking businessman carrying a shiny briefcase and reading *Fortune* magazine. All these people are flying overseas, but there's one minor difference between me and them. Somewhere, deep in the belly of our plane, they all have luggage.

In the food court near the sign that says *International Departures* there sits a woman with three small children. The children are slurping noodles, squabbling, crying and kicking each other in the shins. They'll be on my flight, definitely. The way they kick, probably in the row behind me.

Ruby pulls me aside, takes a fist-full of notes from a cash machine, presses them upon me.

'I'm sorry about the cheque,' I say. 'I'm sorry about everything.'

She is fussing now, straightening my collar, tsk-ing over a broken button on the front of my shirt. 'Wait until you get to the other side, past immigration,' she says. 'Then you don't need to pay the tax. And no horizontal stripes.'

'Tell Dad and Sam and the cousins I'm sorry.'

'They'll get over it. It's time we got rid of that house anyway. Nasty, draughty old thing.'

'Ruby. What will you do?'

'Perhaps you should get some trousers. You've got the hips for it and they're better for travelling. More relaxed. Something with a flat front.'

'Thank you, Ruby,' I say. 'But you can't afford this,' and I try to give her back the cash. 'You need it for you and Dad.'

'It doesn't matter,' she says. 'We've had our whole lives to get it right. Now it's your turn.' I think for a moment she's going to hug me again, but instead she peers into my face. 'And for heaven's sake get some mascara.'

I cannot thank her for all the years of cooking and cleaning and teaching me to read and work and dress, so I don't. I look at her face and see I don't need to. I nod and take the money and fold it inside my bra. The boarding pass is tight in my hand, along with the spare passport I retrieved from the false bottom of my wardrobe before we left the house. Whoever buys that house is going to love the secret passages. I hope they don't tear it down. I hope a herd of children live there and discover all our secrets.

I hear an announcement then: they're talking about my flight. It's almost time to go through. Daniel has stayed this whole time, as involved as if it was his trip.

'I'll pay you back for this,' I say to Daniel. 'For the ticket, I mean.'

He grins. 'Will you? Why?'

I hold my arms out and twirl, as though I'm wearing an emerald cocktail dress instead of the Jervises' old work clothes. 'Can't you see I'm a new woman?' I say.

'I kind of liked the old one,' he says. 'Life's been dull without her.'

People are milling around the door to immigration now. They are hugging each other, tearful goodbyes. The mother has lost something and is pulling everything out of her handbag on to the floor. The kids have darted off to buy last-minute rubbish from the newsagent and one has fallen on the floor and is crying like a car alarm. The businessman is making a final phone call, ordering somebody about and raising his voice. He looks at the crying child like it might explode. For a moment my chest feels so tight that I can't breathe.

'Anyway,' I say, and even as the words come out I know I have been meaning to say this all the way here in the car. 'You're looking quite tired. Are they bags around your eyes?'

'Me? Bags?'

I run my finger over his face, pinch his cheeks. 'Bags. And tired lines around your eyes. I think you need a holiday. A European holiday.'

'Della,' he says. 'This is something you should do on your own.'

I nod. He's right, I know, but I only just found him again. It isn't fair. 'I'll ring you. When I get settled.'

He smiles and says, 'I know.' He runs the back of his fingers down my throat, then with one arm pulls me close. 'Della,' he whispers. 'It's a lovely name.' Then he brushes my hair off my face and kisses me, arm around my waist, lifting me off the ground. It is an old-fashioned farewell from a time when air-travel meant something. I wind my arms around his neck and for a long time I think this trip is the worst idea I've ever had.

'Della,' says Ruby, tapping me on the back. 'It's time. You have to go through.

'Right,' I say, and I untangle my arms as slowly as I can.

There is a disorderly queue forming in front of the sliding doors. In front of me the businessman, now finished with his phone call, cuts in front of the harassed mother and almost steps on one of the children. The child stares up at him, picking her nose. He gives her a look of disdain. The *Fortune* magazine is tucked under his arm and he's waving his boarding pass around like a fan. I can see the seat number: it's in the same row as mine, only a few seats away. 'Della, wait,' says Daniel, and then he puts his hand in his pocket and brings out his wallet. 'You'll need more money than that, surely, for when you get off the plane.'

I'm right behind the businessman now. His shoes are fine leather, polished, new. His suit, I think, is Armani. Silk tie, crisp shirt, solid cufflinks with the monogram of a gentlemen's club in the city. His wrist, the one carrying the briefcase, is heavy with a gold watch. Rolex. It sparkles under the white lights and even from here I can tell it is genuine. The businessman shuffles ahead in the queue. He runs one finger around the inside of his collar.

I smile back at Daniel. 'I'll manage somehow,' I say.

Acknowledgements

This story was inspired by my long devotion to the work of the late Stephen Jay Gould, especially his books *Wonderful Life*, *Ever Since Darwin* and *Eight Little Piggies*. I am also grateful to the real-life monster hunter Paul Cropper, whose patience with my questions and whose books *The Yowie: In Search of Australia's Bigfoot* and *Out of the Shadows: Mystery Animals of Australia* were invaluable.

For information on the profession and lives of con artists, I relied on the the following fascinating books: *The Modern Con Man* by Todd Robbins, *Crimes of Persuasion* by Les Henderson, *Roger Cook's Ten Greatest Conmen* by Roger Cook and Tim Tate, *Scams and Swindles* by the Silver Lake editors and *The Art of the Steal* by Frank W. Abagnale.

For information on the life of the field scientist and the mind of the cryptozoologist, I'm grateful to *Lucy's Legacy* by Donald C. Johanson and Kate Wong, *My Quest for the Yeti* by Reinhold Messner, *Wildmen: Yeti, Sasquatch and the Neanderthal Enigma* by Myra Shackley, *Sasquatch: Legend Meets Science* by Jeff Meldrum, *Carnivorous Nights* by Margaret Mittelbach and Michael Crewdson, *The Origin of Humankind* by Richard Leakey, *Field Adventures in Paleontology* by Lynne M. Clos, and *The Back Road to Crazy* edited by Jennifer Bové.

For their insight and generosity, I am indebted to my early readers Jess Howard, Michael Williams, Jane Sullivan, Kate Holden, Antoni Jach, Alison Goodman, Leah Kaminsky, Simmone Howell, Angelina Mirabito, Lyndel Caffrey, Matthew Hooper and Peter Bishop. For their support and assistance, many thanks go to Anna Nemes, James Reid, Simon Ramsay, Scott and Lee Falvey, Gabrielle Murphy, and to Vickie Lucas, who first made me think of emeralds. To Melissa Cranenburgh, who took me camping for a weekend yet still speaks to me: thank you. At Text Publishing, Michael Heyward and Mandy Brett were encouraging and inspiring, and their advice made this a much better book.

My own zoology studies, culminating in ZL321: Evolution and Zoogeography at the University of Queensland, were so long ago that we studied dinosaurs with live examples. Any errors in fact or theory remain my own, or Della's.